SATAN'S GATE

EXTINCTION SURVIVAL SERIES: BOOK 2

AN EXTINCTION CYCLE STORY

WALT BROWNING

GREAT WAVE INK
PUBLISHING

GREAT WAVE INK
PUBLISHING

Cover Design by Deranged Doctor Design
Edited by Sara Jones

GREAT WAVE INK
PUBLISHING

Foreword
by
Nicholas Sansbury Smith

Dear Reader,

Thank you for picking up a copy of Satan's Gate by Walt Browning. This is the second book in the Extinction Survival series. The first book (Lost Valley) was originally published through Amazon's Extinction Cycle Kindle World. The story transcended to far more than fan fiction, but unfortunately, Amazon ended the Kindle Worlds program in July of 2018. Authors were given a chance to republish or retire their stories, and I jumped at the chance to republish the series through my small press, Great Wave Ink. Today, we're proud to offer the Extinction Survival series in paperback, audio, and to readers outside of the United States for the first time ever.

For those of you that are new to the Extinction Cycle storyline, the series is the award winning, Amazon top-rated, and half a million copy best-selling seven book saga. There are over six *thousand* five-star reviews on Amazon alone. Critics have called it, "World War Z and The Walking Dead meets the Hot Zone." Publishers weekly added, "Smith has realized that the way to rekindle interest in zombie apocalypse fiction is to make it louder, longer, and bloodier ... Smith intensifies the disaster efficiently as the pages flip by, and readers who enjoy juicy blood-and-guts action will find a lot of it here."

In creating the Extinction Cycle, my goal was to use authentic military action and real science to take the zombie and post-apocalyptic genres in an exciting new direction. Forget everything you know about zombies. In the Extinction Cycle, they aren't created by black magic or other supernatural means. The ones found in the Extinction Cycle are created by a military bio-weapon called VX-99, first used in Vietnam. The chemicals reactivate the proteins encoded by the genes that separate humans from wild animals—in other words, the experiment turned men into monsters. For the first time, zombies are explained using real science—science so real there is every possibility of something like the Extinction Cycle actually happening. But these creatures aren't the unthinking, slow-minded, shuffling monsters we've all come to know in other shows, books, and movies. These "variants" are more monster than human. Through the series, the variants become the hunters as they evolve from the epigenetic changes. Scrambling to find a cure and defeat the monsters, humanity is brought to the brink of extinction.

We hope you enjoy the Extinction Survival series and continue to the main storyline in the Extinction Cycle.

Best wishes,
Nicholas Sansbury Smith,
NYT Bestselling Author of the Extinction Cycle

Senior Chief Petty Officer (SCPO)
Rayford "Porky" Shader
Operation Liberty
Five Miles Off the California Coast
USS *Theodore Roosevelt*

Long is the way
And hard, that out of hell leads up to light.
JOHN MILTON
Paradise Lost

Like many of the military's elite operators, Senior Chief Petty Officer Porky Shader loved structure and control, even though his chosen profession brought chaotic situations with each deployment. As a Navy SEAL, Shader was often called on to infiltrate enemy-held territory and do bad things. That meant putting himself into situations that were, by definition, unstructured and out of his control.

But a successful operation was 95 percent preparation and 5 percent luck. In Porky's mind, the results of any well-planned mission were a foregone conclusion, given the time and effort that went into the planning stage. Every conceivable circumstance was practiced, and adjustments made, to maximize the chances of having the desired outcome.

When the outbreak started, it rapidly became evident that this was an extinction-level event caused by a virus that was created by the species it was destroying. The irony of that fact wasn't lost on anyone. Because of the seriousness of the situation, the military responded with a rapid and confused retreat. Shader understood that desperate measures had been needed.

But the Navy ran on a strict diet of rules and regulations, and he knew a counterattack would eventually come, but at a time and place of the military's choosing. Therefore, it was no surprise that almost a month later, news reached him of a nationwide attempt to retake the country's major cities. The mission, dubbed Operation Liberty, was in its final developmental stages. His initial reaction was one of hope. *Maybe they had come up with a way to turn the tide on the viral outbreak.*

After Shader attended his first strategic planning meeting, he began to worry the mission had been doomed from the start, either by inexperienced leadership or out of sheer desperation to save the country.

What made it worse was that most of the information provided at that meeting was unintelligible to everyone without a PhD. No one had a clue what the hell they were being told.

"Our drone overflights indicate the infection has destroyed over 98 percent of the population," Major Poole had said. Poole was with naval intelligence and in direct contact with the remnants of the civilian government. "With their rabid need to feed," he continued, "we estimate that out of an initial count of thirteen million residents, there are now fewer than fifty thousand infected remaining in the greater Los Angeles area. The rest have become food."

The crowd of NCOs and officers let out a collective

groan. The battle group had fewer than fifteen thousand soldiers, sailors, and Marines at their disposal. Of those, less than a third were fighters, while the rest were support personnel.

"How is this a good thing?" asked Admiral Abernathy, the strike group commander. "That's over ten to one against us. I don't think starting a war with those odds is a winning hand to play."

"I understand," the condescending major replied, "but we've been observing the creatures for over a week now, and from what we've seen, it appears that they're not doing well. There are fewer of them and their activity is limited and random."

The admiral looked unconvinced.

"It is our theory," Poole continued, "that the virus causes an epigenetic change that raises their metabolism to an unimaginable level. In short, they need massive amounts of protein to survive, and with fewer sources of food available, they are literally starving."

"What the hell is 'epigenetic'?" Shader whispered to a Marine staff sergeant sitting next to him.

"Like I know?" the man replied. "I need this talk like a bag of dicks. It's completely worthless to me."

The rest of the information the scientist shared flew over the group like a cold winter's wind—neither wanted nor appreciated.

"Well, why don't we just wait them out? Let them die off, and we can walk in and reclaim what is ours?" the admiral finally asked.

"Because, Admiral. Some of the creatures are starting to venture out of the city, looking for more sources of food. Our drones have been sending back pictures of groups of normal, uninfected people hiding outside of the major metropolitan areas. The virus hasn't taken everyone out yet. If we don't stop these things now, the infected will leave the urban areas in search of more food. Those who are safe today will be dead tomorrow."

Admiral Abernathy leaned over and spoke quietly with Colonel Julio Weeks, the most senior surviving Marine Corps officer and the de facto leader of the group's land forces. Almost a thousand men from Camp Pendleton and the 11th Marine Expeditionary Unit had been recovered. However, that represented less than half of the personnel that had been under their flag before the virus began.

After a short conversation, the admiral spoke loudly enough for all to hear. "All right. Let's move forward with Operation Liberty. We need every healthy person possible to rebuild the country, and it's our job to protect those that cannot protect themselves."

Once the decision to go forward had been made, the rest of the confab became a blur in Shader's mind. The confusion and lack of information made his head hurt well before the summit had concluded. The only thing he brought out of that meeting was a headache and a need to get drunk. Unfortunately, getting hammered wasn't an option. Instead, he took his 800mg Motrin, washed it down with one belt of his personal supply of whiskey, and hit the rack.

During the following days of planning, he couldn't shake his feelings of dread. They knew nothing about their new enemy, other than they were strong, relentless, and without fear. Shader didn't trust fighting an enemy he didn't understand.

Now, almost a week later, Operation Liberty had begun. As he sat in the back of a V-22 Osprey, his apprehensions were only amplified by the claustrophobic tube he was crammed into. Fortunately, the flight wasn't expected to take more than twenty minutes.

When they first boarded the V-22, the Marines who had been put under his command marched up the Osprey's rear drop-down ramp and split into two lines. Within moments, the bench seats that ran along both sides of the aircraft had been filled. Every nook was crammed with a warm body and their equipment. He had men smashed into him from both sides, while across the aisle he momentarily played footsies with the squad's corpsman. The man stopped shoving Shader's foot away when he finally looked up, saw the SCPO staring back at him. He wisely gave Porky the space.

Like most operators, Shader didn't like to fly. More SEALs had been killed in helicopter accidents than by enemy fire, and the Osprey seemed even worse. It was like riding inside of an aluminum barrel with no view of the outside world. There were a couple small glass portals that were cut high on the airframe, but these only offered a view of the passing clouds. At least a Blackhawk had an open side door with a gunner strapped behind a Squad Automatic Weapon. The cocoon-like feeling of the vertically launched airplane he presently found himself in only added to his discomfort.

Shader logically knew his chances in the Osprey were no different than riding in a Blackhawk. But having an open helicopter door that allowed the wind to slap at his face was the way he had moved into battle his entire adult life. Now, he was using the Marines' newest toy to lead his squad into the bowels of Los Angeles. It just felt wrong.

Porky marked the time observing the craft he was trapped in. The walls were covered with exposed hydraulic hoses, along with pipes carrying various electronic lines and cabling. Many of the tubes crisscrossed each other as they made their way fore and aft. There had been no attempt to cover the mess with an interior wall. That was an unnecessary and counterproductive luxury. With the computers, switches, and wiring all exposed, maintenance time was reduced, and efficiency enhanced. It was a reminder that the Osprey's passengers weren't worth the extra effort to make the ride more comfortable, and just like a failed component, they were all replaceable.

The Osprey finally began to bank to the right.

"Five minutes," the Osprey's crew chief yelled out.

Soon enough, the drone of the twin Rolls-Royce engines changed in pitch as the machine's propellers began rotating upward. The Osprey started to descend as the craft magically transformed itself from an airplane into a twin-bladed helicopter. The men all looked apprehensively at Shader as their forward movement morphed into a rapid, vertical descent. What they saw was a determined, battle-hardened squad leader who was ready to kick ass. What they didn't see was on the inside—a concerned and confused SEAL who had been given vague instructions along with even more nebulous operational goals.

"We're going to take back the city" seemed to be the only consistent mission objective that leadership provided. There had been little in the way of contingency planning since they had sparse knowledge of the enemy and how it functioned. The few attempts to infiltrate the infected-held areas had all failed. So without on-the-ground intel, how could they prepare to fight a foe they didn't know the first thing about? Aerial surveys did little other than provide a rough estimate of strength.

"Shoot them in the brain box. And, by the way, try not to get infected," was the only guidance the N2 staff had given him. Sound advice.

As the craft began to settle down, Shader adjusted the web gear that was strapped over his battle dress uniform. He felt naked without the CBRN suit and would have normally worn it over his BDU. The biohazard equipment had become standard issue, but unfortunately, their situation was anything but typical. Even with all their scavenging raids, there simply were not enough of them for everyone. He was having mixed feelings about hitting the landing zone without the added protection.

Shader reached down and unclasped his harness just as the Osprey began to settle onto the ground. They had arrived.

The rear of the transport was already dropping down as Shader strode to the back. As he had done for almost three decades, he pulled a full magazine from its pouch, pushed it into the mag well, and slapped the bolt release. He instinctively rolled his rifle to the left and watched as the first .556 round slammed into the chamber. He verified that he had switched his rifle to "safe" mode and let the slung M4 drop down to his side.

With a new group of men under him, he quickly turned back to check on their status. He was gratified to see they were all standing and facing him. As instructed, their rifles were unloaded. "Weapons hot" would be accomplished after they left the aircraft. No one wanted an accidental discharge inside the computerized flying machine. One errant 62-grain hole in the wrong place would end the life of their craft.

Porky stepped off the back and scanned his surroundings. The Inglewood Forum parking lot had been chosen for several reasons, not the least of which was the lack of cars in the lot and a flat asphalt surface. That made an insertion with the Ospreys simple and quick.

Drone video also showed that the arena had many logistic advantages. There were several adjacent plots of land that were undeveloped and gave the Marines a long field of fire, a rarity in the once crowded city. Detritus and some skeletal remains were scattered amongst the occasional abandoned cars, but for the most part, the space was empty. Drone footage of the surrounding neighborhoods also had shown little infected activity over the last week.

The Osprey wasn't the quietest aircraft, and the twin engines were giving off plenty of noise. The blades had rotated and were now facing up. The giant propellers were still spinning, having been throttled back just enough to keep the craft on the ground but fast enough that just a little juice would send it back into the air.

Shader walked quickly to his assigned spot, lifted his battle rifle, and held it at low ready.

The Osprey's engines began to whine at a higher pitch as it started to lift off. Shader turned around and was glad to see that his squad had completed a perimeter around the aircraft and that their battle rifles were loaded and pointed out, creating a 360° field of fire.

The Osprey's crew chief, a Marine gunnery sergeant named Potoski, still stood in the open rear door. He had strapped himself onto the aircraft's bulkhead and rotated a cantilevered metal bar with a SAW machine gun attached at the end. He was now a rear-door gunner. The V-22 would be flying overhead for a while, providing cover and relaying intel on any infected in their vicinity.

"We'll let ya know if we see any of them Variants," Potoski had said in his thick, Brooklyn accent, just before they lifted off for the mission.

"Variants?" Shader asked. "You mean the infected?"

"Yeah. But the eggheads call them Variants now. At least, that's what we were told."

"Shit. I just call them all fucked up. Just let me know when you see them and where they're coming from," Shader said.

"Gotch yer back," Potoski replied.

The giant transport began to accelerate into the sky, and Shader watched the big Pole grab the charging handle of the squad automatic weapon, pull it back, and release. The SAW was ready to fire. The Marine gave a "thumbs up" as his bird rotated away, and Shader had just enough time to give the big Brooklyn grunt a quick wave before he disappeared.

The Osprey began its overwatch flight pattern, and the drum of the engines became a low drone in the otherwise quiet metropolis.

Shader remained still. He gave himself almost three minutes to let the V-22 do a circle around their position before receiving a report that the area was quiet. Given the noise they'd just made, it was a miracle they hadn't been overrun already.

This a good sign, he said to himself. *Maybe the intel guys finally got it right.* That thought gave him some peace.

Another craft landed several hundred yards away, bringing the rest of their unit up to strength. Shader's Osprey brought in twenty-four fighters but only fifteen of them had been put under his command. He was one of three squad leaders, the other two having arrived in the other craft. A second lieutenant was also on that Osprey.

Their platoon leader, a Marine butter bar named Landry, raised his hand and spun it in the air. It was the signal for his squad leaders to gather at his location.

"All right, Fireteam One, take the left flank and use that black Tahoe to set up your SAW," Shader barked and pointed to an abandoned SUV. "Team Two, use the red Honda and Team Three, set up at the white Explorer."

Shader looked at the remaining three men. "You're my QRF. Hold here, keep an eye on the arena behind us, and stay frosty. The rest of you are on my six."

Shader started to trot toward the other Osprey along with eight Marines who were members of the other squads. He suddenly held up his hand and stopped, then turned back to his own fireteams.

"Keep your muzzle discipline," he yelled. "If I see anyone pointing their weapon our way, I'll shove my foot so high up your ass you'll be polishing my boot with your tongue."

Several chuckles followed Shader as he turned and trotted toward the young lieutenant.

"Glad you could join us," Landry said sarcastically as the SEAL joined the three men.

The second lieutenant's offhand comment irked Shader. The kid looked like he wasn't even old enough to rent a car, let alone give a career petty officer some undeserved grief.

Recognizing that any attempt to put the young LT in his place would be counterproductive to the mission, Shader swallowed his anger and nodded.

"Aye aye, sir," Shader simply replied.

The other two non-commission officers, both Marine staff sergeants, gave Shader a knowing and appreciative nod. Obviously, the kid was a problem for them as well.

The lieutenant had moved the group to the back of an abandoned pickup truck. He dropped the tailgate of the GMC and laid out a map of the area.

They had been inserted at the northeast corner of the Forum's parking lot. To their north sat a massive graveyard. That morbid fact was not lost on the men, but it did provide almost half a mile of open space that would be a useful buffer in case of a massed attack. The same situation stood to the south, where the Forum's extended parking lot spread out over tens of thousands of square feet.

Because of the concentration of buildings to the east and west, the Navy had sent waves of F-18 Hornets on bombing runs as well as lobbing hundreds of shells from the fleet's destroyers onto the two densely built-up areas. Each shell generated an explosive radius of nearly thirty yards. Even now, nearly twenty-four hours since the last of the bombs had fallen, wisps of smoke and the acrid smell of burning plastic hung thickly in the air.

The only structure unaffected was the massive indoor arena. It was hoped that the country could be resurrected once the creatures had been eliminated, so any significant infrastructure was spared to facilitate the recovery. This was why the Forum stood untouched while its surroundings had been turned into Iwo Jima beach.

The purpose of the shelling was to create a wide zone around the LZ, giving the Marines a buffer and clear field of fire. The Navy had done their job, leaving behind craters and destruction where there once had been zero-lot houses and multi-level apartment buildings. It was a breathtaking sight.

"I want fireteams positioned in these spots," the lieutenant said, pointing at ten different locations.

Shader immediately noticed that the positioning of the fireteams surrounded the untouched Forum without any plans to clear the building. Shader had pointed that little detail out while helping to plan the mission. He had been shut down by the fleet's N2.

"We've been scanning the building for days including IR and night vision. We haven't seen a thing," the intelligence officer said.

"But, without eyes on the inside, there's no way to know—"

"Your concerns are noted," the N2 barked, effectively ending the conversation.

Now, Shader's fears were amplified by his proximity to the red-and-grey arena. The entrance to the structure was a wide set of stairs that led down under the asphalt. The top of the large downward ramp had once been covered by a white polyurethane canopy. That had been lost some time ago. Only shredded tags of the heavy-duty awning remained, hanging listlessly from the skeletal steel frame that had given it form. At the bottom of the stairwell, the front glass doors had been shattered. Even from a distance, Shader could see pools of dried, blackish-maroon-colored blood.

The dark interior was unaffected by the morning sun, which was still low enough on the horizon to cast its rays down into the opening. The building's entrance seemed to absorb the photons, which created the illusion of monstrous jaws, spread wide open, as if waiting for its next meal. All these thoughts passed through Shader's mind as he cast his eyes on the structure.

Lieutenant Landry, sensing his petty officer's concerns, slapped the tailgate with his open hand.

"Spit it out, Shader!" he commanded.

Shader hesitated, knowing the LT had fully bought into the battle plan. He remained quiet. As far as the lieutenant was concerned, arguing about the dangers of the Forum was settled intel. Challenging that N2 report would only bring Shader grief.

But then Staff Sergeant Russ spoke up.

"Sir. I must agree with Shader. We're relying on some drone jockey to tell us whether our LZ is safe."

"I concur," the other staff sergeant added. "Those guys are wrong as much as they are right."

"Well. We have three men that disagree with the collective intelligence of the United States Navy. I can't tell you how privileged that makes me feel."

The cocky lieutenant stared at his subordinates, daring someone to challenge his decision. The men stood silently as each NCO debated whether to say anything.

"Well, I guess that settles it," Landry said. "Nothing to say? Then do your jobs."

The two Marines gave a half-hearted salute and

grunted, "Aye aye." But Shader stood his ground. He'd been a special operator for almost thirty years, definitely before the LT had even been born. He hadn't stayed alive this long being a wallflower, and he wasn't about to give in to a snot-nosed punk who hadn't fired his weapon anywhere other than a square range.

"It's not settled," Shader said confidently. "We don't have intel on that building, and pretending we do could be fatal."

"Well, Shader. I'm impressed you had the balls to speak up." The lieutenant walked up to the SEAL and jabbed his chest. "If you think the building needs to be cleared, then you clear it."

The young officer turned back to the truck and folded the map. "You can use your QRF *after* we set up our perimeter."

"Just four men?" Shader asked.

"Why? Is that a problem? Anyone who knows more than the Navy should be able to clear a building with a single fireteam. In fact, you could just go by yourself if you wanted to. But I think you'd be smart to take your QRF. That way, you won't get lost."

Landry smiled at Shader and turned away. The two Marine sergeants quietly followed their officer, leaving Shader to curse himself for opening his mouth.

"Stupid, stupid, stupid," he grunted before jogging back to his men. "When in the hell will I learn to just shut up?"

— 2 —

Inglewood Forum
Inglewood, California

Never yield to the apparently overwhelming might of the enemy.
WINSTON CHURCHILL – 1941

The morning flew by. Creating fighting positions was far simpler when the enemy wouldn't be shooting back. The problem was that the Variants were likely going to attack at night, when they were most active, and they would probably rush the defenses en masse. What made things worse was that the creatures reacted to bullets as if they were a nuisance—unless one of the rounds found their brain.

After dropping off the Marines, one of the Ospreys stayed on station, running a racing track pattern around the LZ while the other craft went back to the *Roosevelt* to refuel and pick up more supplies. Then, after dropping off supplies, that bird would take up overwatch while the first Osprey went back to the ship to duplicate the process. By the time midday arrived, the LZ represented a budding FOB (Forward Operating Base). There were two GAU-19 Gatling guns bolted to the asphalt while abandoned vehicles had been shoved and pushed together in spots, creating fortifications for the fireteams.

"At least we didn't have to scrape out any defensive fighting positions," Shader said to SSgt. Russ as he wiped the sweat from his forehead.

15

"Don't put it by Landry to have us try and dig foxholes in the parking lot. I don't think he's got an ounce of common sense."

"Hmmph," Shader replied. "Nothing common about common sense anymore, is there? I wouldn't put it past him."

The mid-May temperature was pushing ninety degrees, and there wasn't a cloud in the sky. Russ handed Shader some water and took a long draw from his own one-liter plastic bottle. After finishing it, he threw it to the ground and let out a loud burp.

"Littering, SSgt. Russ? I hope the UN climate change committee doesn't get hold of you," Shader joked.

"Wait till I fart. CO_2 emissions never smelled so good."

Shader grinned. He liked this guy, even though the man hadn't defended him earlier. Shader understood his reluctance to confront the stubborn lieutenant.

Sensing Porky's thoughts, Russ nudged the SEAL and confessed. "Hey, sorry I didn't stick up for you more. I just didn't see him changing his mind."

Shader nodded. He'd been under the command of too many PowerPoint Rangers himself. It never worked well when you challenged them directly.

With the midday sun beating down, Shader decided to grab a bite to eat with the other men in his QRF (Quick Reaction Force). Nothing was worse than going on patrol or clearing a building with low blood sugar. Then after that, it was into the Forum. Hopefully for a quick and easy search of an abandoned arena.

— 3 —

USS *Theodore Roosevelt*
Off the Coast of California
Combat Directions Center (CDC)

The tactical displays in the carrier's operations room were in perpetual flux. The banks of computer LCDs cast a goblin-green light that bathed the gloomy, cave-like space. Operations specialists, each responsible for one of the many prongs of the group's assets, sat in front of their assigned terminal. Each screen flashed with updated information, and with the remaining Pacific fleet moving close by, the OpSpecs had a lot to monitor.

Some maintained a tactical picture of the surrounding seas, plotting a visual representation of ships, submarines, and aircraft in the area. There needed to be an accounting of the fleet's own massive flotilla to prevent things from running into each other.

Another monitored communication between ships while a third specialist coordinated radio signals with assault forces being inserted on the mainland. There were dozens of them working in the CDC. They all reported their information to the ship's Tactical Actions Officer (TAO), who was the ship commander's eyes and ears. It was a massive and complicated job.

Chief Warrant Officer Kyle Solomon, one of the *Roosevelt's* three TAOs, stood to the side as the admiral paced slowly behind the seated operations specialists.

17

Solomon knew Admiral Abernathy looked anything but comfortable. The TAO was more correct than he could have known.

Against his better judgement, Abernathy committed his Marines and Naval forces to retaking the mainland. Operation Liberty had been initiated on the orders of the Joint Chiefs of Staff, without the input of any of the country's remaining "on-the-ground" generals or admirals. In Abernathy's mind, there were two types of officers—the self-promoters and the performers. It was the former, and not the latter, who had created the mission.

Aside from the paper-pushers planning the op, his discomfort arose from many other sources. The first and most important strike against the whole thing was the lack of preparation and forethought. Half-assed intelligence and almost wishful projections of the Variants' strength haunted Abernathy. There was too much reliance on aerial surveillance because there had been no on-the-ground reports.

Every mission to insert men to gather intel had failed, including the loss of three pairs of Marine scout snipers. That, right there, should have been a warning to take a step back and reassess their assumptions. Marine scout snipers were the crème de la crème of the nation's finest fighting force. If they had failed, the enemy was far deadlier or numerous than was being reported.

The second black mark had more to do with the attitude of the intelligence community. Their almost religious dependence on the United States Army Medical Research Institute of Infectious Diseases (USAMRIID) for scientific information on the virus was obsessive.

Granted, the rapid spread of the epidemic decimated every city on the continent, but there had been additional medical research personnel who survived. Even the Center for Disease Control (CDC) and the National Institute of Allergies and Infectious Diseases had become uncomfortably quiet. NIAID had taken the lead in the initial fight against the spread of the virus, but their voice abruptly disappeared about a week into the infection and was replaced by USAMRIID. Watching the civilian arm of the government shut down so abruptly, then supplanted by its military counterpart, was disconcerting. He now had no counterbalance for the Army medical corps' opinions. Something wasn't right.

The third, and most damning indictment against the plan was their target. Why a major city with no military value? San Diego or Long Beach made far more sense, given their strategic significance. Both had deep water ports where the fleet could service their ships, and there was infrastructure in place to house their personnel.

His arguments fell on deaf ears when he had raised that point with the Joint Chiefs.

"Hell, we still control Coronado Island," Abernathy had stated to the four-star idiots who were now running the show. "Why aren't we using that as a base of operations? We don't even need to fight a battle to take the damn place."

Of course, logic failed to prevail. So here they were, inserting valuable men into an infected city that wouldn't even provide a place for the Navy to park their ships.

"What's our status?" Abernathy asked.

"All teams report minimal contact with the Variants. All five FOBs are on schedule to be completed by the end of the day. Major Jack and his men are inserting into FOB LAX as we speak," Solomon reported.

"Enemy contacts?" Abernathy asked.

"So far, only a few infected individuals have been encountered."

Major Poole then chimed in. "And no losses on our side?"

The Naval intelligence officer already knew the answer to his question.

"No sir," one of the operations specialists replied from his station. "We're green so far. No casualties."

Poole gave Abernathy a smug grin, knowing the admiral's dislike for the entire operation.

"Looks like our intel is correct, after all," Poole said, earning an angry glare from Solomon.

Abernathy, for his part, remained stoic. "It's still early, Major."

"It's been several hours, sir," Poole responded.

"All we've done so far is occupy land that had the shit bombed out of it. Unless you expected the Variants to survive thousands of pounds of ordinance? I'd hold judgement until our men move into the rest of the city."

"The rest of the city is quiet. Nothing significant in two days."

"You mean since we started the bombing campaign?" Abernathy shot back. "You don't think that could have sent them to cover?"

"They aren't that smart. Every computer model of the Variants' behavior, metabolism, and existing food supply shows the same thing. They're dying out unless they find more food. There just aren't any significant numbers of Variants left to cause you problems... sir."

"I'm glad you're so confident," Abernathy said absently as he scanned several of the tactical displays. "I don't have that luxury."

To a casual observer, Abernathy remained stoic. But his internal alarms were blaring as he watched the operation play out on the green-hued screens surrounding him. Right or wrong, they were committed. In the end, all he had left was to do his duty to the best of his ability.

And prayer. He had that as well. He sighed and accepted his job and the fate that would soon unfold before him.

— 4 —

FOB LAX
Los Angeles International Airport
Major Auburn Jack, USMC

"Courage is being scared to death but saddling up anyway."
JOHN WAYNE

"What a cluster," Major Jack mumbled as he watched twenty-four more Marines slog out of the back of yet another Osprey. To the major, it felt like he was trying to fill a bathtub using a soup spoon. His entire company was reliant on squad-sized V-22s to move them from the ship. That would be fine if they were just the leading edge of a normal landing force. But the plan was to create platoon-sized units and push out to FOB Forum. From there, they'd be linking up with FOB Hawthorne, then move downtown. FOB Santa Monica and FOB Compton were to move on their flanks, providing cover as they retook the city.

All of the forward bases, other than the Forum, had been established at existing airports. Once the five FOBs were linked, it would create a line that covered most of the southern side of the city.

But progress was slow. Gone were the days of using the massive C-17 Globemaster transports. The giant aircraft could carry his men in company-sized groups rather than the squads that were landing now. HUMVEEs and MRAPs could have been brought in as well and should have been part of his force. But they didn't have access to those massive transports anymore.

Being unable to bring armor didn't alleviate the fact that they were still needed. In fact, the demand to get transportation was so bad that once the FOB was established, their second assignment was to scavenge vehicles from their surroundings. The entire operation was seriously FUBAR.

"Any word on Freeman?" Jack asked.

"Coms are down," Captain Pavlin said. "T.R. says they had radio problems before they left the deck."

"For fuck's sake. This just keeps getting better and better," Jack grumbled.

"We wouldn't expect to hear anything for another hour, sir," Pavlin replied.

Freeman Park was about a mile south of FOB Hawthorne. Next to the park was a National Guard base that had dozens of IFVs (Infantry Fighting Vehicles) and other transportation.

Six fireteams had been inserted in the park with the goal of retrieving as many of these assets as possible, then drive them to FOB Hawthorne.

Pavlin watched as his CO struggled with the lack of news—not because it was an integral and necessary aspect of their grand mission, but because the major's only son was leading the Freeman operation. Lieutenant Jack was a good kid but was green as hell. He had been out of OCS less than a month when the shit hit the fan.

"Tyrell will do just fine, sir," Pavlin whispered to his CO. "He's got a good head on his shoulders, and you taught him to listen. He has a couple good NCOs under him that will keep him on the straight and narrow."

"Thanks, Dave," Jack said quietly. "I hope he does his job."

"He will, sir. He's his father's son."

— 5 —

40th Brigade Support Battalion
California National Guard
Lieutenant Tyrell Jack
South of FOB Hawthorne

"Good news, sir. We've recovered eight MRAPs, six HUMVEEs and three fuel haulers," SSgt. Michael Braddock said.

"There's fuel in the M970s?" Lt. Tyrell Jack replied.

"Yes, sir. Five thousand gallons of diesel in two of them. The third is about half-full of regular gasoline."

Jack laughed. "Filled 'em up before they left. That was kind of the Guard."

"Almost like they knew we were coming," Braddock countered with a grin.

Thwwwaaaack!

Both Jack and Braddock instinctively looked up to the roof of the two-story armory, where the team's designated marksman had positioned himself.

Thwwwaaack! A second .308-caliber round rocketed from the Marine's suppressed M40A5 sniper rifle.

Moments later, Jack's earpiece crackled to life.

"Perimeter clear," the two-man team's spotter said over the squad radio.

"That's nine since we hit the LZ," Jack said absently.

Braddock's eyes darted to the buildings surrounding them. "Yeah. Well, the air jockeys didn't hit this area, so

I'm sure the stragglers didn't get the memo that we were coming."

"You don't sound too sure of yourself," Jack said, noting Braddock's nervousness.

"How can you be sure of anything? There's nothing normal anymore."

Thwwwaaaack! Thwwwaaaack!

"Sir. We've got a group of Variants four hundred meters east of our position," the spotter barked over the radio.

Jack gave Braddock a concerned look.

Braddock pressed his PTT (Push To Talk) button. "How many?"

Several tense moments went by.

"Half a dozen, Sarge."

"Direction?" Braddock asked.

Thwwwaaaack!

"East. There's five now and they're kind of running around in circles. I don't think they can hear the shots. They look confused. And pissed."

Thwwwaaaack!

"Should I order a defensive perimeter?" Jack asked in a whisper.

Braddock stared around and watched as the men were loading up the various vehicles with salvaged supplies. Not only had they recovered the armored transports, but there was a large supply of CBRN gear, as well as just about any non-lethal piece of equipment they would need.

"Not yet, sir. We're close to done. Then we can button up inside the vehicles and head to the airport."

"Franks! Let us know if you see more tangos. We

should be rolling out of here in ten mikes," Braddock said.

"Aye aye, Sarge," the spotter replied.

Thwwwaaaack!

"Another one down," Franks mumbled, then added, "The last three just bugged out."

"What do you mean, they bugged out?"

"They looked at each other and just took off. Ran like their asses were on fire."

"Together?" Braddock asked. "They took off together?"

"Bosom buddies, Sarge."

Jack gave the sergeant a puzzled look. The Variants weren't supposed to think. According to the intel guys, they acted randomly and on instinct. Unless something drew them away, the last three had coordinated their movements.

"Maybe they heard something nearby," Jack said, sensing his sergeant's concern. "That would explain it."

"I hope so," Braddock replied. "But I'd feel better putting eyes on the perimeter. I'm going up and take a look."

A minute later, the staff sergeant scampered to the top of the old brick armory and had his binoculars up to his face.

The area around them resembled a utility company's lay-down yard. Its sole structure was a glorified brick warehouse surrounded by a parking lot filled with all types of military equipment. The entire area was enclosed by an eight-foot chain link fence topped with concertina wire. The razor-sharp loops of steel provided protection from a normal enemy, but against a determined Variant, it would do nothing more than slow it down slightly. Ripped flesh didn't faze these monsters.

To his east, Braddock saw the Variants his sniper had eliminated.

He pulled out a map of the area and marked the spot over four football fields away. The intersection where the bodies lay was in the middle of a residential area surrounded by nothing but single-story homes.

"Which direction did you say the last three went?" Braddock asked the spotter.

"There," he said, pointing east.

Braddock searched for anything that may have drawn the creatures away. In the distance was a cluster of large buildings rising above the homes nearby.

"Shit!" Braddock said. "Look at this."

The spotter glassed the structures. "Looks like medical offices, Sarge."

Braddock pointed on his map to a group of buildings, about a mile east of the intersection where the dead Variants lay.

"A hospital!" Corporal Franks said, looking at the spot where Braddock had placed his thick index finger.

"Yeah. A place where infected people would have gone to get help."

"Fuck," the spotter spat. "That place must be crawling."

"I'll let the LT know," Braddock said. "Keep a sharp eye out. You see anything unusual, and I mean anything at all, you let me know. Do you understand?"

"Aye aye, Sarge. Anything at all unusual and I contact you, ASAP."

A low thumping began to vibrate the air around

Braddock. He brought his binoculars to his eyes once again and scanned to the west. Off in the distance, a cluster of Ospreys was moving as a group toward Hawthorne airport. The rest of the Marines were on their way.

Braddock nodded to Franks and scampered back to the ground. The arrival of the bulk of their forces along with the increased Variant activity meant they had to double-time their preps and move with a purpose. What's more, command needed to know about the change in enemy behavior. Those three didn't act randomly, and N3 had planned operations based on the premise that the Variants were crazed, primitive creatures and not things that could work together.

"LT," Braddock said over the squad radio. "Do we have coms yet?"

"Negative, Sergeant. Still working on it."

They'd been dark over the fleet's network since their Osprey had taken off. Normally, they would never have begun a mission with broken lines of communication, but these weren't normal times. As it stood, they wouldn't be able to get a message to the *Roosevelt* until they linked up with the rest of the battalion at FOB Hawthorne. If everything went according to plan, that would be almost half an hour from now. And nothing ever went according to plan.

This is not good, Braddock whispered to himself. *This is not good at all.*

— 6 —

Inglewood Forum
SCPO Porky Shader
Quick Reaction Force

"A thing is not necessarily true because a man dies for it."
OSCAR WILDE

"Coms check," Shader said.

The three Marines in the QRF each confirmed that their radios were functioning normally and dialed in to preset two. Preset one was the main squad network, and Shader didn't want their conversations muddling up coms with the rest of the platoon while the FOB was being prepared.

Porky Shader did a final assessment of his men, checking for loose items or missing gear. Each was squared away and eager to get the job done.

When he'd been given the task of leading a platoon into battle, Porky allowed the Marines to choose their own battle buddy then he put two of the pairs together to form fireteams. He held back the best three grunts for the quick reaction force, of which, he'd be the fourth man. He'd had the men for a week of training before Operation Liberty had begun. These three had shown remarkable marksmanship and were quick on their feet. If Porky was going to go into battle with someone, he'd prefer to do it with the best. They may not be SEALs, but they were damn close in proficiency. How they did in actual combat was yet to be seen, but their talent was undeniable.

The four of them were clustered near a ramp that led below the parking lot. It was a truck entrance for equipment and supplies that, just a month ago, used be a private entrance for performing acts along with their equipment. Now, it was going allow Shader's quick reaction force a back entrance into the massive coliseum.

The metal garage door at the bottom had been left open. Paper, along with other trash, was collecting at the bottom of the ramp. The afternoon sun blazed overhead, its rays bathing the path into the underground lot. But like the building's east side main entrance, the sun's rays didn't seem to penetrate the opening.

"Gonzalez. You're on point," Shader said to the short Puerto Rican E-4.

Pablo Ignatius Gonzalez reminded Porky of the diminutive SEALs he'd worked with in the past. Some of the best operators he'd gone into battle with had been closer to five rather than six feet tall. Speed and precision were a more valuable commodity as a SEAL than size, and Gonzalez's hustle and tenacity were legendary among his NCOs. The kid just never gave up, which is a rare quality to find.

Maybe it was his height that made him feel the need to be so unrelenting, or perhaps it was the name his initials spelled. The "PIG" had been molded into an effective Marine. He was the first man Porky chose for the QRF.

"Aye aye. I like being up front," Gonzalez replied with a smile.

"That's good, 'cause you don't have to duck when the

lead starts flying," Corporal Antonio Lazzaro said.

"Secure that shit, Lazzaro," Shader barked. "I don't want to hear a word out of you."

"Copy that. Just like to review our situational awareness."

"Any more sound from your cock-holster, and I'll make you aware of my boot."

The tall Texan quickly lost his smirk but leaned over to the third Marine and whispered, "Told you G-man was gonna take point."

"No surprise there. He is Porky's PIG!" Corporal Keele said, grinning.

"You two are just all kind of stupid, aren't you?" Shader yelled. "We get out of here, I'm putting you both on the short bus. Now tighten it up."

Gonzalez smiled and man-punched Lazzaro in the arm as he walked to take the lead. "Porky's pig," he said, chuckling. "Damn, I kind of like that."

Shader just shook his head. *Marines,* he thought. *They suck out their brains in basic and shove grunt-shit back in.* These three had just proven it to him.

"Line up, gentlemen," Shader barked. "Watch your muzzles and move on my signal. Just like we practiced. I want this clean and quick."

The three stood silently.

"Solid copy?" Shader barked after the three grunts failed to reply.

Three "aye ayes" came back.

"Now, let's move."

The four men strode to the ramp's entrance and started down the slope. About a third of the way,

Gonzalez suddenly stopped and stared at the lower level's black opening.

Shader was next in line, and after a few seconds, he crept forward and put his hand on the young man's shoulder.

"What's the problem?" Shader asked. "You're moving like you're walking to your own funeral!"

"I don't know, Chief. I just got a cold in my spine."

Shader was about to berate the man, but he saw Gonzalez staring intently into the gloom and did the same.

A cool breeze was drifting out. Shader could feel it on his legs as the warm air outside suppressed the cold garage-breeze. It felt like an icy breath was bathing his feet.

Shader stared even more intently into the darkness. He squeezed his eyes tightly, trying to pierce the black, curtain-like opening. It was futile.

Shader noticed for the first time that the tunnel's header was stained. Black, oily liquid had pooled in two spots, giving the opening a virtual pair of inky eyes.

"Shit," Gonzalez said as he made the sign of the cross. "This is all kinds of fucked up. Do you feel it, Chief?"

"Yeah, Gonzalez. I feel it. Now let's get moving. Standing here ain't getting the job done."

"Copy that."

Gonzalez began walking again, but with a great deal more caution. At the bottom, he gingerly stepped into the shadow of the garage and stopped at the threshold of light. He turned back and looked at the rest of the QRF.

"Fuck it," he mumbled. Then he brought his M4 up and strode into the inky black hole.

Shader followed quietly behind, about ten steps back. The darkness was abrupt and complete.

Shader flipped his NVGs down and pushed the "ON" button twice on his rifle-mounted laser, generating a continuous infrared, pencil-thin emerald beam. It was invisible to the naked eye and could only be seen through their night vision monoculars.

Ten yards ahead of him, Shader saw Gonzalez creeping forward, his head scanning quickly from side to side as he cautiously moved into the bowels of the massive garage.

Shader looked behind and saw that the last two men had entered the dark zone. He tapped the push-to-talk button on his neck mic and whispered. "Hold here. Let's get our bearings."

Their visibility disappeared about twenty yards away. The NVGs only intensified existing light, and the blackness of the underground garage was complete. Shader had no doubt that moving another fifty feet further meant even less light to intensify as they put more distance between them and the garage door.

Shader continued his assessment. The space was mostly empty with a smattering of abandoned vehicles. Nothing big enough to move military gear and supplies, rather more like golf carts or small electric flatbeds.

Shader had underestimated the size of the garage. It was massive.

"We have to clear this space first," Shader whispered. "Gonzalez, move left. You two take the other side."

Shader moved up to Gonzalez and put his left hand on the Marine's right shoulder while Lazzaro and Keele did likewise.

"Let's go," Shader said.

Deeper into the garage, the darkness began to thicken. Visibility through the NVGs was becoming a problem. With fewer photons to intensify, even the night vision goggles were having a problem creating an image.

"Turn on your intensifiers," Shader reluctantly ordered.

Their monoculars were equipped with an infrared flashlight. It would dramatically improve their field of vision, but it ate away at the NVG's battery life. With no more batteries being produced, Shader was hesitant to use them, but it was necessary.

Immediately, the garage was bathed in four infrared beams that turned the space into a green-hued stage. Emerald light danced on the surrounding surfaces, revealing a vast space filled with electric vehicles and a few civilian cars. They all needed to be checked out.

"Unless a car door is already open, don't worry about the inside. These things aren't supposed to be able to operate door handles," Shader whispered into his mic.

Shader tapped Gonzalez on the shoulder and pressed forward and to the left. Like leading a horse, he steered the young Marine to the first vehicle.

The process was tedious. Space was tight and the underside of each vehicle had to be checked along with everything around them.

"Chief!" Lazzaro hissed. "Over here."

Shader and Gonzalez stopped their progress and moved to the other two men. They were standing outside of a large Lexus.

"What is it?"

"Check it out," Keele said, pointing into the car.

Shader leaned close and stared into the driver's side window.

A man, his dead body disintegrating from the decay of time, lay back against the driver's seat. His head was canted back and mouth agape, staring at the ceiling. His forehead had a hole near the center. In his right hand was a revolver.

"Died of lead poisoning," Shader mumbled. "Hell of a way to go out. So, why'd you bring me here?"

"Check out the rear seat."

Shader moved to the back window and looked in. He jumped as a Variant, no more than a toddler, had its face smashed against the window, its eyes wide and sucker-like mouth attached to the glass. The creature's razor-like teeth were exposed, searching for its next meal.

Shader brought his suppressed rifle up and aimed, but the thing didn't move.

"It's dead," Lazzaro said quietly.

Shader stopped, willing his heart to slow down. He moved to the window and looked in again. The back of the infected child's head was gone, blown away by a single gunshot.

"Shit. He had to kill his own kid," Gonzalez whispered.

"That explains the suicide," Keele added.

The four men stood quietly for a moment before Shader began to move.

"Let's just get this done."

Fifteen minutes later, they cleared the left side of the garage and moved to the right. With fewer vehicles, they finished this area even more quickly. Finally, having taken nearly half an hour to make sure the front of the garage was safe, they were back moving toward the entrance to the Forum. The venue's double metal doors still lay a good hundred yards away, but most of the vehicles in this area were open-bedded electric carts, the kind that transported supplies along the walkways of an airport or, in this case, an entertainment venue.

The QRF continued their sweep of the area, rapidly approaching the entrance to the Forum.

"Hey, Chief, check out the car to the right of the doors," Keele whispered.

Shader looked through the monocular to where Keele was pointing his infrared laser. The green dot from Keele's battle rifle was bouncing around on the windshield of a passenger car parked a few yards from the building's entrance. Something was moving inside.

"Hold here," Shader whispered into his neck mic.

The SEAL slid forward, rifle up and laser pointing at the moving object. The infrared beam was invisible to anyone not wearing a monocular. To Shader and the other three men, it was a solid-green, pencil-thin line that he was painting on the shadowy apparition within the car.

It was a Variant. And it was very much alive. The creature was strapped into the car with a seatbelt that it hadn't figured out how to unfasten. The creature sensed Shader's presence. It let out a blood-curdling, high-pitched scream so alien and frightening, it froze the SEAL in place. Then it jammed its face against the driver's side window and attached its sucker-like lips to the glass.

Shader stood, transfixed at the horror. The Variant's tongue snapped around inside its mouth and onto the window, leaving a trail of thick, mucinous saliva tinged with dark speckles of some unknown calcification. Shader stepped back as the Variant detached itself from the glass and began thrashing to get out of its bindings. It reared its head back again and let out another primal cry.

This time, there was an answer from behind the double door entrance to the Forum. The giant entertainment venue could hold tens of thousands of people, and naval intelligence had assured them that there were no Variants inside of the structure.

Shader aimed his laser onto the rabid creature's head and pressed off three quiet shots. The driver's side window erupted as wisps of smoke trailed out of the end of his suppressor. Beyond the window, Shader saw what was left of the Variant's head. Only the attached mandible remained as the rest had exploded, splashing black-speckled goo across the other side of the car. Gonzalez ran forward and scanned the front window for signs of any more of the creatures. There were none.

Another scream came from behind the double metal doors. It was then followed by silence.

"Everyone, freeze. Defensive perimeter, now," Shader whispered.

The four men took position in a circle, each looking outward, scanning their piece of the pie. They stayed that way for over five minutes. Sweat dripped from each of their faces, collecting in small puddles on the concrete floor. Even though the underbelly of the Forum had started out feeling like a refrigerator, it now felt like the threshold to hell.

After five minutes, Shader gave the all clear and moved the men away from the double doors.

"Did you see that?" Gonzalez whispered.

"It had to have been strapped into that seat since the beginning," Keele added. "That was not a weak and dying Variant."

"Chief. You need to report this to the LT. These things ain't starving," Lazzaro said.

"I know," Shader said. "Nothing to eat in a month and it sure wasn't near death."

The implications of this intelligence fuck-up were enormous. If they could stay animated for weeks without food, then all the estimates of the Variant population were seriously flawed.

Shader switched his radio to pre-set channel one. "Red One, Red One. This is Blue One actual. Over."

Shader waited for a full thirty seconds. Nothing but static.

"Red One, this is Blue One. Do you copy? Over."

Again, nothing.

"Too much concrete between us," Shader mumbled.

Shader hesitated. The afternoon was passing by and the night was a few hours away. If he turned back now, just yards from the Forum, he'd never be allowed to return. After a few moments of deliberation, Shader decided he needed more information. They had to, at least, check out the building before reporting back. The lieutenant wouldn't accept a report about one Variant kicking up a storm in the front seat of an abandoned car. He needed more.

"All right," Shader said, "let's get this done. Let's clear the building."

"What about the one we just smoked?" Lazzaro asked.

"It'll still be just as dead in an hour. Let's finish what we started and get back before dark. We'll make our report then. Do you copy?"

Shader watched the three of them nod through his NV monocular.

"Jesus. Is that a solid copy?" he said forcefully, after no verbal response.

"Copy that," they finally replied.

Gonzalez took point, and they returned to the double metal doors.

Shader took a moment to search the grounds nearby and found a broken wooden palate. He cut one of the broken planks down to a wedge with his KA-BAR knife then ordered them forward.

Gonzalez stopped at the door and gently checked the opening lever. It depressed without a problem.

"Not locked," Gonzalez whispered.

Shader pointed at Keele, the last man in line. The corporal dropped his slung M4 to his side and moved up to the door. He grasped the handle and prepared to open it.

"Slow at first, Keele. I don't want any noise."

Shader gave him the wooden wedge and whispered. "You're the last man. Wedge this under the door after we're through."

Keele nodded, and Shader ignored his lack of verbal response. They were all on the edge.

Gonzalez positioned himself in front of the door and brought up his rifle.

"Ready, Gonzalez?" Shader whispered.

"Ready."

"Remember, slow and steady… Now."

The Marine gently drew the door back, only the faintest of sound coming from the well-oiled hinges.

About a third of the way open, Shader whispered. "Let's go. Move."

Keele brought the steel panel back and wedged it open. Gonzalez strode inside, then banked to his right. Shader, Lazzaro, and Keele quickly followed, each man taking a pre-determined path into the bowels of the Forum.

Moments later, they were staring at an empty hallway. The silence was oppressive. The air hung heavily around them, and the stench of rotting food or some other degenerating flesh was overwhelming. Lazzaro nearly retched from it.

They waited for several minutes. It helped them adjust to the stench and gave Shader a chance to listen for any sounds. He knew there was at least one more of these things in here, and he didn't want to accidentally stumble across it. No sense rushing things when winning a battle wasn't about speed but creating the best angles to gain the greatest advantage.

The hallway was wide, with a padded carpet that would let them move silently. That would help mask their movements.

Shader tapped Gonzalez on the shoulder, and the short Marine turned right and began to move. Heel-to-toe strides kept his rifle's barrel level and steady. He swept his view from side to side, scanning the space ahead.

To their right, the outer wall had recessed alcoves with Formica-covered counters about three feet off the ground. Each kiosk was about thirty feet wide. Many were permanent food vendors with idle refrigerators attached to the back wall. Cash registers anchored the left side of the counter. Still others were empty, likely used by the many performing acts to sell their merchandise. All the openings had to be addressed and cleared.

The four moved gradually, and about thirty minutes into their sweep, they had covered nearly a quarter of the circumference of the building.

In the distance, the sound of V-22s could be heard approaching the area. The noise Shader heard was not so much the high-pitched whine of the engines, but the thump of the craft's twin propellers. The *WHUMP, WHUMP, WHUMP* of the compressed air created by the giant blades sent out low frequency sonic waves that penetrated the walls of the large building. By the sound of the heavy shuddering, multiple Osprey were landing outside. The vibrations made the air around them shudder, and the squad stopped to wait for this to pass. Many minutes went by before the aircraft took flight, allowing the building to fall silent once again.

After resuming their mission, Gonzalez suddenly froze and held up a closed fist, stopping the rest of the fireteam.

"You hear that?" he whispered to Shader.

The SEAL bent his ear out, closed his eyes, and held his breath, searching for any sound he could find.

There! Something ahead and to the right, he said to himself.

"Heard it," Shader whispered.

"Sounds like it's coming from the head," Gonzalez said, pointing his laser at a restroom sign about thirty meters down the hallway.

"Agreed. Keep going and stop short of the opening."

Gonzalez crept forward, continuing his clearing ritual. Stop, look left, then slowly scan to the right. Quickly swing the rifle left again then look forward and take two strides, heel to toe. Then freeze and listen. After a few seconds, start the process all over again.

Twenty meters further, and the noise coming from the bathroom area was becoming louder. What had started out sounding like the faint scratching and squeaking of a rodent in the walls now became more distinct. Shader listened to the wheezing and grunting of what had to be a trapped or injured animal.

"I think we found our screamer," Shader whispered into his neck mic. "Lazzaro, you're on me."

Lazzaro moved up to Shader as Gonzalez and Keele set up overwatch, each taking opposite sides of the hallway.

"I'll go first," Shader said. "You break right. Weapons hot. Put this thing down before it can make a noise."

Both men stacked up at the bathroom's opening. Shader crept forward until he came to a ninety-degree bend to the left. The sounds became more pronounced. Whatever was on the other side of the turn was struggling mightily.

"Move," Shader whispered.

They turned the corner as a pair, and both men brought their weapons up and at eye level.

Urinals lined the left side of the space, with toilet stalls and sinks on the right. Movement at the end caught their attention. The shape in Shader's NVGs didn't make sense. It was a mass of flesh moving and churning against the wall. Shader hesitated, then took a step forward. He could see three, no four arms and more than two legs. Whatever it was, it needed to be put down.

Lazzaro, his hand still on Shader's shoulder, froze in place. While Shader struggled to understand the misshapen form writhing on the floor in front of them, Lazzaro knew immediately what it was.

"Oh, fuck no!" Lazzaro said as he put the green IR laser dot onto the creature's head. Before Shader could respond to the corporal's sudden movement, Lazzaro's rifle spat out five bullets. Seeing the young Marine move and kill so quickly surprised the SEAL. He watched as Lazzaro walked up to the mass and sent three more lead pills into the pile of infected tissue.

"What the hell?" Shader hissed.

Lazzaro just stood, dumbfounded. The Marine turned back to face the SEAL and took two unsteady steps before lunging into a stall and dumping his lunch. Lazzaro puked with such force that he made more noise than the suppressed shots he'd just taken.

Shader moved behind the man and waited for the nausea to subside.

"You squared away?" Shader asked after a half a minute of retching.

"Yeah," Lazzaro mumbled as he continued to hover over the porcelain bowl. "That was just wrong."

Shader turned and took another look at the creature Lazzaro had just killed. Staring at the pile of infected tissue, forms and outlines began to take shape.

It was then that Shader realized the futility of Operation Liberty. Humanity was not going to survive simply by waiting for the eventual starvation of its infected brethren anymore. There wasn't going to be a mass die-off. The future of the Variants wasn't just spreading disease to non-infected humans because what Shader saw told the SEAL that they were truly and utterly fucked.

It was a pair of very healthy-looking Variants, and they had been mating.

"Jesus help us," Shader said, staring at the dead eyes of a female Variant that looked very strong, and more than capable of bearing offspring.

"Chief," Gonzalez's voice crackled over the team headsets. "We've got movement out here."

"Be right there."

"You'd better hurry. We've got a lot of noise coming our way."

Shader grabbed the back of Lazzaro's chest rig and pulled him from the stall, dragging him along until they were out in the hallway.

Once out of the confines of the public bathroom, he could hear multiple grunts and chirps coming from the Forum's main floor. Across the walkway from them was an open tunnel with stairs that led into the venue's arena. The noises were coming from there.

"Holy shit. We woke the dead," Shader grunted.

"I don't know," Gonzalez whispered. "You didn't make that much noise."

"Whatever stirred the pot, I don't want to be here when those things come squirting out," Keele said in a panicked voice.

Movement from their left froze the team. Several Variants lumbered out of a tunnel at the bend of the circular walkway. Fortunately, they turned away from the team and quickly disappeared. Unfortunately, they were moving toward the entrance to the underground garage. Their way back had just been compromised.

"This just gets better and better," Shader said. "Let's keep moving and find a place to hole up. Keep your eyes open for something to the right, and we better do it now."

Gonzalez began to practically fly down the hallway. The sound of restless Variants was becoming more and more pronounced as they passed several more tunnels that led to the main floor.

"Up ahead. Take a right," Shader said.

A large hallway opened, and the team glided swiftly down it, leaving the main concourse behind.

It quickly became clear that they had entered a service tunnel. Heavy-gauge electric conduits ran along the seam where the ceiling and walls met. Doors with placards that marked the offices of various venue departments were all closed and locked. Every knob or lever was checked as they scurried away from the expanding cacophony of screeches and grunts that were coming from behind them.

The end of the tunnel approached, and Shader turned back toward the concourse. He saw movement. In the pitch darkness, he could only make out shadows as the creatures spilled out of the tunnels that led to the venue's main floor. He lost count, as the Variants became so numerous that they appeared as one massive organism in his NVG monocular. Even the infrared flashlight couldn't give him a clear image.

The team kept moving away from the growing threat, checking the locks on each door they passed. None were open.

The end of the hallway rapidly approached. It was a service elevator. Its oversized metal doors stood silent as the men drew near. With no electricity, the lift would prove as impenetrable as the locked office doors that lined the hallway.

"Shader. To the left," Gonzalez whispered into his neck microphone.

Shader turned to see the little Marine disappear down a side passage that almost magically appeared at the end of the tunnel. Porky rushed ahead and cut around the bend just as several Variants began to probe down the service hallway. He didn't know whether it was the sound of the Marines' movement or the smell of their sweat that got the creatures' attention, but something triggered this group to turn in the team's direction.

Shader looked down the short dead end and saw his men checking the knobs of three more rooms. Just like the rest of the hallway doors, they were locked. There was nowhere left for them to go.

Shader dropped to his knees and bent his head around the corner, looking back toward the concourse. Three Variants, two males and a female, were moving their way. The creatures' yellow eyes lit up in the infrared beam as they crept toward him and his men.

If the Variants kept their pace, they'd be on the team in just a few more seconds. He could only hope that their suppressed shots would silently put the creatures down. But if they failed to take these three out quietly, it would be Custer and the Alamo, all rolled up into one glorious last stand.

"Gonzalez and Keele, set up a firing line. Lazzaro, start working on that lock," Shader said, pointing at the last door down.

The men quickly responded, and Shader stood behind the two Marines who had taken a kneeling position while Lazzaro began to work the lock just behind them.

"They can't see us in the dark," Shader whispered. "Hold your fire until I set it off."

The sounds from the three Variants were quickly becoming louder as each doorway they'd passed was bumped into or slapped as the creatures moved closer to them.

Shader could hear Lazzaro quietly cursing as he fumbled with his lock pick set and started sliding the metal rasp back and forth in the keyhole.

"Make it fast, Lazzaro," Shader said quietly as a Variant threw itself against a door just around the corner.

"Fuck, Shader," he replied loudly. "It's not like I'm playing with myself here."

Shader was about to dress down the Marine for being so loud, but the sound of a chirp and grunt from the hallway grabbed the team's attention.

The creatures had heard Lazzaro's voice. Not that it would have made a big difference in the grand scheme of things. The infected would have gotten to them anyway. The three Variants exploded forward, sprinting around the corner and right into the hail of bullets from two terrified Marines and one startled SEAL. They dropped instantly as multiple rounds tore into their diseased flesh as well as the wall behind them. The bullets hit the concrete block, creating miniature explosions that sounded like a hammer smashing brick. Small sparks erupted as the lead hit the hard, cement surface. The combination of sound and light was the last thing the team needed, and within seconds, the combined noise of an inestimable number of Variants came from down the hall. Hundreds of screams reached the four men. The fireteam had been found and there was no way out.

Shader knew instantly that they were screwed, but maybe they could buy enough time to get inside one of the doors.

"Follow me!" Shader barked loudly. "Lazzaro. Keep working on that door!"

The time for stealth had passed. Shader grabbed Gonzalez by his webbing and flung him ahead.

"FIRING LINE. NOW!" Shader yelled as he stood next to the small Marine.

Keele, Shader, and Gonzalez formed a line facing back to the main concourse.

"Kill those bastards!" Shader yelled.

Three M4s began firing at a very angry and hungry-looking pack of Variants. The creatures pushed and shoved each other, their tongues flicking and slapping about as they rushed toward them.

Shader grabbed a grenade from his webbing.

"FRAG OUT!" he called, as he tossed it in front of the advancing horde.

The three men turned and crouched as the hallway erupted about twenty yards away.

WHUMP!

A muted flash followed by a small cloud of smoke hung down the hall where the M67 fragmentary grenade erupted, sending shards of metal into the advancing creatures. Several high-pitched "*zings*" sung in the air as multiple chunks of metal flew past the team.

The pause was only momentary, as those behind the wounded Variants pressed forward, crawling over the pile of bodies the team had put down.

"Frag out!" Keele yelled, sending another green, metal ball down the hallway.

Another explosion rocked the building, creating an even higher pile of bodies.

"Lazzaro! Tell me you're through the door," Shader barked.

"Fuck, I can't get it."

"Get up here! I'll do it," Shader yelled.

Lazzaro sprinted to the hallway and stared down at the carnage.

"Jesus Christ! They can climb the fucking walls!" Lazzaro yelled as a couple of Variants had taken to the ceiling.

Shader watched the pile of bodies slow down the mass, but now they were climbing the walls like crazed insects.

"Keep shooting! I've got this!" Shader yelled as he ran back to the last door in the hall.

Shader cursed himself for not picking the lock to begin with. Breaching barriers was standard training for a SEAL, not a Marine. But Lazzaro had claimed to know this skill. Obviously, not a trick he'd practiced under stress.

The sound of battle raged, each man taking shots one at a time to preserve ammunition and to be as precise as possible. They needed to sever the spine or hit them in the brain box to be effective. As long as Porky heard semi-automatic fire, he knew he still had time.

Shader took his tension wrench and shoved it into the lock, then began to work the tumblers with one of the set's hooks.

Ten seconds passed, then twenty, before he felt the tumblers drop.

Shader triumphantly twisted the knob and was

rewarded with a full turn.

"Got it!" he yelled as he pulled the door open. Or at least he tried.

The door didn't move. It was bolted from the inside.

Just then, automatic fire began. They had run out of time. The Marines wouldn't be spraying unless the Variants got within ten yards.

Shader cursed loudly, then brought up his M4 to his shoulder and placed the green laser onto the advancing horde.

"Rally on me!" he yelled, and all three glanced at him. Their shoulders slumped when they saw the closed door.

The three men turned and began to run down the hall toward Shader.

"FRAG OUT!" Lazzaro barked as he threw his grenade forward before sprinting toward the SEAL.

Shader raised his rifle and spat out several rounds, hitting a Variant that was crawling around the corner on the wall over six feet above them. His bullets struck the creature in the neck, sending it to the ground screaming, but paralyzed.

Shader knew they were done. He'd gone through six of his nine magazines and not even put a dent into the oncoming creatures.

"Make 'em count," Shader said as he raised his rifle for one last fight.

"I wish I could blast that bastard lieutenant just one time," Shader said quietly. "Nothing in the building, huh? That son of a bi—"

Shader felt himself being grabbed from behind and flung back. He dropped his battle rifle and instinctively reached behind him to cushion his fall, but there was nothing but air. He landed on his back and hit his head with a heavy thud. If it wasn't for his helmet, he'd have been knocked out.

Shader reached for his sidearm and whipped it out, his head still ringing from his collision with the floor. He saw a shadow in the doorway he'd just been pulled through. The sound of automatic fire from outside the room shook the air around him.

Shader jumped up just as Gonzalez was thrown next to him. Shader realigned his NVG, which had retracted up on its cantilever hinge when he'd been thrown back. The eyepiece came to life.

Keele sprinted into the room just as another grenade erupted outside. A painful cry came through the open door. The shadow disappeared and came back, dragging a struggling Lazzaro with it, leaving a thin smear of blood on the concrete floor.

The shadow slammed the door closed just as a mob of infected flesh crashed into its steel frame. Then the apparition turned toward the fireteam. It was a normal, uninfected man.

Their savior dropped a metal bar down in place. With an outside swing to the door, there was no way for the creatures to force their way in.

"Who are you?" Shader asked.

"Don't worry about me. You better take care of your man."

Shader saw a small pool of blood forming next to Lazzaro, who was sitting on the floor a few feet away.

"Flashlight!" Shader said, and the four men lifted their monoculars off their eyes, shutting down the NVG. If they exposed the intensifier tube to normal light, it would burn the monocular out, rendering the device useless.

"We all clear?" Shader asked.

"Aye," they replied, including Lazzaro.

"Let's have a look at that," Shader said.

Lazzaro had taken shrapnel to his leg.

Shader produced a folding blade and cut Lazzaro's BDU. He spread the slit open and gently wiped the wound. It bled freely but didn't pulsate. No arterial tears. That was good.

The wound was a four-inch gash, just above the knee and was about an inch deep. Muscle spread easily as he flexed the man's leg. They'd have to splint his knee to keep the wound from re-opening once Shader had sutured it closed.

"He gonna be all right?" Keele asked loudly.

"You have to be quiet," the shadowy man said. "They won't stop if they hear you."

The screams and pounding were deafening as Shader pulled an IFAK off of his web gear. He had learned to carry a basic suture set-up and although he wasn't a squad medic, he was trained in advanced first-aid. Going behind enemy lines, like the SEALs were oft to do, meant they had to be their own doctor.

"Embrace the suck, Lazzaro. This is going to hurt."

Lazzaro pressed his lips together and nodded.

Five minutes later, the pounding diminished slightly, and Lazzaro was sutured and bandaged, with an improvised splint in place. It was only then Shader had a chance to shine his SureFire flashlight around the space.

They were in a large utility room with HVAC air returns and compressors anchored to the floor. Duct work snaked in and out of the walls, while the back of the room had an open doorway with a dim, flickering light spilling out of the other side.

"Come on," Shader commanded.

Keele and Gonzalez bracketed Lazzaro and helped him move. The four men hobbled to the door and stepped in. They stopped and stood in silence as they came face-to-face with the man who had saved them.

"My name is Alejandro Morales. I am supervisor of maintenance for the Forum," he said. "And these people," he added, "are the rest of the survivors."

The room was lit by several makeshift candles. People were huddled against the far wall. Shader counted over a dozen. Many were frightened and weak-looking, their faces gaunt and their eyes sunken into their sockets.

"How many?" Shader asked, after introducing himself and the men to Morales.

"Fourteen, including me."

"You've been here how long?"

"Since the beginning. Most of us were Forum employees when the infection started. I brought as many as I could in here."

"Find a place for Lazzaro," Shader said to his Marines.

Gonzalez and Keele moved to the left and put the wounded man on an empty metal table.

"Do you have any food?" a weak voice croaked from the group.

"Not much," Shader replied. "Just a few snacks. We weren't supposed to be here very long."

"The little girl could use something," Morales added. "She's awful weak."

Shader dug out an energy bar and handed it to Morales. He walked over to the crowd and picked up a frail girl who had been sitting against the wall. He placed her in a nearby chair and broke off a small piece and gave it to her. Her eyes were vacant, and she barely moved her lips. Eventually, she managed to chew and swallow the piece of peanut butter bar. She washed it down with some water. Her eyes began to respond, and she took another piece, chewing it more aggressively than the first.

"We've been without food for a couple of weeks. We've eaten everything we could scavenge, now all we have left is a bunch of vegetable shortening. That and some newspaper make good candles, but we haven't been able to eat it. Every time we try, most of us just puke it out. Then we're weaker than before."

The others began to ask for food, and Shader distributed all of their edibles. From their appearance, they didn't have much longer to live. Many could barely move unless some of the stronger ones helped.

"You've done well," Shader said to Morales as they gave out the last of the food. Shader noticed he hadn't eaten any of their meager supplies.

"I used to be fat," he replied with a smile, pointing at his sagging pants.

"That's a hell of a way to lose weight," Shader added.

Morales broke the last bar in half and gave it away.

"Can we speak?" he asked as he nodded to the other side of the room.

"Are you four the only ones?" he asked Shader after they had crossed the room.

"No. We have a full platoon of Marines forming outside."

"Are they here to rescue us?" he asked incredulously.

"I hate to break this to you, but no one has a clue

there is anyone alive in here."

Shader gave the man a quick summary of their predicament. Morales just bowed his head and shook it back and forth.

"This place is crawling with the infected," Morales said. "Many of them have been using this place as a home for weeks. That's why we couldn't leave. Then, when the bombing started, the place filled up even more."

"How many are here now?"

"I don't know. Hundreds. Maybe thousands. They just kept coming in. I haven't taken a look in days."

"You go out there?" Shader asked incredulously.

"Sí. I used to have a flashlight to see where I was going, but that died a few days ago, right after the explosions started outside. We were sure that the building was going to drop down on us, but the bombs never came."

"You didn't just walk around, shining the flashlight?" Shader asked.

Morales began to chuckle, his droopy facial skin jiggling from the laughter. "No. I suppose not," he replied sarcastically. "I didn't walk out onto the concourse and shine the light around. I used the ducts." Morales pointed back to the utility room where they had first entered.

"Ducts? They're big enough to crawl through?"

"Some of them, yes. The main return is huge and runs under the Forum. It's wide and tall enough to squat and walk through. It will take you to the main floor. At least four of the branches off of it can be navigated as well, but you have to crawl through those. That's how we rescued the little girl."

"Rescued her?"

"Yeah," Morales replied with a grim frown. "Rescued. It's horrible. You can't imagine what these things do to the people they catch."

"What do you mean, 'catch.' Don't they just eat them?"

"Oh, yes. They do. But some people, they don't eat right away."

Morales stopped and caught his breath.

"You don't understand, Shader. Sometimes, they bring them back here alive. They keep them like cattle until they're hungry, then they feast on them."

Shader couldn't comprehend that. Having a human farm inside the Forum couldn't be possible. How could they manage a farm? They weren't supposed to have the intelligence to do something like that.

"I don't get it. How do they keep the people they catch from escaping?"

"They glue them to the walls," Morales whispered. "They vomit out some kind of sticky, crusty paste that hardens and keeps people stuck to the walls or floor. Then they just grab who they want, when they want, and eat them."

Shader couldn't believe what he was hearing. If true, it meant there were groups of Variants clustered throughout the city.

"The storm drains," Shader said quietly after several moments of silent thought. "There must be nests all over the city's storm drains."

"No doubt," Morales replied. "They love the dark. I thought about the same thing. The drains could hold hundreds of thousands of these things."

"Do any of the ducts lead outside?" Shader asked.

"None of the returns do. They're all from the main floor and smaller ones are from the concourse. The only thing that goes to the outside are electric runs. And most of those are too small to get through."

"You said most of them. Are there any that someone could navigate?"

"I never gave it much thought because I'm too big to even try," Morales said as he pulled at the extra fabric on his now too large shirt. His weight loss had been staggering.

The big man stood silently in thought, mentally walking himself through the schematics of the building's arteries and ductwork.

"There is one conduit," he said tentatively. "But no one much bigger than a child could get through. It goes to the garage and ends next to a large panel on the wall near the service entrance. But it's a real narrow tube. I wouldn't want to try it."

Shader looked back at his men and nodded in their direction. "What about Gonzalez?"

Morales looked him over and shook his head. "The short one? He's too wide."

"Gonzalez. Come over here," Shader commanded.

The diminutive Marine jogged to Shader and reported.

"Strip off your gear. Nothing but pants and t-shirt," Shader said.

"Chief?"

"Just do it."

Gonzalez shrugged and removed his loadout. By the time he'd put the gear on an adjacent table, he was nearly fifty pounds lighter and showing off his wiry body.

"Hell, I didn't realize how much stuff you guys carried around," Morales said.

"You've no idea," Shader replied. "Sometimes, we're humping over a hundred pounds."

Morales looked Gonzalez up and down then walked around the confused Marine.

"It would be very tight. I don't know, but it's possible he could make it."

"Possible is good enough for me," Shader said. "Let's do this."

"Do what, Chief?"

Shader had an idea. It was the first time since they entered that God forsaken underground garage that he felt somewhat in control.

"Okay," Shader said with a smile. "Here's the plan…"

$$— 7 —$$

Underground Ducts
The Inglewood Forum
SCPO Porky Shader

"If you're going through hell, keep going."
WINSTON CHURCHILL

Shader's quads were burning. The Forum's main return duct was large enough for a man to squat and walk through without hitting his head. But Porky was on the downslope to the big five-oh, and his legs were letting him know that he was playing a young man's game in an old man's body.

Duck-walking his way through the tunnel required several stops where the SEAL would stretch and shake his legs, trying to get the building lactic acid in the muscles to move on through his bloodstream. In years gone by, recovery time from any physical exertion took mere moments. Now, he had to wait almost a minute to prevent leg cramps from disabling him.

Morales had estimated it was about a hundred yards before he'd hit a turnoff in the duct. Shader could have sworn he had to have passed it by now, but his NV monocular was working, and the IR flashlight shone brightly. Regardless of how it felt, he still hadn't made it to the branch off.

The sounds of the Variants were becoming more distinct with each passing stride. Shader knew how to count steps. Every SF operator had a set of Ranger beads they could use to estimate distances, but that didn't work when you were squatting and walking rather than taking normal paces.

Shader wanted to curse, but he couldn't afford the noise. So, he did what he had been trained to do; he pushed on.

Twenty more steps ahead and the branch off came into view. The duct sloped upward at a slight angle but not so bad that the SEAL couldn't get traction and continue. This was the way Morales had come when he had rescued the young girl. The tunnel would take him up to a higher level, where he could get a better view of the main floor.

By Shader's estimate, he still had an hour before dusk. Morales told him about several holes in the roof where bomb fragments had penetrated the dome. It allowed the sun into the building, and Shader wanted to get a look before he lost what light there was.

As expected, the return duct began to narrow, forcing Shader to crawl on his knees. Up ahead and to his left was the heavy metal grate that sat halfway up the Forum's stadium seating. The same one that Morales had quietly unbolted to get to the entrapped little girl.

Shader slowed down and caught his breath. Stealth was his friend, and he needed to be under control. After thirty seconds, he slid quietly to the grate and gazed out.

The light was minimal, but it gave his intensifiers plenty to work with.

There were literally thousands them. The main floor was packed with Variants, many standing and swaying like they were in a trance. Some moved around, almost acting like sentries. The seating area was mostly filled as well, with the creatures clustered in groups of varying numbers. Each small faction seemed to have a leader that was treated almost like a rock star. Some of their clan groomed the chosen one, while others stayed on the perimeter and stood watch.

Shader took his eyes off of the Variants and scanned the walls. Dozens and dozens of cocoon-like patches clung to just about any open space you could find. Some were broken open with pieces of crystalized glue sitting under the open cavity. Others were full. It was these that Shader had the most difficult time with. He could see that people were encased by the crusty secretion. Most of the humans looked dead or unconscious, with their heads exposed and the rest of their bodies trapped in the hardened slime. Some weren't so fortunate. Moans and the occasional whimper drifted into the grate. It took all of Shader's will power to not tear open the metal cover and begin shooting every Variant he saw.

After steeling himself, he began to count, estimating the enemy's numbers.

Almost six thousand Variants! And that didn't include the ones that were still at the utility room door.

Shader was about to turn and leave, when he noticed the monsters becoming restless. A high-pitched whine could be heard from outside. The creatures began to huddle together, their chirping and barking transforming into a low-pitched growl.

It was incoming ordinance. One or more of the destroyers were sending shells into the city, with the explosions landing a short distance away. The Variants looked skyward, staring out of the cracks and holes left by the prior bombardment. A few minutes later, F-18 Hornets shrieked overhead, their supersonic boom rattling the rafters of the building. The rumble of several more explosions shook the floor, eliciting panicked grunts from the assembled creatures.

Shader had to respect these things. With many days of death raining down around them, they'd learned to hide from the bombing runs of the Navy jets. That explained why they hadn't left the building with the Marines right outside. It wasn't fun being at the working end of an artillery barrage, and they'd adapted to that reality.

Shader turned and silently slid down the duct and made his way back to the utility room. The entrance to the duct was on the floor of the utility room, and Morales helped him crawl up and out of the access opening. The maintenance chief then dropped a metal hatch down and locked it in place. Then they rolled a golf cart on top it to keep any Variants from following.

"Where's Gonzalez?" Shader asked, as he brushed off the dust and hairballs that were clinging to his clothing.

"Coming, Chief," Gonzalez said as he scampered from the back room. "Hey, you look like a feather duster," he added while watching Shader picking debris out of his tight beard.

"I'm going to enjoy this. You think I'm covered in crap? Just wait," Shader replied as he finished grooming himself. "Have you memorized the schematics?"

"Aye. It's not too hard. Just one turn. But Shader, I don't think I'll be able to get through the choke point. It's damn tight."

"That's why we're coating you with shortening."

"Say what?"

63

"You heard me. You're going in with nothing but skivvies and a pistol. We're going to paint your ass with as much shortening as we can."

"Fuck, Shader. You ain't kidding."

"No, I'm not. Now let's get going. It's almost dark, and I don't want you taken out by friendly fire because your jarhead brothers think they saw a ghost."

— 8 —

Van Ness Avenue
South of FOB Hawthorne
Lieutenant Tyrell Jack

"If you can fill the unforgiving minute
With sixty seconds' worth of distance run,
Yours is the Earth and everything that's in it,
And – which is more – you'll be a man, my son!"
RUDYARD KIPLING
"If: A Father's Advice to His Son"

The point vehicle ripped off a burst from its mounted Ma Deuce. The fifty-caliber machine gun tore through yet another Variant that had sprinted at them from one of the houses they were passing.

Sergeant Braddock gripped the wheel of the HUMVEE he was driving as the fuel hauler to his front bounced over the freshly killed creature, sending pieces of rendered flesh flying to the curb.

"Nice," Lieutenant Tyrell Jack said. "Like having a snowplow clear the way for us."

"I'd feel better if we didn't need to clear the road," Braddock replied. "We're not even halfway to the airport, and that's the ninth Variant we've taken out."

"Yeah. I noticed," Lt. Jack said, staring out the window. "Not as quiet as I would have thought."

Braddock saw that they were, appropriately enough, approaching Marine Avenue. That was the road where their sniper had taken out a half dozen Variants. It was also the avenue that went to the local hospital.

"What's up?" Lt. Jack asked as Braddock pulled out of the convoy.

"I want to put eyes up the road, make sure we don't have any Tangos coming our way."

The vehicle behind them began to slow down, but Braddock jumped out of the driver's side and waved him on. The sergeant jumped up onto the back of their HUMVEE and stood on the roof. Bringing his binoculars up, he looked east.

The street was lined with older single-story businesses and strip malls. The road was void of vehicles, but in the distance, Braddock could just make out the outline of the community hospital. Everything was clear, other than a shimmering mass out in front of the building.

"Hey sir, take a look at this."

Jack stepped onto the back of the vehicle and glassed to the east. Both Marines stared at the distant building. There was something peculiar about it that neither could quite grasp.

"Able One, this is Panther Thirty," Corporal Franks, their designated marksman said over their squad radio. "I've got Ladder Three on their squad radio."

Whoever had programed their handhelds had screwed up with the main battle net frequency. But as the convoy approached the airport, they were able to get FOB Hawthorne on their local channel.

"This is Able One actual," Jack replied. "What's your pause?"

"We just rolled past 135th Street, coming up on Rowley Park."

"Any activity around you?"

"Negative, Able One."

"Wait one. I may need you to relay messages for me."

"Solid copy that, Able One. Over," Franks replied as he pulled his MRAP off to the side of the road to await further orders.

The lieutenant turned to SSgt. Braddock and continued. "I don't like what I'm seeing down there. I want to put eyes on that hospital."

Braddock nodded his approval. "Good idea, sir. Maybe Panther Thirty can relay our situation and we can get a drone to take a look."

The rest of the vehicles finished passing them by, and soon the convoy became a low-pitched rumble in the distance.

"Shit, Sergeant. Take a look!"

Braddock glassed east once again. The blurry image that had been clustered near the hospital suddenly became clear.

"Holy mother of God," Braddock whispered. "It looks like the whole city is out there."

"Yeah… and they're coming our way," Jack said. The lieutenant jumped down, grabbed his map from the front seat, and laid it down on the hood of the HUMVEE.

"Panther Thirty, this is Able One actual. Do you copy? Over."

"Send your traffic, Able One. Over."

"Adjust fire. Over."

"Solid copy, Able One. Adjust fire."

The coms went to static as Franks switched frequencies. He had to alert Hawthorne to contact fleet. Hawthorne would, in turn, call in an artillery strike from the battle group. There were several people relaying information, and Jack would have to take that delay into account. It took some time to coordinate it all.

"How are we doing, Sergeant?"

"Not good. Those things can really move."

Jack looked again through his binoculars and was shocked at the speed of the Variants. Hundreds of them were sprinting down the road, directly at the two Marines.

Braddock raised his pistol and let off several shots.

"What was that for?"

"I saw some of them branching off. We need to keep them from splitting away from the group."

Jack nodded. The sergeant's plan was working, but he didn't like the idea of being the bait for a throng of hungry Variants.

"Able One, this is Panther Thirty. Ready for coordinates."

"Panther Thirty, Grid 134235, altitude zero-five-zero, direction 8774 mils. Over."

"Solid copy, Able One. Adjust fire at grid 134235, altitude zero-five-zero, direction 8874 mils."

Several seconds passed. Jack had anticipated the delay and called a single strike a hundred meters west of the mob. Hopefully, he led them properly.

The whine of an incoming round whistled through the air. The explosion was just short of the advancing creatures and almost fifty meters behind them.

"Panther Thirty. Left two hundred mikes, add fifty mikes. Enemy in the open. VT in effect. Fire for effect."

"Copy that, Able One. Left two hundred, add fifty, VT in effect. Fire for effect."

Ten seconds later, it began. VT, or variable timing,

meant that the warheads would explode above the target, sending shrapnel into the enemy. Round after round erupted just overhead of the advancing horde. With the five-inch shells falling every five seconds, the results were devastating. Several minutes of constant bombardment left each and every creature ripped apart. Nothing moved when the smoke finally drifted away.

Braddock look on with satisfaction. The lieutenant may be green, but he called a perfect artillery strike. He couldn't have done better himself.

"Well, LT, looks like we stirred up a hornet's nest."

"That we did. Now let's get to the FOB and get the party started."

"Aye aye," Braddock replied.

— 9 —

FOB Forum
Sergeant Paul E. Russ

"If ignorant both of your enemy and yourself,
you are certain to be in peril."
SUN TZU
The Art of War

The setting sun was just beginning to touch the surrounding buildings. The QRF had been gone most of the afternoon, and there had been no radio contact with Shader since he and his men had entered the underground garage.

When he reminded the lieutenant of the quick reaction force's absence, the man didn't seem to care one way or another.

"He's probably lost," the LT said dismissively before Landry turned his attention back to the rifle company's commanding officer.

Over the last few hours, over a hundred more Marines had been inserted, bringing the Forum FOB up to rifle company strength. There was now a captain in charge as well as five lieutenants commanding their respective platoons. With four other officers vying for the captain's attention, Landry was now busy sucking up to his CO. He couldn't be bothered by the temporary absence of one of his squad leaders, especially one that wasn't even a Marine.

On the positive side of it all, as long as Landry was busy shoving his nose up the captain's ass, he was staying away from the rest of his men. That allowed Russ to run his squad properly.

But the absence of the QRF weighed heavily on Russ's mind. He'd been monitoring the squad channel, even wandering over to the mouth of the service ramp and occasionally transmitting Shader's call sign. He'd stopped doing that about an hour ago when the lieutenant dressed him down over the open channel. Every grunt and officer in the company heard the verbal beating.

"Green One is a big boy. He can take care of himself. Now, clear the channel," Lieutenant Landry barked.

Russ was furious. The kid had a hard-on and didn't listen to a thing his NCOs told him. The two staff sergeants and SEAL who were directly under him had over fifty years of combined experience. The LT had zero. Maybe the brass on his collar made his brain malfunction.

"Fuck him," Russ said under his breath. "I'm doing what's right."

Russ had repositioned one of the fireteams close to the ramp in case Shader needed help. Even more frustrating was that Landry was clueless about how to set up a defensive fighting position. Russ wasn't going to let the young LT screw up their lanes of fire because he wanted the defensive positions looking symmetric on a map.

Russ checked his men, making sure they stayed hydrated and alert. He casually strolled over to the ramp and stared into the black abyss, shuddering at the thought that four of their own had voluntarily entered that nightmare.

SSgt. Russ pulled out his tin of Skoal and took a healthy pinch, placing it in the fold of his cheek next to his remaining left lower molar. The nicotine rush hit him instantly, calming his nerves. He'd sure miss the tobacco when he ran out.

POP! Russ heard from the tunnel.

It was an M9. The Marine sidearm's sound was so familiar that he dreamed about it during his many restless nightmares.

Russ brought his M4 up and began to tactically walk down the ramp. He switched his mounted flashlight on and pressed his PTT button.

"Red One, this is Blue One actual. Contact in the garage." Russ ignored the lack of reply from his lieutenant and could only hope that the rest of the company had been alerted. Instead, he ran into the inky darkness.

POP! POP! POP!

The blasts from the handgun exploded from the far end of the garage, but Russ's flashlight couldn't penetrate the distance. Without NVGs, his world was limited to the reach of his rail-mounted flashlight. He fast-walked toward the bursts of light. Gone were his fears of the unknown. Variants be damned, at least one of his brothers was in trouble.

The size of the space was unexpected, and the sergeant became disoriented as he moved past several vehicles and concrete support pillars. After a frantic minute, Russ stopped his forward motion, realizing he had pushed himself too quickly. He turned to try to find the ramp but was met with only blackness. How had he lost the light? He began to feel panic welling up within.

A sound broke the stillness. The padding of bare feet slapping on concrete.

"Fuck me sideways!" Russ hissed.

With less than a hundred feet of visibility, he began to spin, shining his light around in search of the creature bearing down on him.

A flash of white briefly popped into view, and Russ let off a burst at the apparition.

"FRIENDLY! FRIENDLY!" came a scream from the blackness.

"Identify yourself!" Russ shouted, aiming through his ACOG.

"Blue Two, Blue Two! It's Gonzales!"

Russ dropped his rifle to low ready and stared into the dark. After ten seconds, he shouted out.

"God damn it, Gonzalez. Get your ass out here."

Russ saw movement from behind a pillar, but instead of seeing a Marine in full battle rattle striding up to him, he watched in amazement as a white ghost appeared.

"What the fuck!" Russ yelled as he brought his rifle up and drew down on the young Marine.

"Stop!" Gonzalez said as he continued to walk forward, hands raised. "It's me."

The kid had stripped down to his underwear and was coated in something white and pasty.

"Where is your gear and what the hell is that shit on you?" Russ said.

Gonzalez, holding an M9 and wearing nothing but his skivvies and an NVG on his head, stepped up and held his arms out as if saying *Look at me!*

"It was Shader's idea, but he was right about the Crisco."

"Tell me about it later," Russ said. "I heard four shots. Any more of those things I need to worry about?" Russ asked.

"You've got no idea, Sarge," Gonzalez replied. "I need to report to the LT."

"We've got a captain now. We're saved," Russ deadpanned. "Just answer me, are there any more in this garage?"

"No, Sarge, but we better move. I blocked the door with a delivery car. It should hold, but there's a shitload of those things in the Forum."

"How many?"

"Too many," Gonzalez replied. He flipped his monocular over his left eye and turned to their right. "This way to the ramp, Sarge."

Russ shook his head and followed the young Marine. He'd never have thought he'd gone in the direction he had. Without the night vision monocular, Russ decided he'd likely have died of starvation before finding his way out of that damned crypt.

— 10 —

Captain Virgil Kane
11ᵗʰ Marine Expeditionary Unit (MEU)
Commander, FOB Forum

"Therefore the clever combatant imposes his will on the enemy
but does not allow the enemy's will to be imposed on him."
SUN TZU
The Art of War

The night was close at hand. The sky was turning a greenish-purple color as the final rays of the sun beamed through the Pacific Ocean, creating a prismatic display in the sky. But with the Variants preferring the night, there was no time to enjoy the show. Because there was so little time before dark, Gonzalez immediately reported to the captain. Covered in white vegetable shortening, he made a dramatic impression.

"That's quite a story," Lieutenant Landry said. "I find it hard to believe that Chief Shader counted over six thousand Variants inside the Forum."

"Sir, I can only speak to what Chief told me. He crawled through the vents and did a headcount inside the auditorium. I can personally attest to many hundreds in the concourse area."

"Intel has been clear that the Forum was clear of Variants," Landry countered.

"Excuse me, Lieutenant," Captain Kane said. "I am curious why you'd doubt your own men, especially your squad commanders?"

"Sir, I'm just going on what N2 told us. They're assessment is…"

"I'm quite aware of intel's assessment," Kane interrupted. "But let me clue you in on something, Lieutenant Landry. Intel isn't here, we are. If your men tell you something, especially an old salt like one of your squad leaders, I'd expect you to believe them."

Kane turned back to Gonzalez. "Well done, Corporal. Report back to your men. Staff Sergeant Russ will be in charge of your fireteams until we get Chief Shader and the rest of them out of there."

Russ gave the diminutive man a nod, then they both saluted before leaving the officers.

"Grab your ruck and have "Bones" check you out. I assume you have spare BDUs in your sack."

"Aye, Sarge. But I left 'Roxanne' back with my team. I just need to dig up another rifle and loadout."

"You call your rifle Roxanne, huh?" Russ chuckled.

"Yeah, like the song."

Russ gave the man a quizzical look.

"You know, Sarge. The lyrics. 'I loved you since I knew you, I won't share you with another boy.'"

"Huh. That actually makes some sense," Russ replied. "Now get moving. We're going to need every rifle tonight."

"Copy that, Sarge."

— 11 —

The Battle of the Forum
Inglewood, California

"Big things have small beginnings."
THOMAS EDWARD LAWRENCE
Lawrence of Arabia

It wasn't supposed to start yet. The ambush had been hastily planned to kick off at midnight. But about eleven that evening, a wandering Variant and a tired Marine chanced upon each other, and the Battle of the Forum quickly ensued.

The unfortunate Marine had been securing one of the building's emergency exits when the creature decided to investigate the sound of metal chains on a metal door handle. Although the unfortunate grunt killed the Variant, its screams alerted the rest of its brethren and all hell was unleashed.

The captain had planned to funnel the horde out of the main entrance. All the emergency exits except that one, had been secured.

"Here they come!" SSgt. Russ yelled to his men.

His fireteams had been rushed to the open emergency door, and a hasty ambush was created. By the time the first three rifle teams had positioned themselves, the double doors exploded and scores of infected began to pour out. They were cut down instantly. The dead were quickly replaced by dozens more and the bodies began to stack up. The corpses began to clog the entrance as the Variants tried to get over the fleshy mound.

The team's radio channel was thick with men yelling and cursing. Trying to give specific orders over their coms was next to impossible, so Russ took to doing things the old-fashioned way. He yelled. Russ was good at yelling. It always worked.

He had two SAWs set up within a minute, each bringing automatic fire onto the Variants.

"They can't get out!" Russ said to himself. "We want them to get out."

"Red One, this is Black One actual. Over," Russ transmitted.

"Black One, this is Red One. Hard Copy. Over."

"Red One, our doorway is blocked with bodies. Tangos can't get out. Over."

"Black One. Stand by. Over."

The Variants weren't happy. The sound of their screams was louder than any crowd he'd ever heard before. The World Cup finals couldn't have been as intense as what was coming from behind the Forum's walls.

"Black One. Hold position and continue mission. We're sending a SMAW team to you. Over."

"Red One, this is Black One actual. Confirm continue mission. Confirm SMAW team. Over."

Minutes later, two Marines jogged up to Russ. The SMAW rocket was designed to punch through walls and bunkers. Their job right now was to make a new hole for the Variants to use.

"I want a hole to the right of the emergency door," Russ told the rocket team.

"Copy that, Sarge."

Russ began to move his men back, leaving the rocket team to cover the clogged opening. Thirty seconds later, they were nearly a hundred meters away. The Variants were just starting to push the bodies forward. They were over a football field away, but barely in the safe zone from the coming explosion.

"DIRECT FRONT," Russ screamed.

"DIRECT FRONT," the rocket team yelled.

The MK 153 fired a ten-pound warhead. It was also equipped with a side-mounted rifle which fired a tracer round that had the same ballistics as the rocket. It was a crude method of aiming before shooting. The team let loose a tracer and the green streak hit the building's wall five meters to the right of the clogged door.

The rocket team's assistant gunner raised up his right hand with a "thumbs up."

"Range 100 meters!" Russ yelled.

"Range 100 meters," the rocket team answered in unison.

"On my command!" Russ shouted.

Russ saw that the top bodies in front of the double doors had been pushed aside. A Variant was struggling out of the opening, its sucker-like mouth hissing at them. In a few seconds, there wouldn't be anything left of that creature's smirk.

Russ loved this shit. He was a good ten yards to the side of the rocket launcher. He looked behind them to make sure no one had wandered into their back-blast zone. It was clear.

"Back blast area, secure!"

The rocket team was ready, and the rest of his squad was down behind cover.

"SEND IT!"

The 83mm rocket exploded from the tube, sending the ten-pound warhead hurtling at the building at over 250 meters per second. The back-blast from the rocket tube felt like a gorilla had slapped Russ on the side of the face. Less than half a second later, the HEDP (High-Explosive, Dual-Purpose) warhead erupted on the wall of the building, sending fragments of steel and chunks of the wall into the massed creatures within.

"ADVANCE!" Russ screamed.

The fireteams popped back up and advanced to their prior positions. The smoke and dust from the rocket ballooned out onto the parking lot, blocking anyone from putting eyes on the new hole in the structure.

"Holy shit!" one of his men yelled. "They're climbing the fucking walls!"

Shader looked above the settling dust and could see dozens of Variants racing up the side of the building. Creatures were pouring out of the new hole and onto the top of the domed structure. It was like a fire ant mound had been kicked as thousands of the nasty bastards erupted from the nest.

"FIRE!" Russ yelled at the stunned Marines.

Variants fell from the walls as the Marines began to respond. But too many of them made it to the roof and out of sight.

"Red One, this is Black One actual. Do you copy? Over."

"Hard Copy Black One. What's your sitrep? Over."

"Red One, we have a jailbreak. Tangos are climbing

walls and up onto the roof. They're above our line of fire. Over."

"Repeat Black One. Did you say that tangos are climbing the walls? Over."

"That's an affirmative, Red One. Tangos are scaling the walls. It's like a nest of spiders just broke out. I'm seeing hundreds of the damned things. Over."

"Hard copy, Black One. Wait one. Over."

"Solid copy, Red One."

Russ brought his M4 up and began to fire on the climbing creatures. The Variants were quick, with their disjointed limbs working to grip and climb the walls.

They had just made it back to their original position when movement from the dust cloud caught Russ's attention as hundreds of Variants flooded out of the opening.

"Enemy front!" someone yelled into their mic.

The SAW machine guns opened fire on the rushing creatures, tearing into the diseased flesh. But Russ knew within moments of engagement that they were fighting a losing battle. The Variants just kept pouring out of the brown fog.

Russ watched as several of the leading creatures took multiple kill shots to the torso with no seeming effect. And when they did get a head or spine shot, there were five more of the damned things that took the dead one's place. It was a tsunami of infected monsters that seemed to have no end.

"FALL BACK!" Russ yelled, then punched his PTT button.

"Red One. This is Black One. We're falling back."

Before he could get an answer, a Variant suddenly

landed not ten meters in front of him. The creature hit the pavement with such force, that its torso exploded, sending infected blood and goo flying in every direction.

Confused, Russ looked up in the air, trying to figure out where the body had come from.

"Shit! RUN!" Russ screamed.

The Variants on the roof, under strafing machine gun fire from a newly arrived Osprey, were throwing themselves out at the Marines.

Russ ran, putting as much distance between the Forum and himself as he could. Looking over his shoulder, he watched as three of his men were overrun by the advancing horde, and one of them was crushed by a suicidal Variant that came crashing down from the roof.

Marines turned and fired, but there were too many to stop. Russ and his remaining men made it to a second line of vehicles. They had lost one of their SAWs to the horde and expended half their ammunition. It was a futile battle, but there was nowhere left to go.

Headlights suddenly lit up from behind them, casting long shadows onto the Variants. Russ looked back and saw almost a dozen HUMVEEs and MRAPs rushing across the parking lot.

FOB Hawthorne had arrived!

Vehicles screeched to a stop behind Russ and the Marines inside pushed forward, their guns firing at the Variant throng. It felt like the stage at a cheap theater. Headlights from the vehicles shone brightly at the building. The elongated shadows of the advancing Marines danced across the walls of the Forum. The horde paused as the intense white beams temporarily blinded them. A couple HUMVEE-mounted 50-caliber, M-2 machine guns as well as dozens of M4 battle rifles opened fire, sending tracer rounds into the Variant mob.

The results of the heavy caliber barrage were spectacular as the creatures were ripped into multiple pieces. Often, the large bullets from the Ma Deuce would pass through several of the creatures, tearing each body apart. Eventually, a Variant four or five back would die as the last fragments of the exhausted projectile found them.

Entire rows of the creatures fell and within seconds, and the Marines were back on the offensive.

WHUMP!

An explosion in the middle of the infected throng erupted, throwing several Variants into the air. Russ watched as multiple grenades landed within the mass, ripping them apart. One of the Humvees was throwing 40mm grenades from its roof-mounted MK-19 grenade launcher.

He could hear the explosive fragments shooting by. The high-pitched whines of the metal shards caused him to flinch. Russ and his men were danger close, but the only other option was to be overrun.

A second Osprey began to hover over the top of the dome, machine gun fire raining down on the trapped creatures and within twenty minutes, the battle was over. At least on the outside the building.

"That was a rush," a new lieutenant said.

The young officer was standing next to Russ, his battle rifle smoking from the sustained gunfire. Russ had lost count of how many rounds he'd unleashed.

"Well done, Sergeant," the young LT said.

"Thank you, sir," Russ replied. "We'd be dead without you guys."

"Maybe. But it would have been glorious."

Russ smiled at the lieutenant's humor until he glanced at the man wistfully gazing at the dead. He realized the young LT wasn't joking. Russ looked at the lieutenant's name taped to his breast pocket. It read "Jack."

The major's kid. Russ had heard of him. He had been told by some of the other sergeants that Jack was green as hell but a good officer who listened to his NCOs. The kid was just a little too inexperienced to realize that combat, regardless of the outcome, always sucked.

"Sir, you've been ordered to report to the major," a sergeant named Braddock said to his lieutenant.

"He's here?"

"The major should be rolling up in five mikes," the sergeant replied. "He wants all of the officers at his location when he arrives."

"Lead the way, Sergeant."

Russ gathered his remaining fire team members. Of the fifteen men under his direct command and the additional twelve from Shader's group, he had nineteen Marines left. Six grunts were somewhere in the pile of rendered flesh that lay in front of the Forum, while two had been evacuated for wounds suffered during the battle. One E-2 had been struck by shrapnel from the massive grenade barrage. The other Marine had broken his arm during their hasty retreat. The man had managed to stay in the fight but was flown out on a helicopter for his wounds.

The screams from the Variants were still reverberating from within the building, but the noise from the creatures had changed. The volume was now more diminished, and the anger had been replaced by pain. The Marines had kicked their asses, but Russ had no illusions. They'd be back once they'd licked their wounds, and the sergeant was determined to have his troops ready for the next round. He immediately began to organize the men under him, sending small groups back to resupply while others kept watch.

It had been nearly an hour since the last bullet had been fired, and the Forum was still quiet. Russ had his men rotating between guarding the hole in the wall and resting a hundred yards back, where they could eat and hydrate.

The Ospreys had been replaced by three AH-1 SuperCobra attack helicopters. They were flying cover for them, darting and weaving around the perimeter.

With the Marines from FOB LAX joining FOB Hawthorne at the Forum, they were nearly at battalion strength. Over seven hundred rifles and squad automatic weapons now surrounded the structure while another three hundred Marines were moving on their flank.

FOB Santa Monica was sending their grunts up Route 10, providing cover on the main unit's left side, while FOB Compton was taking the 710 to the east. A classic pincer movement that Russ was having doubts about. The enemy wasn't massed in one location like a traditional army, they were just everywhere. Splitting their platoons didn't make a lot of sense now that they'd had some experience fighting this enemy force. But the military was structured on momentum, and once a plan was put in motion, it rarely deviated from its pre-ordained path.

"Sergeant Russ!" Lieutenant Jack yelled.

"Sir," Russ replied, jogging over to the lieutenant.

"We've got a mission," Jack said. "You're going in to get our men."

The Forum was going to be leveled once they'd retrieved Shader, his fireteam, and the civilian survivors. Then they'd move downtown to secure the city. Russ was to put together a squad, including Gonzalez. They would use the service entrance to affect the rescue mission. The rest of the Marines were going create a diversion at the above-ground entrances, hopefully distracting the creatures.

It would all kick off in thirty minutes.

— 12 —

Service and Utility Room
Inglewood Forum
SCPO Porky Shader

"We men and women are all in the same boat, upon a stormy sea.
We owe to each other a terrible and tragic loyalty."
G.K. CHESTERTON

"It's been too long," Morales said. "He didn't make it."

Shader was prone to believing him. It was well past dark, and the sounds of the battle outside were deafening, even in this insulated room. It wasn't looking good.

Even if Gonzalez had managed to get out, there were far too many Variants to try a rescue mission. Because of this, Shader had already begun to plan their own escape, but their options were not good. Most of the survivors were too weak to run, and any chance of getting out would require that. Lazzaro was another factor. His wound would likely open up if he tried to use the leg. He needed an AMPT, or stretcher, to be moved.

With no food and the survivors in an ever-weakening condition, Shader was without any good choices.

"Shader," Keele whispered. "Something's up."

The constant screeches from the Variants in the hallway had only slightly diminished since the battle had started. Shader had hoped the firefight would have helped pull some of them away, but it was not to be.

Shader strode into the duct room and drew next to the

door. The screams and pounding were fading.

There were definitely fewer creatures trying to get in. But were they just waiting quietly outside, standing in the trance-like state he'd observed through the air duct grate earlier that day? Or, were they leaving for other reasons?

"Blue One, this is Blue Two. Do you copy? Over."

Shader heard Gonzalez faintly over his squad radio.

"Keele. Lazzaro. Coms on, now!" Shader hissed.

He had made the other two Marines turn their radios off to preserve the batteries.

"Blue Two, this is Blue One actual. I read you. Over."

"Blue One. We're on our way. Prepare for evac. Do you copy? Over."

"Blue Two. That's a hard copy. Prepare for evac. Over."

"Blue one. Good to hear your voice. Hold on. We're five mikes out. Blue Two out."

Shader couldn't believe it. The Marines were coming. "Lazzaro. How's the leg?"

"Ready to move the fuck out of here!"

"All right, everyone. The Marines are coming. Leave everything here. And I mean, everything. The only thing walking out that door is your body," Shader said, pointing into the front room where the Variants continued their assault.

Three of the civilians, along with Lazzaro, needed help ambulating. They would slow the group down, but no one even thought about abandoning them. It was all, or nothing. They would survive as a group or die as a family.

They gathered at the back of the room, waiting for a sign or signal that it was finally safe to open the door.

Explosions erupted right outside. Shader recognized

the distinctive sound of flash-bangs detonating. Three loud *pops* echoed through the steel door, followed by a hail of gunfire. It sounded like the "mad minute" at the end of live-fire exercises at the range, where the entire line would shoot their remaining ammunition as quickly as possible. It wasn't unusual for Shader to empty four 30-round magazines on semi-automatic in sixty seconds and sometimes all eight on automatic fire.

"Blue One, this is Blue Two. You're clear. Begin evac. Over."

"That's a hard copy, Blue Two. Goddam glad to hear you."

Shader and Morales went to the door and cautiously opened it. Shader had his M4 up and ready as Morales tried to push the door out. It wouldn't move more than an inch.

"Blue One. You've got bodies blocking the door. Put some muscle behind it."

Keele joined the other two and they pushed through the bodies, creating enough room for the survivors to pass through.

"Be careful!" Shader yelled. "Don't touch anything! The blood is infectious. Don't let it get near any cuts or open wounds and keep your hands away from your eyes and mouth."

One by one, the haggard survivors were led out of the room.

The Marines had their weapon-mounted lights shining on the scene, their beams nearly blinding the group as they illuminated the hallway.

It was utter destruction. Shader lost count of the bodies. There had to be at close to a hundred.

"Over here," Gonzalez yelled, pointing at a flatbed electric cart.

They put the three sick survivors on the back, along with Lazzaro, his M4 raised and ready for a fight.

"Let's move," Shader heard.

It was SSgt. Russ.

Over a dozen Marines turned back down the hallway and retraced their steps to the underground garage. The team bracketed each tunnel that led to the main floor, protecting the passing survivors from any creatures within.

If need be, flash-bangs were tossed into the stairwell, stunning the light-sensitive creatures. It was proving to be an effective strategy.

Shader was finally feeling good about their chances as the flatbed turned toward the double doors that led into the garage. His euphoria, however, was short-lived.

A cacophony of pain, anger, and hunger exploded from down the hallway. The combined sound of screams and roars hit the group like a sonic wave. The squad assigned to that flank began to fire on full automatic as confused and frightened voices jammed the squad radio.

As best as Shader could tell, there were hundreds, if not thousands of creatures flooding down the hallway. All of them furious at the beating they had already taken and ravenously insane knowing that several dozen fresh and uninfected slabs of meat were just within their reach. Shader knew they'd been found and were to be the next course on the Variants' planned dinner party.

"MOVE!" Shader yelled as a tsunami of creatures deluged the concourse. Walls, ceiling, and floor were thick with the infected mass, the popping sound of their deformed limbs loudly announcing their arrival.

The flatbed careened around the corner of the hallway and shot into the garage. Headlights popped on and Shader watched as the four injured shot away to safety, closely followed by the remaining survivors who were slogging behind the electric transport.

"Protect the civilians!" Shader barked, pointing at Gonzalez and Keele.

"Fireteam Charlie. Stay with the survivors," Russ added.

The remaining Marines poured automatic fire up the hallway as two flash-bangs detonated in front of the screaming mob. It stunned the creatures long enough for the Marines to slam the doors close. Shader pushed against the doors while the rest of the Marines and ambulatory survivors retreated.

A high-pitched whine approached from behind Shader. Russ pulled up and slammed an electric vehicle into the doors, just as the frame buckled from the weight of the Variants as they hit the outside. The doors split open slightly, and Russ responded by accelerating the large flatbed, closing the door once again.

"Move it!" Russ yelled. He set the parking brake then jumped out of the open driver's side. Then both men began sprinting toward the receding lights of the Marines ahead.

Shader didn't need any encouragement. He was quickly on Russ's heels and fifty yards away from the door when he heard a crash from behind. It was the Variants. They had breached the barrier. Their screams were all Shader needed to know they had just a few seconds' lead. It was a race to the ramp, and Shader could only hope that his old legs wouldn't fail him now.

As if reading Shader's thoughts, Russ looked over at the old SEAL.

"I'm too old for this shit," the Marine grunted as they watched flashlights disappear up the incline ahead.

Shader didn't have the breath to respond and from the sounds coming from behind them, it was going to be close. Really fucking close.

"Roaarrrraaaa," Shader heard as he started running up the ramp. A hand brushed on his heel, followed by a thud. A Variant had thrown itself at him, landing just short of grabbing his leg.

Shader flew up the ramp, Russ just a step ahead.

Several screeches of frustration sounded from below as a couple Variants stumbled over the downed creature that had tried to grasp Shader.

"Move it!" someone screamed from above.

Shader was halfway up when over a dozen rifles opened up, creating a wall of lead that rained down on the Variants at the bottom.

But the echoes of many hundreds more of the infected blasted back at them.

Shader dashed out of the opening.

"FIRE IN THE HOLE!" came a cry from the lot nearby.

Someone grabbed Shader by the shoulder and flung him down and away from the ramp.

Shader heard the high-pitched *zing* of a spring being tightly wound. It was a detonator being twisted, sending an electric pulse down into the garage.

Multiple muffled explosions sounded from below. Shader stood up and watched as over half of the parking lot, from the ramp back toward the Forum, collapsed with a giant flop. The Variants that had been chasing them were now properly buried beneath tons of asphalt. Shader glanced over at Russ and gave him an appreciative nod. Russ smiled and nodded back.

It was finally over.

Or so they thought.

— 13 —

The End Begins
USS *Theodore Roosevelt*

"Only Burnside could have managed such a coup,
wringing one last spectacular defeat from the jaws of victory."
ABRAHAM LINCOLN, on the Union defeat
at the Battle of the Crater (1864)

"That went well," Major Poole said with relief. The naval intelligence officer had been on the chopping block with the admiral when multiple reports of Variant hordes began hinting at their true numbers. The successful rescue of a dozen survivors mitigated the failure in intelligence. At least it did in Poole's mind.

"Stow it, Poole," Admiral Abernathy scowled. "We've lost good men today, and we sure as hell don't have the bodies to replace them."

Abernathy strode back and forth in the Combat Directions Center. The room was normally bustling with activity and muted conversations. Abernathy's dressing down of the major had put a stop to all that background noise. The room was oppressively quiet as the two men sparred.

"The Joint Chiefs will still want you to proceed," Major Poole confidently said.

"I know what they want, Major," he replied with an emphasis on "major."

"All I can do is relay messages, Admiral. This isn't personal, sir."

"Don't put lipstick on a pig, Major. You don't just relay messages. I know they rely on your assessment."

"Sir, I am just one of many. There are over a dozen operations ongoing. We aren't the only ones."

"And, how are those going?"

"I'm not privileged with that information, sir," Poole immediately replied.

Abernathy scowled. He knew they'd been lucky, so far. It was just a matter of time before something went fatally wrong. He could feel it in his bones.

"Sir, we have a situation with Redwood," one of the operations specialists said loudly.

Abernathy strode over to the man and watched as the OpSpec listened intently into his headphone.

"Copy that, Redwood One," the man said into his mic. "We'll send air support immediately."

"What is it?" the admiral asked.

"Sir, Captain Nancee is reporting contact with a large Variant force. He's requesting air support."

"Admiral," one of the other OpSpecs said, "we've got reports from Angel Two and Four that they can see Redwood in the distance. Sir, they're lighting it up. Looks like a real battle going on out there."

"Angel Two and Four are over FOB Forum, sir," CWO Solomon informed the admiral.

"They're on overwatch?" Abernathy asked.

"Yes, sir," Solomon replied.

"Can they detach and engage?"

"It's quiet enough now. At least one could be spared," Solomon said.

"Do it."

The OpSpec in charge of air support relayed the order, sending one of the SuperCobras to the east. The men from FOB Compton were in trouble. The helicopter would be there in under a minute.

The CDC sat quietly, waiting for any word from Nancee.

"Redwood One. Repeat again," the OpSpec said loudly into his headset. "Redwood One. I did not copy your last transmission. Repeat. Over."

"Redwood One, do you copy? Over," he repeated.

"Redwood One. Redwood One. Do you copy? Over."

"Redwood One."

Nothing.

"Sir," one of the other OpSpecs said, "I have Angel Four. He's over Redwood One right now."

"Is he engaging the enemy?"

The OpSpec seemed to ignore the admiral, listening intently into his headset. Abernathy stood silently behind the man, allowing him to do his job without distraction. Poole slid up behind them both.

"Repeat again, Angel Four."

The OpSpec began to somberly nod, as he listened to the pilot's report.

"That was a hard copy, Angel Four. Pause for orders."

"Well?" Abernathy hesitantly asked, knowing somewhere deep inside, the answer would not be good.

"They're gone, sir."

"WHAT?" Poole shouted in disbelief.

"Angel Four reports that Redwood One was overrun. There were no survivors."

"Did he try the radio?" Poole stupidly asked, begging

for a different response.

"Yes, sir. Squad channel went dark, and the Variants were thick in the area. Angel Four could see that the vehicles had been overrun."

"Did they report on enemy strength?" Abernathy said as he glared back at the cowering major.

"Too many to count, sir. That's all he said."

Abernathy did all he could to keep from striking the intelligence officer.

"I just lost over one hundred Marines!" Abernathy barked, pointing at the disgraced major. "Get this piece of shit out of my sight!"

Two sailors flanked the major and escorted him out of the room.

"Sir. It's Angel Two. They've sighted a mass of Variants moving towards Big Pine."

FOB Santa Monica, also known as Big Pine, was moving on the Forum's west flank.

"Alert Big Pine. Warn them that they will be getting company," Abernathy ordered.

"Yes, sir."

"Where are they now?" Abernathy asked.

"What's your pause?" the OpSpec asked their Big Pine contact.

After a moment, he replied to Abernathy. "They're one mile east of the 405."

"Have them return to Santa Monica Airport. We'll pick them up there."

Abernathy turned to his TAO. "Get my men back. NOW!"

CWO Solomon jumped into action, unleashing multiple orders to a cluster of operational specialists. The room lit up with dozens of voices while others scurried in and out of the door, taking their assigned duties to the next level.

Admiral Abernathy watched with both pride and apprehension as the Combat Center reacted to his order. The men were working flawlessly, which brought him some satisfaction. But he just didn't know if it would be in time to avoid more casualties.

"Sir," one of the OpSpecs said. "I have information from Major Jack. He insists that it's important."

"Very well. Let me have it." He'd lost an entire company of Marines in a matter of moments and he wasn't about to lose the rest of the Battalion as well.

— 14 —

SCPO Shader
Inglewood Forum

"100 per cent of us die, and the percentage cannot be increased."
C.S. LEWIS
The Weight of Glory

Morales dropped to his knees and kissed the ground. The night sky shone through the headlights that were illuminating the Forum, at least the brighter stars made it through. The rest of the survivors were in various states of shock. Pairs of Marines guided each of the recovered civilians back to the idling vehicles, where they were checked over by one of several Navy corpsmen who had been inserted with their companies. Most were immediately hydrated with vitamin water or intravenously.

"Shit, that was intense," Gonzalez said as he drained a full liter of bottled water. "That place is fucking crawling."

"Well, it won't be standing much longer," Russ replied. "Plan is to evacuate the civilians then push north, downtown. The air jockeys are going to level the building after we leave."

"That's a hard copy," Gonzalez said. "I don't ever want to go back in there again."

"I need to speak to Gold One," Shader said. "There's some fucked up shit going on in there."

"Good luck with that," Russ said. "Captain's knees deep in shit right now. But if you want to try" —Russ pointed to the right— "he's over there next to the MRAP."

Shader nodded and made his way to the mobile command center. One of Hawthorne's armory vehicles had been upgraded to the major's personal carrier.

Porky stood back and watched the chaos of war unfold. Every officer was there, along with communications and a number of grunts who were either guarding them or being used as glorified gofers. After a few minutes, Shader decided there would be no lull for him to use to catch the major's attention. So, he did what any door-knocker would do, he did a hard breach and muscled his way past two lieutenants and a captain. He found himself at a folding table, standing across from Major Jack.

One of the lieutenants grabbed Shader by the shoulder and tried to spin him around.

"Stand down, Chief!"

Shader glanced back and saw Lieutenant Landry looking up at him, his face beet red and snot bubbling out of one of his nostrils. The man was furious at being pushed away from his seat at the throne, but Shader decided that he really didn't give a fuck how the lieutenant felt at that moment.

Shader grasped the lieutenant's fingers and squeezed them. Twisting Landry's hand away from him, Porky brought a yelp from the lieutenant.

"What's going on?" Major Jack barked.

Shader spun back to face a very angry and tired battalion commander.

"Sir," Shader said, releasing Landry's fingers from his vise-like grip. "Senior Chief Petty Officer Shader reporting."

Jack looked Shader up and down, measuring the SEAL like a horse broker assessing a stallion for purchase. After just a moment, the major must have deemed Shader an asset worthy of his time.

"As you were, Chief. What's so important that you'd barge into my planning meeting?"

"Sir. I just got out of the Forum. There's a lot you need to know before you go forward."

"Shut it, Shader. Get the hell out of here," Landry barked from behind. Shader ignored him.

"So, you're the SEAL that opened this can of worms?"

"Yes, sir."

"And who is your C.O.?"

"I am, sir. It was against my better judgement, but the man is persistent," Landy barked.

"The lieutenant was against it, sir. I felt that we had to clear the building."

"You did right, Chief. Now, what is it that's so important?"

"It's about the Variants, sir. I can explain why there are so many of them."

"This should be interesting," Jack said. "Go ahead, Chief. I'm all ears."

After five minutes of a non-stop narrative that included the mating pair and the farming of the civilians, Shader finished with his estimate of enemy forces.

"You're sure about all of this?"

"One hundred percent, Major. They're not dying off like the deuces say they are. And they don't need any more humans, other than for food. They're self-sustaining, and they're everywhere."

Jack's face became pale. The implications were enormous. He had to run this up the ladder to the top.

"Well done, Chief. I want you to escort your civilians back to the fleet."

"Sir. I'd like to stay here, if that is possible."

"You'll get your turn, Chief. Don't worry about getting some payback. You'll get your chance."

Jack started barking out orders, and Shader felt his time had come and gone. The press of the officers around him soon had him one or two layers back from the commander, so he spun around to return to the civilians. That's when he came face-to-face with Lieutenant Landry.

"You fucking bastard," Landry hissed. "Your ass is done."

Shader was taken aback by Landry's sudden appearance, but his red face and meaningless tirade brought a smirk to his face.

"Sure, LT. Whatever you say. I'll see you later and we can discuss the matter."

Shader tried to move around Landry, but the lieutenant stepped in front and put his hand on Shader's chest.

"You're not going anywhere!" he screeched.

"You're going to stop me?" Shader loudly flared. "Get your hands off me before I remove them. Sir!"

"Stop!" Jack yelled.

The major strode around the table and stood toe-to-toe with them both.

"Disabling the lieutenant would be a real bad idea, Chief."

Then he looked at Landry. "Are you serious, Lieutenant? You're going to take on a senior petty officer? A SEAL? I should let him break you in half. Maybe that would put some sense into your shit-for-brains skull."

Major Jack started to leave, then went back for one more beatdown.

"Lieutenant, I've never seen such stupidity. You failed to listen to your men to begin with, then you want to punish him for being right? Jesus, Landry. What did they teach you in OCS?"

Major Jack turned to Shader. "Chief, return to your men. And if I ever see you disrespect any of your superiors, I'll personally break your ass in half. Do you understand me?"

"Aye aye, sir!" Shader replied, bringing his large frame to attention.

"Dismissed, Chief. Tell your squad leaders that a new commanding officer will be coming your way soon."

Shader nodded and spun on his heels. The crowd around him parted, and he walked briskly away.

Russ should be happy to hear this, he thought as he strode past the machine gun emplacements and firing positions. His steps quickened, and his gear seemed a little lighter. Strange how sometimes bad shit turns out good.

"Get Sequoia for me," Jack said to his radio operator.

Sequoia One, or Admiral Abernathy, needed to know this information.

"Sir, I have Sequoia One actual."

Jack took the radio phone and reported. What he heard back in reply shook him to his bones. He returned the phone to the R.O. and walked back to the table. Dozens of eyes watched as he composed his next words.

"All right, everyone. We're being extracted. Redwood is gone. The enemy overran them less than five minutes ago."

Before the officers could react, Major Jack began planning a protected LZ for the incoming Osprey. The problem of the Forum would have to wait, at least until his men had been removed. Then they could do with the building whatever they wanted. That was up to people breathing a far higher atmosphere than him.

Their call sign was Sycamore, a stately tree found throughout central California. Their original mission called for them to be the anchor of the operation. Now, like their dendritic namesake, they were shedding their skin and leaving the city behind. The Sycamore survived by dumping its bark as it grew, and so too would the Marines. They'd lost a few men but hopefully became stronger because of it.

— 15 —

Archangel Three
SuperCobra Attack Helicopter
Just South of Downtown Los Angeles
Captain H. F. Everly

"Once we have a war there is only one thing to do. It must be won. For defeat brings worse things than any that can ever happen in war."

Earnest Hemmingway

Captain Howard Everly had been given a helicopter ten years prior. When he'd graduated from flight school and was assigned to become a rotorhead, he felt like he'd been demoted. Every kid wants to be Top Gun and fly a fixed-wing fighter.

But that changed the first time he flew his SuperCobra. The blend of foot and hand controls was as complex as any orchestral movement. All four limbs moved in concert as his eyes were fed a data stream through his head-up display (HUD) as complicated as any musical sheet from Bach, Beethoven, or Ravel. The feel of the craft jumping at every move of his arms or legs, no matter how minute, was addictive. Add the destructive power of the attack helicopter, and Everly justifiably felt like a god. He wielded death at 180 mph to man and machine alike.

He had spun his props in Afghanistan, fighting the rarified atmosphere of the Hindu-Kush mountains while raining Hydra rockets and 20mm bullets onto the enemy. The fear and death he and his Apache helicopter brothers had created earned them the nickname "Monsters in the Air" from the Taliban. Now, he was using the infrared camera to scout out the Variants of Los Angeles.

He spotted a few here and there as he began the evening run. The Variants were definitely not the living dead. According to the movies and TV shows he'd seen, zombies were the walking dead and assumed room temperature. They would have been indistinguishable from the background through his IR glasses. The Variants lit up like a flare in the night. They were hot and there was no doubt what he was looking at when they showed up on his HUD.

When word came through that Operation Liberty had been cancelled, Everly had been running over the north side of the city. Once the Marines had been recalled, that part of town was no longer a concern. Now, he was to watch for Variants much closer to downtown and immediately report any large groups.

He'd been flying for about half an hour, shooting above the skyscrapers. It was exhilarating, given this was restricted airspace when life had been normal.

"Hey, Everly. Think you can spot the Nakatomi Building?" his front seat gunner, Lt. Mark Cowley, asked.

"I've got it marked."

Fox Plaza was actually used as the iconic building in the first *Die Hard* movie. It was about four miles to the west of downtown, just north of Route 10. That was the road Big Pine was using to return to Santa Monica Airport.

"Let's head over there. I've always wanted to see that place."

"It ain't Christmas until Hans Gruber falls from the Nakatomi building!" Everly deadpanned.

"Yippee ki-yay, mother fucker."

With no designated flight plan now that the invasion had been scrubbed, Everly shot low above the downtown high-rise buildings. He continued south then began to bank west toward Big Pine. It would take them over Fox Plaza.

"Hey, you want to go in close, just like the movie?" Everly asked.

His gunner didn't reply.

"Hey! Cowley."

"Shit! Look left," the gunner gasped.

Everly swung his weapon's camera west and looked out toward the Forum. Halfway between the FOB and their position was the Los Angeles Coliseum. They'd passed over that spot not fifteen minutes before. It had been dark. Now it was lit up like a shopping mall at Christmas.

Everly banked and accelerated. A few seconds later, they hovered over the giant stadium. Inside, tiny points of fire ignited in their IR image. Thousands of them popped up, spreading out from the center of the field and into the surrounding seats.

"Holy mother of God," Everly said.

The stadium was full. The Variants were appearing at a terrifying rate, their metabolism suddenly shifting into overdrive. The heat from this transformation glowed in the infrared lens.

"We don't have enough ordinance," Everly whispered.

"Sequoia, this is Archangel Three. Do you copy? Over."

"Archangel Three, this is Sequoia Two-niner. We copy you. Over."

The mass of Variants began pouring out of the Coliseum, rushing toward Inglewood.

"Sequoia Two-Niner, I have a mass of Variants moving toward Sycamore One. Estimated strength in the tens of thousands. Do you copy? Over."

The band remained silent for a moment. Then a different voice came through the radio. "Archangel Three, this is Sequoia One actual. Do you copy? Over."

Admiral Abernathy. Everly was stunned. "Yes, Sequoia One. We copy. Over."

"Archangel Three. Are you sure about that number? Over."

Everly gave the admiral the bad news. Within minutes, FOB Forum would be overrun by the infected. "Sequoia One. If anything, I'm being overly cautious on that estimate. Over."

Everly received orders to dump his ordinance on the advancing horde then bug out north. The fast-movers would be on station in two minutes, followed by a naval bombardment. They needed to slow the Variants down to allow for an evacuation.

Everly did as he was told. He made two runs, expending all of his rockets and Gatling gun rounds into the mass. It had no effect. Two minutes later, three flights of Hornets dropped their massive bombs on the front of the group. Then the naval barrage began. Explosions were happening almost every second. Everly and Cowley watched through the helicopter's gun camera as each detonation whited out their screen, then as the image reconstituted, another wave of Variants flooded through the devastated spot. Hundreds of creatures were dying, but it didn't slow them down as thousands more took their place.

The fleet's coms were thick with radio traffic, but Everly could pick enough information out of the cacophony to estimate the rescue crafts' arrival time. The majority of the Ospreys and the few Sea Knight utility helicopters at their disposal were still three minutes out.

Everly watched the flood of creatures glow brightly in his IR camera. Their amoeboid movement flowed like fast-moving batter. They oozed around craters and buildings, enveloping the land and consuming anything in their path. The horde was moving at an incredible rate.

"Jesus!" Everly muttered as he watched the scene unfold before him.

"I think Sycamore's going to make it," Cowley whispered hopefully into his mic.

"No, they're not," Everly somberly replied. "We're gonna lose them all."

16

FOB Forum
SCPO Shader

Explosions erupted in the distance. The concussive blasts were beginning to be felt as the fleet walked their rounds onto the leading edge of an advancing enemy. The ground shook, and the air buffeted with bombs landing less than a mile away.

Shader and Russ were guiding the survivors onto the first aircraft to arrive. This particular Osprey had been on station when the order to retreat had come. It was the same craft that Shader had ridden on that morning.

"You know how to throw a party, don't you?" Sergeant Potoski barked as Shader helped the civilians move up the rear ramp of the V-22.

Shader strapped several of the weaker ones into their jump seats while Keele and Gonzalez carried Lazzaro and deposited him onto the craft.

Sergeant Russ and one of his fireteams stood outside, forming a perimeter around the landing zone.

"Come on," Shader said to Gonzalez and Keele. "We've got work to do."

The three Marines lumbered out the back and came face-to-face with Lieutenant Jack.

"You're their escort," Jack said, pointing back into the Osprey.

"Sir, you need our rifles. They don't need us now."

"Neither do we," Jack replied somberly. "I'm ordering you to take your team and evac."

"But Lieutenant, we can't—"

"That's an order, Chief."

Jack turned to Russ, who stood to the side. "Take your team as well."

The detonations of the five-inch shells were now erupting on the buildings that stood at the edge of the graveyard to their east. The Variants were close.

"But, sir!" Russ screamed.

"I don't want any arguments. All of you. On board. NOW!"

Shader grabbed Gonzalez, who stood defiantly in front of the officer, and shoved him back to the Osprey. Russ and his four men joined them and the V-22 slowly began to lift.

Potoski rotated his SAW back in place and left the ramp down. He spoke into his mic, and the Osprey hovered in place, its rear ramp facing the graveyard. Potoski flipped his NVGs down and over his eye. Shader did the same, joining the big man at the back opening.

Shader watched as hundreds, then thousands of creatures flowed out from the destruction. Potoski's machine gun began to fire. Every fifth round was a bright streak, as the SAW's feeding belt was peppered with tracer rounds.

Shader joined the fight, emptying his magazines on full-automatic. They were over a quarter mile away but aiming wasn't needed because the infected bodies were so thick.

In the end, it really didn't help. Two more Ospreys had made an emergency landing and recovered as many

Marines as those craft could hold. The rest of the rescue flight held back when Major Jack called them off, right before the FOB was overrun. The Marines' final act of defiance was to detonate the gasoline fuel truck. It was a glorious death. Russ instantly knew who had done it. He only prayed that the lieutenant was with his father when it happened. It seemed only fitting.

Watching the death of the 11th MEU through their NVGs from just over a mile away was a cold and humble experience. No one spoke a word as the Osprey lumbered back to the *Roosevelt*.

In the end, nearly a thousand Marines had perished. They sacrificed their lives for a dozen civilians and less than a hundred of their brothers. And even though they likely killed tens of thousands of the creatures, they hadn't made a dent in their massive population.

There was now no doubt that the country had been lost. Their next move was beyond Shader's exhausted brain. He fought back a tear and took a deep breath. Then he did the only thing he could do to keep from losing his mind. He closed his eyes and shut down his brain. The last thing he wanted to do was to think.

Sitting next to the SEAL, Gonzalez was stunned when he turned to speak to his squad leader and found that the man was asleep.

"Fucking SEALs. How do they do that?" he said to no one in particular.

The drone of the twin propellers was the only answer he got back.

— 17 —

John Eric Carver
Schoepe Boy Scout Camp
Lost Valley

*A real friend is one who walks in when
the rest of the world walks out.*
WALTER WINCHELL

Carver's nap on the veranda was interrupted by silence. The ex-SEAL was tuned into his surroundings at all times, especially when he was sleeping. It was both a curse and gift.

Carver's eyes fluttered open, and he dropped his hand down to his side, reaching for his faithful battle buddy. The Belgian Malinois had been on the wooden porch floor, gently snoring next to the patio couch. But Shrek wasn't there. That's when he realized the dog's breath sounds were missing. That's what woke him from his afternoon slumber.

Carver was interested, more than concerned, in what or who drew his faithful friend away. He stretched and slid out of the old plastic sofa, his exposed skin peeling off of the vinyl surface as he extracted himself.

He wandered around the corner and found the offender. Kyle Torrence sat on the front steps, and the faithless dog sat in front of him, allowing the young teen to rub and scratch his head and neck.

Carver wandered over to the pair and rubbed Shrek's snout.

"Traitor," he said, smiling.

"He likes to be rubbed," Kyle said appreciatively.

Shrek, for his part, continued to lean into the teen, letting the young man massage his upper body.

"Hey, Mr. Carver. My mom wants to know if she can talk to you," Kyle finally said.

Shrek looked up at the boy with a chastising look, as if to reprimand the youth for losing his fur-rubbing concentration. He nudged Kyle's hand, demanding that the young man continue to ply him with attention.

"Sorry, boy," Kyle dutifully responded and began to scratch the dog's back.

Carver shook his head. The kid had been co-opted into the dog's personal massage therapist.

"Where is she now?"

"She's at Beckham," Kyle replied. Beckham Hall was one of three fixed structures at the camp. It was a gathering lodge and kitchen for the three-thousand-acre facility.

"Thanks. I'll head over after I take a shower."

Kyle absently continued his attention to Shrek while Carver gazed out over the massive camp property. The two-bedroom cottage was the home of the camp's park ranger, Harold Kinney. He was a retired Marine and Carver's best friend—at least of the ones he knew were still alive. They'd bonded over the last couple years when Carver had volunteered at the camp after retiring to a nearby forty-acre farm.

Kyle and his single mother, Hope Torrence, occupied a house at the end of the dirt road that led to Carver's

114

place. After the viral outbreak, Carver had rescued Hope from her job at a resort an hour's drive away and brought both mother and son to the Boy Scout facility.

"Sir?" the boy asked, interrupting Carver's quiet moment.

"Yeah, Kyle?"

"Are you going to ask my mom out on a date?"

Carver blurted out a laughing snort, then caught himself before further embarrassing the young man.

Hope had been unavailable throughout his time at the ranch. After a bad marriage that left her financially fragile, Hope had been forced work unending hours for a failing desert resort that paid her just enough to survive. Carver stepped in to fill the hours that she'd been forced to work, becoming Kyle's de facto parent. During all those many months of sharing Kyle's upbringing, he and Hope hadn't spent more than an a few hours together, always talking about the young teen and how he was developing. They both just did what they had to do.

Even if Hope had expressed an interest in forming a romantic relationship, Carver hadn't been ready. He'd spent years in the Navy, bouncing around the Asian continent, never settling back in the States for more than a year.

Besides the lack of opportunity that this life presented, a SEAL was always at the tip of the spear. He couldn't imagine putting someone he loved into a situation where every deployment meant months apart and every knock at the front door could be the Navy's death notification team calling. Because of all this, it didn't make sense to get that involved with someone else while he had been active.

Kyle was suspiciously quiet. Carver's reaction had been taken the wrong way.

"Hey, Kyle. I'm sorry I laughed. I like your mom. I really do. It's not that I wouldn't like to take your mom on a date. But there really isn't anywhere I could take her. You know what I mean?"

Kyle perked up. He nodded and resumed rubbing the dog's neck. Carver glanced at Shrek and could have sworn the Malinois was scolding him with his eyes for hurting the young man.

"My mom likes you," Kyle said absently.

"I like her," Carver replied, not knowing what else to say.

Several minutes passed by, neither man nor beast inclined to break the awkward silence.

"You know," Kyle said. "She takes me on picnics when we have time. I think she likes that."

"I like picnics, too," Carver replied, even though he hadn't been on a picnic since his childhood in northeast Iowa. Back then, a picnic was a rare Sunday treat from a life that rarely had a day off.

"I think I'll go visit your mom now. Find out what she wants."

"I think it's about her friend Randy," Kyle replied, without taking his attention from Shrek's thick coat of hair.

Carver just nodded.

Randy Thomas was her co-worker back at the resort. He'd distracted a horde of the infected, allowing him and Hope to escape after they had been trapped in a storage room. They never found out what had happened him. Hope said he knew the resort inside and out, having been there since its beginning.

"I'm sure he found a place to hide," she'd said, driving back to the camp after their escape. That had been a few weeks back. She had sounded like she was trying to convince herself that he hadn't sacrificed his life for theirs.

Carver understood her feelings. There was no guilt more consuming than having someone die so you could live. John had experienced that once or twice before. It haunted his dreams and often woke him up at night. The shame of surviving was a permanent stain that time failed to wash away. Maybe that's why she needed to talk.

Carver decided to forgo the shower and began to walk to Beckham Hall.

"Blijf!" he commanded to Shrek in the dog's native Dutch tongue, ordering him to "stay." The war dog had been raised in Germany but, like many European kennels, they trained the Belgian Malinois using Dutch. Carver had to learn these commands in Shrek's language to interact properly with the animal.

Shrek just sat in place, barely acknowledging Carver's order. A simple glance was all the response Carver got back. That wasn't going to stand!

Carver stopped and pointed at the dog. "We're going to have a talk when I get back!"

Shrek seemed to understand. The dog sat at attention and turned his head toward Carver. The SEAL used his "handler voice," and Shrek knew he'd somehow earned the man's ire.

Carver's eyes bore into the Malinois's, then he turned and walked to Beckham Hall to find out how he could help Hope once again. Not that she or Kyle had ever been a burden. It had just become their life.

Carver strode through the canopy of a nearby cluster of Sweet Acacia trees, their branches still laden with their fragrant, golden puffballs. Carver slowed down, enjoying the cool underbelly of the stand of drought-tolerant vegetation. The trees' aromatic smell had diminished over the last few weeks as the puffballs began to drop off. They'd all be gone soon enough, so Carver was going to enjoy this brief and welcome respite to the apocalypse that was occurring around them.

After a minute, he reluctantly left the copse of trees and entered Beckham Hall. He walked to the back of the large, open building and hesitated at the swinging saloon doors that separated the kitchen from the rest of the place. He looked through the circular portal window and watched Hope standing at the kitchen's large sink.

She swayed back and forth gently to some unknown song, smiling and humming as she washed the morning's dirty pots and pans. She wore an old apron, the kind commercial dishwashers wore. Her hair was pulled back into a ponytail. She wore no makeup. She was on the far side of thirty and had lost the luster of youth years ago, likely because of her contentious marriage and the stressful divorce after.

Despite all these "shortcomings," she radiated something that was lacking in the few females he'd known in the past. She exuded a comfort and stability that was hard to find.

She felt like home.

Kyle's words came back to him. *My mom likes you.* Carver told the boy that he liked her too, but it was more than that. He couldn't even define his feelings for Hope to himself. How else could he have responded to her teenaged son?

Carver pushed through the door, the squeak of the hinges alerting Hope that she had company. She jumped slightly, like many women did when their concentration was broken by a nearby man.

"Oh! John," she said, blushing at his presence.

"Hi, Hope. Kyle said you wanted to talk to me."

"Oh, yeah," she stammered as she tried to push a few stray strands of hair back from her face. Then she laughed at the futility of it. "I'm a mess."

Carver stared. Her apron was covered with splashes of water, and a few soap bubbles clung to the side of her head. Her disheveled appearance only made her more attractive.

Before he realized what he was doing, he stepped closer to her. Hope's eyes dilated and color rushed to her cheeks. Seeing her reaction, Carver realized this was the first time the two of them had been alone together in a very long time. She blushed at his approach. He liked the feeling.

He slid next to her and gently brought his hand up, brushing her hair back and wiping the bubbles from above her ear. "No, Hope. You look perfect."

John smiled and Hope loved that it lit up his face. She didn't see him do this often enough. His normally serious demeanor seemed to vanish when he grinned. His eyes twinkled and the hard, facial lines that defined his military career disappeared into the wrinkles that bordered the corner of his eyes.

They both stood transfixed. The silence was intoxicating.

John felt himself falling for her. He brought his hand up to Hope's face again and brushed it softly. He reached behind her head and tenderly pulled her face forward to his. Their lips touched, and she lost herself in his embrace. His arms were like velvet tree limbs, strong and forgiving. She couldn't have imagined that she could ever feel like this again after her horrific divorce. Who would have thought that an apocalypse would bring her soul back to life? They kissed until it felt better to embrace.

"I'm sorry," John whispered as he hugged her.

Hope pulled back from his arms, a questioning expression on her face. "Sorry? For what?"

"That I took this long to let you know how I feel."

Hope smiled. "I didn't help things that much."

"You had a lot more on your plate than I did," Carver said. "I guess that's why I never even thought that something like this could happen. I'm not too experienced with relationships, you know."

"Come on. A man like you? I'll bet there are women all over the world that have your mark on them."

Carver smiled.

"Not really. I've never lived anywhere long enough to make a relationship."

Hope gave him a sideways glance. "Come on, John. Whoever you have out there isn't interested in going out with you for dinner anymore. Unless you're interested in being the main course."

Hope regretted her dark humor immediately when Carver raised his eyebrows at the comment. "That was harsh."

Hope blushed again, turning away and breaking their grasp. She walked to a stack of clean, dry pans and began to put them away.

Why did I say that? she asked herself. *What the hell is wrong with me? He's probably the last available man in the world, and I'm pushing him away?*

Then she realized that if John was the last man on earth, then she was the last woman as well. *What if he is attracted to me because there's no one else? After all, what man would want a middle-aged woman with a teenage boy? Why would he want someone who looks the way I do? Old, wrinkles forming, and no future. He's settling. He doesn't know what love is.*

Carver stood, dumbfounded by her attitude. They'd just kissed, and if he was any judge of it, they'd connected as well or better than any woman he'd kissed before. She seemed to melt in his arms. What more was there?

Hope saw his dismayed look. *He's a man,* she thought. *He doesn't even know his own feelings.*

"John. You're sweet," she began. "I don't want you to settle for me because there's no one else."

"Settle?"

"Yeah. It's not like you have a lot of other options. I just happen to be the last one on the dance floor."

Carver began to chuckle. It was all clear now. "Hope. How long have we known each other?"

"Over two years."

"And, in that time, how many women have I had a relationship with?"

Hope knew the answer. She had just chalked it up to PTSD, or some other personal issue. At one point, she thought he might have been gay. Not that it mattered, other than thinking at the time what a waste it would have been for the female persuasion.

"I take it by your silence that you know the answer.

None. I didn't have any relationship with any woman. A few dates in town, but nothing that was serious or lasted more than a week."

"So, you have attachment issues. All the better."

"If I had attachment issues, it must have been because of you," John said.

He slid up to her once again and held her hands.

"I realize now that it was because the only person I could show my love for couldn't love me back. I loved her son, instead," he whispered. "I love Kyle because he's a great kid and his mother was not available. It was the best way I could show her that I was there. That I wasn't her ex-husband. That I wasn't going to abandon her like he did."

"Oh, John," she sighed, flinging her arms around him once again.

"I love Kyle, because I love you. I just realized that. You and Kyle gave me purpose. I won't lose that."

Hope grabbed Carver and pulled him down to her face. She greedily smothered his lips with her own and ran her hands up under his shirt. His belly rippled, and his chest was like a rock. He was all man, and she hadn't realized how good that felt until just now.

"Mom?"

Kyle was outside. *How long had he been there?* she thought, ripping herself from Carver's arms.

The doors swung open and Kyle, along with the Gringleman boys, walked into the kitchen. They gave no indication that they'd seen anything.

"We're hungry," Kyle said.

"You just ate a few hours ago," Hope facetiously complained. Teenage boys ate their own weight in food.

She was glad the camp had stored supplies for hundreds of campers. With so many ravenous teenagers running around, she was going to need every calorie if they hoped to survive.

"I could use some food too," Carver deadpanned.

Hope leaned in close and put her lips up to his ear. "I'll feed you later," she said slyly before brushing her lips against his neck.

It was Carver's turn to blush. Hope gave him a knowing look and turned her attention to the stove.

"How do eggs sound, boys?"

"Great!" they all replied, including Carver.

The saloon door gently swung open and Shrek slid into the room, staring at the group.

"What do you want, Shrek?" Hope asked.

The dog sat down and looked expectantly at Hope.

"Another man to feed?" She sighed. "Don't worry, boy. I've got plenty for you, too."

Shrek seemed to understand. He sat back on his haunches and let his tongue loll out. A slight smile cracked from the corner of his mouth.

The four of them grabbed plates and silverware, then Shrek followed the boys out to the dining area.

She lit the burners of the industrial stove. The shouts and laughter of John and the three young men made her smile. Somehow, in the middle of the end of the world, she felt a contentment she hadn't experienced in many years.

Soon, she had reconstituted eggs and TVP bacon bits sizzling in a lard-greased iron skillet. It all seemed so right, and the outside world soon faded into the background. That was when, looking back at it all, Hope finally gave in to her feelings. She was in love, and it was time to trust once again.

The men stopped their banter when four plates of eggs and bacon and a stack of recently made flour tortillas came out the swinging kitchen door. Hope beamed as she set the food in front of each one of them.

"Oh. I forgot Shrek's plate!" She spun around and quickly went back to the kitchen.

Kyle leaned over to Carver and put his hand on the SEAL's arm. "Thanks," he whispered.

"For what?"

"For making my mom happy. She's hasn't been like this in forever."

Carver sat back and looked at the kitchen doors. The muffled sounds of Hope singing an old Whitney Houston song wafted out of the saloon doors.

He looked down at Shrek, who sat expectantly next to his chair. *What do you think?* he silently asked the dog with his eyes.

Shrek stared back and gave Carver an approving look.

"Of course," John said to the dog after a moment or two.

Carver sat up and turned to Kyle. "I haven't been this happy in a long time either," Carver said as he absently stroked the Malinois's head.

Kyle beamed, thinking it was about time the two of them quit being so stubborn and started dating. He'd been waiting for this day ever since Carver first moved to the farm down the street from their house. He knew after the first day they'd met, that he wanted Carver in his life. Now, it looked like he'd finally be getting his wish.

An hour later, with the boys running around outside

and the kitchen clean, Hope and Carver sat at a table, sipping some newly brewed coffee.

"This is nice," John commented, as they sipped the warm java. "But I sort of forgot to get an answer earlier. Kyle said you wanted to talk to me about something."

Carver's comment jolted Hope from her stupor. The last hour had been a whirlwind of happiness, and now, she'd have to face the real world once again.

"It's about Randy," she began. "I need to know if he's all right. Can't we go back for him?"

Carver sat back. He thought she was going to tell him about her guilt. Now she wanted them to return to the resort and face an unknown number of the infected, without knowing whether her friend was alive or not.

Carver sat silently. He'd mentally divorced himself from re-entering the outside world. They hadn't seen or heard a thing in weeks. Their isolation was complete, and the odds of a significant number of creatures stumbling on their camp were slim to none. Leaving the camp could only increase the chances that they'd attract trouble.

Now Hope wanted to risk everyone for the off chance they could save someone. It was the old conundrum. Do the needs of the many outweigh the needs of the few? For Carver, it was simple. You don't risk everyone to save just someone. He'd expect them to do nothing less if he'd been in Randy's shoes. The man had been a hero, but that didn't mean they should risk everything to find out what had happened to him. If Carver had done the same as Randy, he'd be outraged if they tried to come back for him.

"Hope. I don't know if that's a good idea," he began.

He stopped immediately when he watched Hope's face

collapse. Her eyes drooped and her mouth saddened into a slight frown. In some ways, she'd expected Carver's response. But it hurt, nonetheless.

"I can give you many reasons that just *leaving* the camp is a bad idea. I can add a ton more if we're going out to attack an infested, multi-building compound."

"I know," Hope replied. "But I just know that he's still alive."

"Alive and infected?"

"No. Alive and normal. I know I can't explain it, but he's all right. But I don't think he has much more time."

"Hope. This sounds like survivor's guilt. It's common. I've had experience with it. You're trying to make it better by rescuing someone who's probably dead. You'll only make things worse if we lose anyone else in the process."

"I thought about that possibility," she said. "But I really feel like he is alive and needs our help."

Carver sat silently. It was hard to argue about a feeling. Feelings had no logic, even though they drove many decisions and could define a life. He respected that much and let Hope spill her emotions.

They talked for many minutes, Hope arguing her points and Carver gently shooting each of them down. In the end, it boiled down to his original definition of the problem. Rescuing Randy Thomas would put the whole camp at risk, and that was something that made no sense to the analytical SEAL.

"John, I can't make an argument that logically makes sense."

"Should I agree with you?" John hesitantly asked, hoping that she'd take the question as a humorous, but accurate, reply.

Hope smiled and clasped his hand in hers. "I love you, John Carver. I'm sorry I didn't let 'us' happen before now."

Carver was about to respond, but Hope's eyes told him not to. Maybe it was his training with Shrek that heightened his emotional awareness, but he wisely stayed quiet.

"But if you're going to love me back, you need to respect my feelings. I know that every reason I can come up with to find Randy has an equal or greater counterargument. But, there's one thing I can say that you have no rebuttal for."

"And what is that?"

"It's the right thing to do."

Compassion. You couldn't argue with that.

"You talk about the needs of the many. That sounds like something a Communist would say. That's not who we are," she said, spinning her pointed finger in a circle above her head. "If Randy isn't as important as all of us, then who are we? Are we just a mindless mob, like the infected?"

"I don't know," Carver replied. "I'm just trying to keep us safe."

"I know. But if we don't try to help him, then we aren't any better than those things out there. They do everything for themselves. They don't do anything for each other. That's what makes us human. We take care of each other. That, John Eric Carver, is why we need to try and help Randy. Because it is the right thing to do. It's the human thing to do."

Carver knew he couldn't win that line of reasoning, even if it was emotional and not logical.

"We need to run it by the group," he finally replied. "They have to approve it because it will affect us all. We can bring it up at dinner."

"That's all I could ask," Hope said, her eyes popping back to life. "Thank you."

Hope slid her chair next to his and leaned over, giving him a deep and passionate kiss.

"Wow," John said, catching his breath. "That was unexpected. Do I get one every time I agree with you?"

"No," she said as she stood. "You can get one of those anytime."

She tugged on him, pulling him from the chair.

"What are you doing?" he said smiling at her playfulness.

She just grinned and led him to a back room.

"I told you," she purred, "that I'd feed you later."

She closed and quietly locked the office door.

— 18 —

Jennifer Blevins
Director, Schoepe Boy Scout Camp
San Diego Naval Base

The next morning, Jennifer woke with a start. The makeshift shades of their converted office glowed dimly around its edges. Jennifer glanced over her sleeping boyfriend at the bedside clock. It was a little after five.

Garrett Jacobs lay quietly at her side. She'd twice put her arm around her fiancé that night, his restless sleep interspersed with nightmares unknown.

He'd arrived back at their building after midnight with tales of thousands of Variants staring back at them as he and his friends gazed across San Diego Bay. His normal joy at coming home after a long night on patrol never materialized. His restless night only cemented her fears that their time on Coronado Island would soon come to an abrupt end.

Jennifer rolled onto her back and stared at the acoustic tiles above her. She reflected on the circumstances that had brought her to this bed, on this island, and at this time.

She absently twirled the engagement ring that hung around her neck, a gift from Garrett on the night the infection started. Called back to the base when the virus had become an emergency, he had run out of the restaurant before she could give him an answer to his proposal. She'd finally said "yes" after several days of hiding in the Manchester Hyatt, followed by her rescue by Garrett and his Shore Patrol friends.

Unfortunately, the offer to wed had been a surprise, and the big dunce didn't get the ring sized correctly. It was too big. It now hung around her neck until they could find a jeweler to size it properly. When that would happen was anyone's guess.

Commotion from the large common area outside startled Jennifer. Garrett woke as well. Throwing the covers off, he dropped into his boots and stomped out the door. He had been sleeping in a clean pair of Navy working uniform pants. The blue-and-grey patterned khakis were anything but comfortable, and she had wondered why he'd been doing that. Now she knew.

Jennifer slept in one of Garrett's long t-shirts. She began to put on a pair of shorts when several women cried out in anguish. She rushed to the room, where the rest of the people bunking in the converted office stood in shock.

"What is it?" Jennifer asked as she slid up to Garrett's side.

"The Marines," he said quietly. "The entire 11th MEU was destroyed last night."

"What?" Jennifer hissed. "Everyone?"

"Less than a hundred survivors. The rest were overrun by Variants."

"I still don't understand," Jennifer said. It was all too overwhelming.

The sun hadn't risen, and they had been torn from their sleep to the news that the fleet had just lost most of its warriors.

Garrett led her back to the room and closed the door.

"All I know is that they were in Los Angeles and were overrun on some operation sanctioned by the Joint Chiefs," Garrett said. "As to why and how? I haven't a clue."

He began to dress, putting his gear back on as Jennifer sat in silence on the bed. Their protectors had been wiped out in just one night.

"Garrett," she suddenly said. "All those creatures you saw last night."

Garrett recognized the panic in her voice. He felt the same way. But his job denied him the chance to let it out. He had already pushed his fears down and put them into a box in the back of his head. Now was not the time to open that container.

"You'll be all right," he said more stridently than he felt. "I'm going to get Gardner. We'll figure this out. I promise."

Jennifer knew he was placating her. But he said it so confidently that she almost believed him. Looking into his eyes, she saw that he needed her to trust what he'd just said.

She faked confidence as best she could. "I know. Let me know what to do."

Garrett hugged her and gave her a kiss.

"I love you, future wife."

"I love you too, future husband. See you soon."

Garrett smiled and left. As she looked around, the room suddenly felt small and insignificant. If the creatures got into the building, they wouldn't last for long. She remembered when she was trapped in the hotel. Those doors were more substantial than the thinner, government-approved piece of hollow wood that separated her from the rest of the office.

She shook those thoughts from her mind and began to clean their bedroom. When that was done, she decided to organize and fill the backpacks Garrett had procured for them a while ago.

"Just a precaution," she said herself, as most of her clothing went into a camo-patterned assault pack.

Soon after that, she had Garrett's things put away in his own ruck. She stacked both packs against the far wall and sat down. With nothing to do but think, she lay back on the perfectly made bunk. The world pressed heavily on her soul and she began to quietly sob.

Garrett Jacobs got to the armory a few minutes after the LT had begun his impromptu brief. By the end of the hour-long session, he'd learned two things.

First, the Variants were in far greater in numbers than the intel community had estimated. He laughed out loud when the lieutenant made that statement, earning him a stern look. Garrett had seen the increasing threat firsthand on his evening patrols. He watched the Variant population grow each night, their eyes blazing back at him in ever increasing numbers, every time he glassed across San Diego Bay. Garrett had reported this to their CO, but it obviously never made it to the people in intelligence. Naval intel personnel, or N2, were often called "deuces." After hearing the implied surprise in their report, Garrett thought that the two must represent their I.Q. as well.

The second thing he'd learned was that the entire island was to be evacuated. They were sending one of the

Marines' Amphibious Assault ships, the USS *Boxer*, to pull them all out as quickly as possible.

The *Boxer* was a massive troop transport. It was a combination aircraft carrier and boat garage. It had a giant door on its tail that dropped open, releasing its three air-cushioned hovercraft. Each LCAC (Landing Craft, Air Cushion) could hold almost two hundred people.

On top of the *Boxer* was a big, flat top that could launch the transport ship's two dozen or so Osprey aircraft. Between the hovercrafts and Ospreys, they'd hoped to have everyone off the island within the next twenty-four hours.

Garrett lingered after the brief had ended to meet up with John Gardner and Manny Polodare. Both were master-at-arms that he called his friends. They huddled together at the back of the room as the rest of the personnel funneled past them.

"Just one more night," Garrett said quietly, as if saying it loudly would curse them all. "We can do this."

Polodare began to say something, when Gardner stopped him. "Stow it. We all know what you think."

Manny was a confirmed pessimist. The other two could tell he was just dying to get it out. He tried to speak up once again, and both Garrett and Gardner cut him off.

"NO!" they said in unison.

"Just saying," Manny griped, knowing his friends were aware of his dire predictions.

Everything he'd said so far about the Variants and their odds of winning the war against these creatures had come true. It seemed that pessimism was the new realism and, practically speaking, if anything could get worse, it did. Who could have predicted that the Marines would be wiped out in just one night? Why Manny, of course. He'd made that call over a week ago. He had been eerily correct so far and neither of the other two wanted to get his take on their chances of getting off the island alive.

"I missed the first part," Garrett said.

"LT says we're here till the end," Gardner said. "Pack your shit up and get it back here by 1500. They'll haul all our gear on one of the landing craft, and we can pick it up when we get to the *Boxer*."

"LT said to make sure you put a nametag on your bags," Polodare added.

Being master-at-arms meant they were the Navy's onshore police force. The evacuation was expected to take most of the night and the *Boxer* wasn't going to be offshore until evening.

"I'm going back to my room to get Jen. I want her on the first transport out of here," Garrett said.

"Yeah. Well, I want a back massage from Ariana Grande. Don't mean I'm gonna get it," Manny shot back. "You ain't gettin' her on anything till the officers and their families are off this rock."

Garrett knew his buddy was correct. There was a definite pecking order in the military, and Garrett and Jen were not at the top. She'd have to go to the island's naval air base where the families were to gather. She'd be assigned a number, just like the others, that would determine her place in line.

"We better get going," Garrett said. "I've got to pack my shit."

"I'm already done," Manny said. "I knew we'd have to do this."

"Bullshit," Gardner replied. "You're just too damn

lazy to unpack. I know your ass. You've been wearing the same two pair of NWUs since we've been here."

Manny was about to reply, then thought better of it. He smiled and nodded. Gardner was correct. He hated to unpack. But it wasn't because he was lazy. He didn't unpack because he didn't have anything in his duffel bag that he needed, other than a change of clothing.

Manny shrugged. "I like to do laundry."

"Yeah, right," Gardner sarcastically replied.

The real reason Manny left his possessions packed away was, like most truths, more complicated than a simple answer could provide.

Manny didn't have much of a history outside the Navy. He was raised by an aunt who didn't want him there. His mother had abandoned him with her as a baby, turning her attention to drugs instead. Ultimately, like most poor life decisions, it led to pain and eventually, her death.

Manny found structure and acceptance at his high school where the Navy had set up a junior ROTC program. He had already chosen his NEC (Naval Enlisted Code) six months prior to graduation. Manny wanted to be a cop, and the MA (master-at-arms) would pay him and train him to be a naval security specialist. He'd have been out of the Navy six months from now, having his pick from most any police department in the country, if it hadn't been for the apocalypse.

The second reason was that, at least while they were on shore, he did enjoy doing his laundry. The thumping of the washing machines and hum of the driers were strangely soothing. He would bring a book or iPad and sit near the bank of machines, watching the other sailors launder their dirty clothes. The guys would dump everything into a machine, turn it on, then disappear. The women lingered. It was a good way to meet girls without being creepy.

"You guys wanna meet up for breakfast?" Manny asked as they made their way out of the armory. "Might be the last hot meal for a while."

"Give me a bit," Gardner said. "What do you say we meet at 0830?"

"Solid copy on that," Manny said. "Give me a chance to do one more load."

Polodare smiled and left quickly, leaving the other two to decide if he was yanking their chain. In the end, it really didn't matter his reasons. The man liked to do his laundry. It might be the last time he'd have a chance to do this on land, possibly for the rest of his life.

"See you at 0830," Garrett said.

He left the armory as well. Only this time, he was toting his M4 battle rifle and a full loadout of nine 30-round magazines. Normal protocol was for their firearms to be returned after each patrol. But they'd all been issued their weapons and ammunition before the meeting had adjourned. It was an ominous sign of things to come.

A few minutes later, Garrett silently entered their room. The common area was eerily quiet. The gravity of the threat had hit home.

Jennifer lay on their bed, her arm folded over her face. Her rhythmic breathing let Garrett know that she was asleep. Her lips were downturned into a pouty frown. Streaks of dried tears lined her cheek.

He set his rifle and loadout onto a nearby table and quietly rolled into bed next to his fiancé. Jen's eyes fluttered and she turned to Garrett, then smiled weakly.

"Back already?"

"It's been over an hour."

"Oh. I didn't know it's been that long."

"That's all right. We just need to pack up."

"Already done," she said. "First thing I did when you left."

Garrett loved that about her. She always seemed to know how to help without being prompted. She just went about her life and brought stability and happiness wherever she went.

"We're meeting the guys in about an hour," he said in a whisper. "Anything you want to do before then?"

Jen looked back at him. He made her feel safe.

"I don't know. What's the plan after we get off the island?"

"No idea. Probably sail somewhere secure and start over."

"We're going to be on the ship for a while, aren't we?"

"Yeah, and no one has any idea of how long it'll take to find a safe place."

Jen smiled and pulled him to her bosom. He lay against her chest and listened to her heart beat. She pushed him back and grinned.

"An hour. That's plenty of time."

She pulled his face to hers. They gently kissed. It soon turned more passionate as his hands began to wander. She struggled to grab his belt. The damn NWUs were buttoned in front instead of having snaps and zippers.

"I hate those things," she said, after unsuccessfully trying to loosen his pants.

He laughed. "How do you think guys feel about bra straps?"

They both disrobed and slid back into bed.

It was their last day on dry land. They had no idea how long they'd be on the ship, crammed into spaces shared by many.

They lost themselves in each other, neither of them worried that their cries and moans could be heard by their neighbors. Once they left the island, they might not have a room to themselves for many months to come.

— 19 —

SCHOEPE BOY SCOUT CAMP
BECKHAM HALL
SHREK

"To his dog, every man is Napoleon."
ALDOUS HUXLEY

I can smell the humans' fear. They talk to Carver like they're strong, but they aren't. They lack the warrior mentality. Carver has that fighter attitude, and so do I. The only other one to come close to us is Kinney. He was a Marine and still caries that swagger.

The rest of them are all weak, but I am proud that they still prepare to fight. They've been strengthening their buildings with bars of steel and heavy wood bolted over the windows.

The asps are still out there. I pick up their acidic scent every once in a while. My ears lay back on my head and my neck hair stands high. But then, the scent disappears, and I know I've scared them away once again. I am Shrek, the ghost in the night. I will kill any of them that get in my way.

Carver is planning to go to the mansion with the giant driveway and all the lights. It's where we rescued Hope. They want to find another human that they left behind. Whoever it is, is probably dead, but they want to try.

Normally, I can tell the direction and number of any creature just by the intensity of their scent and which nostril it smells strongest in. But when we were at the place where Hope worked, there were so many asps that my nose was overwhelmed. This is not a good idea to go retrieve the human, but I understand loyalty. It is the driving force in my life.

The humans had talked about this last night at dinner. I quickly ate my food and sat under the table in front of Carver. Like always, I had lain on his feet, guarding him and letting him know he is the leader of our clan.

"Then it's settled," Carver had said. "Me and Kinney will take my truck and go to the resort. I only want to make one trip, so there'll be no recon. If we see the place overrun, we head back and call it a day. We don't have the manpower for a stand-up fight."

Now I notice that Carver stays close to Hope. They'd mated yesterday and again this morning. It's about time. Humans are so slow to understand their own feelings. I could tell that they would be together the first day we met her and her cub. She had given off a smell that left no doubt what she thought of him. I can't believe he hasn't done this until now. But I'm not surprised. Humans have no clue about how each other smells. I wish they could be like me. It would save so much time and effort.

"When are you leaving?" Hope asks.

Carver looks at his watch. The sun had already passed overhead but was still high in the sky. It would be light for a while.

He looks at Kinney. "Harold, how long to get ready?"

"I'm ready now. Got my gear already packed."

"We have six hours of light and less than an hour's drive each way. Now is as good a time as any," Carver says. "Let's move."

That is my cue. I jump up and stand at Carver's side. I never go more than five feet from his right leg. It's like I have a tether tied from his thigh to my neck. When we go to war, I only leave his side when he commands me to. We are a team.

We had been the best, back in the mountains, fighting the enemy called the Taliban. They were fierce fighters, but we were better. We are Carver and Shrek, and we are back fighting in the mountains once again. I look up at my master. He is calm and committed. We are going out to kill the asp. I can't wait.

— 20 —

Coronado Island
San Diego Naval Air Station
Jennifer Blevins

"By failing to prepare, you are preparing to fail."
— BENJAMIN FRANKLIN

Jennifer woke with a start. Something had jolted her from a deep sleep. She struggled to find coherence as a frightful dream lingered, just beyond her conscious grasp. Then she heard what shook her from sleep, the distant *thump* of an Osprey landing at the nearby airstrip. The evacuation had begun.

The room was alit by the midday sun filtering through the makeshift curtains. She moved her arm to touch Garrett, but only found an empty, sheet-covered mattress. Before she could panic, she vaguely remembered him kissing her on the cheek before he geared up and left.

How long ago had that been?

Her body lay exhausted, legs still rubbery from earlier. She struggled up to one elbow and found her watch.

"Wow," she said softly. It was nearly one o'clock. She'd slept for over three hours. They had bypassed breakfast with his friends and stayed in bed, eventually falling asleep from exhaustion. Combine that with all the worrying and lack of sleep over the last week, and it wasn't surprising that she'd needed to crash like that.

Jennifer lay back and began to think. She'd need to

find a duffel bag and pack all the non-essential items she'd left out of the two assault packs that were sitting on the floor nearby. One duffel should do it. She thought of other supplies that she might need as well. She mentally brought up a list that the Boy Scout camp gave out to their kids, items they'd need for their extended stay at Schoepe.

Jen rolled out of bed and shuffled to the room's desk. She brought out a pad of paper and pencil then began to catalogue the items she'd need. It was more extensive than she'd realized. Hygiene products were near the top, along with over-the-counter medications and other things found in a typical drug store. But with no pharmacies available, she'd have to see what was left at the naval base's store.

Jen put on her clothes and hurried out of the building. She walked to the NAS base exchange and entered. She stood dumbfounded when rows of empty shelves stared back at her. There were plenty of canvas clothing items and luggage remaining, but the OTC meds and hygiene items were gone, along with every food item that used to fill the store. The place had been cleaned out. With nothing available, she left without getting a duffel.

The base's pharmacy was next. The fifteen-minute walk began with a degree of panic and ended with her jogging the last hundred yards. She turned the final corner and was met with a line out the door. Scores, if not over a hundred people, stood silently. Their eyes glancing about nervously as if they expected a Variant horde to appear at any second.

Jen gave up. Fear welled up inside her, and she hurriedly walked in the direction of their private room.

She struggled to think coherently as the panic began to take hold. In her self-absorption, she turned a corner and ran headlong into one of the other wives, nearly tripping over her three-year-old daughter.

"Oh Jeez, Ellen. I'm so sorry!" Jen said, after catching the little girl, preventing her from tumbling to the ground.

The contact between the two had been slight, but the sudden appearance of a large adult and their near impact frightened the child. She began to cry.

"Oh baby," Ellen said, picking up the toddler. "You're all right. Miss Jennifer didn't mean to bump into you."

The girl dropped her head onto her mother's shoulder and put her thumb in her mouth. She looked unconvincingly at Jen and snuggled into her mother more deeply.

"I'm so sorry," Jennifer blurted. "I'm just not myself."

"Honey," Ellen said, in her thick South Carolina accent. "Aren't we all? I'm as nervous as a long-tailed cat in a room full of rocking chairs!"

Jen tried to stroke the little girl's arm, getting a squeal and "harrumph" in return.

"Now, baby. Be nice. You're just fine," Ellen said to her daughter.

Ellen turned to Jennifer. "What's got into you?"

"Ellen. It's everything. Garrett has to stay here until the last person is evacuated, and they have me scheduled to leave without him. I just tried to get supplies from the commissary and the pharmacy. They've either cleaned out or the line's out the door. I should have thought of this before today, and I'm pissed at myself."

"Well, bless your heart."

"Seriously, Ellen. I'm not usually this stupid."

Ellen stared off to the east where soldiers and sailors guarded the lone bridge to the mainland. "I know," Ellen said. "I haven't felt safe since this all started."

Ellen put the little girl down and brushed her cheeks.

"I'll tell you what," Ellen said as she straightened out the little girl's shirt. "I'll bet there are tons of supplies in those homes south of the base."

While the Navy owned the north end of Coronado, that side of the island was thick with residential buildings. Single-story houses, a few hotels, and even a golf course were sitting empty. The area had been evacuated and cleared of any humans or Variants.

"We're not allowed to leave the base," Jen replied.

"Who's going to stop you?" Ellen asked. "We've got less than a day left here, and there's no shore patrol in that area. They're all guarding the bridge."

"How do you know that?"

"All I'll say is that there probably isn't anything left to scavenge north of Cabrillo Avenue. At least, that's what I've heard," Ellen said with a wink.

"Thanks, Ellen."

"Good luck, Jen," Ellen said, walking away as she pulled her daughter along.

Jennifer stood silently, her fears slightly relieved. She needed a number of things, and with thousands of extra people to support, the Navy's supply chain couldn't be relied on. Her scout training kicked in. She would take care of herself and Garrett.

"Be prepared!" was the scout motto. She was going to do just that.

Jennifer hurried back to the base's exchange and grabbed two duffel bags. She made it to their room just as

Garrett returned from duty.

"Two duffels?" he asked. "Are you planning on bringing our mattress?"

"No. I've got some personal supplies to pick up. Lots of girl stuff, if you know what I mean."

"A duffel for girl stuff? You not telling me something?" he said jokingly.

"No babe, you've seen it all," she said back with a grin.

"Whatever. You know what you're doing. How about a bite to eat? I've got an hour before my next patrol."

Jen glanced at her watch. It was almost two. She was scheduled to leave in three hours and had been struggling whether to make that trip without him.

"Come on. You've packed already. Let's spend one more meal together," he said, his eyes finally betraying the anxiety he'd been hiding from her.

One more meal together, Jennifer repeated silently to herself. That was apocalyptic.

She never let on that he'd dropped his guard, exposing his fears. She nodded eagerly at his suggestion. Garrett smiled and gave her a hug. His embrace felt desperate and final. It was at that moment she made up her mind to miss her flight. She'd stay with Garrett until the end. Whatever fate awaited him, she would share it as well.

They left the bedroom and began walking to the base's cafeteria.

"For better, or worse," she whispered to herself, twisting the engagement ring hanging from her neck.

"What did you say?" Garrett asked as they jogged down the building's stairwell.

"I love you," she lied, just two steps behind. "I said that I love you."

USS *Theodore Roosevelt*
Thirty Miles West of San Diego
Porky Shader

"For the want of a nail the shoe was lost, For the want of a shoe the horse was lost,
For the want of a horse the rider was lost, For the want of a rider the battle was lost,
For the want of a battle the kingdom was lost, And all for the want of a horseshoe-nail."
— BENJAMIN FRANKLIN

Shader moved silently through the massive ship. The *Roosevelt* was designed to hold about five thousand souls under normal conditions. Now, the massive carrier was struggling to house over double that number. Because of this, the ship's filtration system was being pushed to its limits, and both the air and water produced were tinged with contaminants.

Shader ducked through a portal and snaked around clusters of civilians who had been rescued over the last month. Spaces that normally sat unoccupied were filled with both people and their detritus. The decks looked unkempt and stains from unknown liquids spotted the floors. It was so unlike normal that Porky could have been convinced he was in a college dormitory or dirty apartment building rather than one of the country's elite fighting ships.

Shader ducked through another opening, and the distinctive smell of a cigarette hit him. Smoking was forbidden. A fire aboard a naval craft could find a critical cable or ship component. With no more ports to call on, a broken part could permanently cripple the large craft.

The stress of the Forum and loss of the Marines had the SEAL on a tightrope of emotions. Shader followed the stench. It led to the head.

The shower and toilet facility contained over a dozen stalls and sinks. The burning tobacco odor was strong as Shader passed by several civilians taking a leak into the urinals. A door opened in one of the stalls to the right, and a woman came out, tucking her shirt into her unbuttoned pants. Men and women were no longer segregated, other than designated times in the morning and night where they could use the communal showers by the assigned gender. Otherwise, the water to the bathing facility was shut off to preserve the desalination equipment and filters.

Midday wasn't one of those times as Shader marched into the shower room. His capacity for patience had long run out.

A group of men and women were standing in the tiled room, passing around a bottle of schnapps. Alcohol was prohibited, but these idiots had smuggled two liters of the stuff onboard. One of the men was smoking, his back to Shader. As the SEAL strode up behind them, the others suddenly went quiet. The smoking man, sensing Shader's presence, spun around to face the unknown visitor. Before he could even remove the burning cancer-stick from between his lips, Porky smashed his jaw with an explosive right cross, knocking him instantly unconscious and onto the floor. His cigarette rolled out of his mouth and settled over a shower drain. The remaining civilians stood in stunned silence.

"You stupid bastards," Shader hissed. "You could start a fire. Just what the hell were you thinking?"

"We're sorry. We thought it was safe to smoke in here," one woman stammered as she looked around the all-tile room.

"There's no safe place to smoke on a ship," Shader hissed back. "I should report you to the XO."

The Executive Officer was responsible for the maintenance and function of the carrier. One of their responsibilities was to police and inspect the ship. When the civilians had been brought on board, they'd been given a set of rules. These included the no smoking policy as well as the requirement that any alcohol was to be surrendered for the length of the voyage. An infraction of any of these rules would lead to confinement in the brig or even a one-way ticket back to the mainland. Discipline was paramount on a craft with over five thousand people. It was even more important when you doubled that amount.

"No!" the woman pleaded. "You can't do that."

Two of the men made a move at Shader, earning them a low chuckle from the SEAL.

"Oh. That's just rich. You two against me?"

Shader stepped toward the two and spread his hands to his side.

"Go ahead. After I break your arms, I'll take you to the flight deck and personally put a bullet in your heads."

The two stood down, dropping their gaze away from Porky and to the deck. Their alcohol-enhanced bravery didn't last but for a moment.

"Names and billet," Shader said, demanding their identification.

Shader took their issued ID cards and gave them one last look.

"We just lost a thousand Marines. For people like you. And you stand in here, having a party. Putting almost ten thousand people in danger for a cigarette and a whisky buzz. It makes me want to vomit."

No one met his gaze and Shader turned and left.

Little things mattered. If there was anything he'd learned in his decades of military service, it was that a broken firing pin or even an untied shoelace could turn an operation on its head. Shader strode on, turning up a set of metal stairs.

"Make a damn hole!" he shouted at civilians who were blocking his way. They were sitting on the steps, using the space as a gathering spot.

They moved to the side as Shader pushed through them.

It was all just too much. Too many people. Too much garbage, and in the end, too little appreciation for what he and his fellow warriors were doing. He looked around at the idling civilians and saw nothing worth saving. He was fed up. Last night, he watched men and women worthy of his enduring gratitude and appreciation, overrun by a horde of creatures that had once been these ungrateful and purposeless people around him. In his own jaded mind, he began to realize that the only difference between the Variants and the listless civilians surrounding him, was a tiny virus. One group would kill you instantly with an infection-laced bite, while this group would slowly suffocate you by sucking the life from your surroundings.

"Why are we killing ourselves for this rabble?" he said to himself.

His mind was moving into a terrible place, but Shader didn't care. He was over it all.

Porky stomped up the stairs and moved more freely as he got closer to the bridge. He'd find out where the XO was and turn the identification badges over to him.

"Hi Mr. Shader!" he heard from behind.

Porky stopped and turned, finding the young girl from the Forum he'd rescued the night before. She was walking with Morales, who held an IV bag that was attached to the frail girl's right arm.

She was stick thin, her newly issued shorts and shirt hanging loosely over her gaunt frame. The Navy didn't have anything for such a small and frail body. Morales fared far better. His weight loss was now camouflaged by properly fitted garments. Both of their shirts had a crest on the front. A circular image of the carrier with "USS *T Roosevelt*" printed in gold letters above the image of the ship and CVN-71 printed below.

"Thank you," the girl said. She limped forward and gave Porky an unexpected hug. She could barely get her short arms halfway around him as she lay her freshly washed head on his stomach. Morales beamed.

"Thank you, my friend," the Puerto Rican man said. "You came for us. We'd be dead if it wasn't for you."

Porky's sour mood changed, transformed by a weak and tiny girl whose hug he could barely feel along with a few thankful words from a man who, just a month ago, was a faceless and invisible cog in the working class of a now-dead city.

Shader was without words. He struggled to reconcile the dichotomy between the leeches living just a deck below and the two survivors he stood with now.

"What are you guys doing up here?" Shader finally asked.

"Bella needs to get out and move," Morales said. "We thought we'd come up here and see if there was anything we could do."

"I told the sailor that I could serve food," the girl said, looking up at the big SEAL.

"We went to the cafeteria to see if they needed help. It was her idea. She wants to do something other than sit on her butt," Morales said.

"It's my tushy," she said, giggling. Then she looked up at Porky and smiled. "I sat enough. I don't ever want to have to sit again."

"I don't imagine you do," Shader said. "A month is more than sufficient."

Morales put his arm around the girl and turned her away. "She needs to rest now," he said.

"What about you?" Shader asked.

"Maintenance. The ship needs me. I'm going to help keep the filtration system up and running."

Morales leaned into Shader and whispered. "Bella doesn't have parents anymore. I need to watch out for her."

"You're going to be a good father," Shader replied.

Morales beamed and nodded. "Come on, little one. You may not want to sit down again, but you need your rest."

"Okay, Mr. Morales," Bella replied.

The two of them shuffled away, Morales hovering

over the child as they disappeared through the portal.

Shader felt renewed. At least these two were worth fighting for. He patted his front pocket, feeling the identification cards.

Shader resumed his mission to report the infraction.

"Those two might be worth it, but those idiots down below need a reminder of just what the United States Navy is all about," he said to no one in particular.

Rules had a purpose. Breaking them wasn't an option. The punishment might be mitigated given their circumstance, but the infraction needed to be addressed.

Shader found the bridge and reported to the XO. It was now out of his hands, and he felt no guilt in identifying the culprits. Little things mattered. Little things often turned out to be the lynchpins of success or the reasons for failure.

For the want of a horseshoe nail, the kingdom was lost.

He left to find Gonzalez and Keele. They needed to check on their wounded battle buddy and make sure he was taken care of.

Shader checked the two Marines' assigned quarters, but it was empty. After failing to find them in the mess deck, Porky was directed to the carrier's hangar bay. There, he found the two working out. Gonzalez, all one hundred twenty-four pounds of him, was bench-pressing his weight while Keele spotted him.

Shader stayed back, leaving the grunts to continue as the two men switched spots. Keele left the weight the same but ran off more reps. Shader approved. By not adding more plates to his routine, Keele accomplished two things. First, it sped things up—there were other people standing in line, waiting for their turn to use the equipment. The second thing it did was keep the two of them on even terms. Keele could likely bench more than the more diminutive Gonzalez, but he didn't shove it in the man's face. They were battle buddies. They were equals.

When the two surrendered the bench to the next pair, Shader made his presence known.

"Hey, you two," he said from behind.

Gonzalez turned and smiled. "Hey Chief! Why're you slumming down here? Need someone to spot for you?"

"No. But maybe if both of you spotted for me, I'd be able to do my reps."

"Ha!" Keele snorted. "In your dreams, straphanger."

Shader let out a loud laugh. He hadn't had a good chuckle in a long time. Straphanger was a pejorative for men who passed through special ops training but were of little value in combat. They held onto the other operators' straps, being pulled along like dead weight.

The three men smiled and Shader good naturedly slapped Gonzalez on the shoulder.

"You two would have made good SEALs," Shader said.

"Aw Chief, now you're just being mean," he replied, earning another laugh.

"I just wanted to know if you two wanted to go check on Lazzaro. I'm heading down to sickbay right now."

"Oh, Chief. They moved him to the *Boxer*. They medevaced him this morning."

"What happened?" Shader asked.

"They were worried about infection, and the *Boxer* has a better facility to handle that. Plus, it was a deep cut, and they told him it needed internal sutures to close the wound properly."

"I did what I could," Shader replied, feeling guilty that he'd done less than an adequate job on the injury.

"No sweat, Chief. You stopped the bleed. Let the docs make it pretty. Right, Keele?"

"Copy that. You got us out of there, Shader. We owe you."

Porky felt better. These two could run with him anytime.

"You eat lunch yet?" Gonzalez asked. "We're heading out to get some chow."

"I haven't eaten yet," Shader replied. "Sounds good."

"You think they'll let a squid eat with us, G-man?" Keele asked with a smile.

"Yeah. He's earned it," Gonzalez replied.

Shader didn't say a word. Eating with Marines was always an adventure and one that, a few months ago, he'd have passed on. The Navy and Marines had a contentious relationship, one born of both disdain and respect.

Shader used to scoff at the Pavlovian way the Marines were trained. If they were told to do something, it was a mindless response. They followed orders, regardless of the danger or likelihood of success.

When SEALs were given an order, they spent days planning the operation, each person having near equal input into the final decision.

But as Shader walked with the two jarheads, listening to them banter back and forth, he realized one important thing. They were incredibly loyal and devoted to both each other and their mission. It reminded him of a quote from Eleanor Roosevelt—both the wife of President

Franklin D. Roosevelt and the niece of the ship's namesake.

"The Marines I have seen around the world have the cleanest bodies, the filthiest minds, the highest morale, and the lowest morals of any group of animals I have ever seen. Thank God for the United States Marine Corps!" she had said.

"Thank God for the Marines," Shader mumbled to himself as Keele and Gonzalez shoved each other.

"What was that?" Gonzalez asked as Keele pushed him playfully against the bulkhead.

"No better friend and no worse enemy," Shader said.

"Oorah," the two Marines chanted.

"Oorah," Shader replied as they entered the mess deck, joining the few remaining men of the 11th MEU. He was surrounded by Marines and Shader was happy to have them.

— 22 —

USS *Boxer*
Marine Amphibious Assault Ship
Off the California Coast
Corporal Lazzaro

"Beware of little expenses. A small leak will sink a great ship."
-BENJAMIN FRANKLIN

Lazzaro lay back on the medical cot. It was nice to finally relax after the prior day's events.

After his debrief on the T.R., the medical bay decided to helicopter him to the *Boxer* for further care. The sick bay on the aircraft carrier was swamped by civilians, and Lazzaro's injury wasn't enough of a concern to warrant bumping an emergency appendectomy or a compound fracture from the surgery schedule. With a supply run scheduled only thirty minutes after the debriefing had been completed, Lazzaro was ordered to hobble onto the craft and report to the *Boxer's* sick bay.

The sick bay was designed to handle mass casualties. It was, after all, a Marine assault ship. With multiple empty beds and a full complement of medical personnel, Lazzaro was feeling rather special. He was one of three Marines being taken care of. All had been injured during what was rapidly being called "The Battle of the Forum."

The other two Marines were bunked at the front of the room, while Lazzaro had been assigned a cot near the back. Why they hadn't been put together was, like most rules in the corps, a mystery to be obeyed and not challenged.

That was fine by him. The last thing he wanted to do was talk about the Forum. The debrief and the constant demands to tell his story to everyone he'd met since he'd arrived left him emotionally exhausted.

Now he was recovering from a re-do of his sutured wound. Apparently, the surgery went well. The doc had taken a look at his chart and nodded in an approving, medical sort of way before he moved on to the other two Marines. Five minutes later, the three of them were alone.

One of the other Marines was ambulatory and began to pace back and forth after the doc had left the room. His left arm was in a cast that went from his shoulder down to his wrist. He was not comfortable and let everyone know it. He didn't have an IV, and the oral meds he'd taken weren't cutting it.

"Come on!" he complained to a hospital corpsman who sat at a desk nearby. "My arm is killing me!"

"Doc prescribed Tramadol," the corpsman replied.

"I need more."

"Not for another two hours."

The Marine's buddy was asleep on his bed, an IV was attached to both arms. "Jesus. Lender's got an IV. Why don't I?"

"Your buddy had shrapnel removed from his bowels. He's had major surgery and has three drains pulling shit out of his gut. He needs it. You don't."

"For fuck's sake. Get the doc."

The corpsman shook his head and left the room. Lazzaro wasn't sure if it was to get the doctor or get away from the complaining E-2.

Having undergone general anesthesia seemed to put Lazzaro in the more critical category. He was hooked up to an IV bag with antibiotics and some kind of wonderful narcotic. His own pain was a distant background noise in the back of his brain. More than manageable with the drugs that were being pumped into his arm.

A low buzz suddenly grumbled from his computerized infusion pump and a warm glow began to creep over him. The synthetic opioid began to saturate his brain. With no rest over the last twenty-four hours, Lazzaro happily allowed himself to pass into a deep, drug-induced sleep.

One of the side effects of the drug was active and vivid nightmares. Lazzaro was no exception. He was constantly jolted into semi-consciousness as images of the Variants consumed his dreams. One time, he was at the Forum, where he watched Gonzalez devoured by the creatures. He had another nightmare where Shader and Keele had been bitten. They turned on the survivors and slaughtered them all. The hours he spent in that drug-infused sleep brought little rest.

So, when the sounds of a Variant screaming nearby assailed his ears, he simply rolled over and tried to ignore his overwrought imagination. But a second cry, this time from someone not infected, forced Lazzaro to turn and make sure he was truly dreaming.

Lazzaro froze. It wasn't possible. It had to be another dream. He slowly pinched himself, digging his fingernails into his thigh, just above his shrapnel injury. His wounded leg exploded with pain. He was awake!

Lazzaro glanced up the room and saw the Marine who had been hooked up to the two IVs hovering near the corpsman's desk. He was hunched over something on the floor. Lazzaro raised himself slightly to get a better look. What he saw froze him with fear. The first Marine, the one with the stomach wound, had turned. He was a Variant.

The second Marine, the one with the broken arm, was lying akimbo across his bed. His neck had been ripped open, the blood spatter on the wall behind him leaving no doubt that he was dead. He'd nearly been decapitated.

Grunting and slurping sounds came from the Variant. Lazzaro slowly lowered himself back down and rolled to the side of the bed. He pushed the IV line back and dropped down onto the ground.

The sounds of the creature feeding continued. Lazzaro looked under the rows of bunks and saw the thing feasting on the body of the dead corpsman.

As the minutes went by. Lazzaro could barely breathe. The Marine, now Variant, stopped his meal and stood up. Lazzaro could see his feet moving about the room. The creature was becoming agitated as it hobbled back and forth at the far end of the bay. Lazzaro pressed his eyes shut as the footfalls of the infected thing began to come closer. Creaking and popping from the Variant's joints became louder. The creature howled. It flipped over a bunk in frustration. With the door to the room closed, Lazzaro knew it didn't have the ability to manipulate the door handle and get out. Eventually, it would find him. With a splinted knee and an IV hooked into him, there wasn't much hope of him fighting the creature off. He slid further under the bunk and began to say a silent prayer.

The creature was getting closer. It sniffed at the air, becoming more and more agitated. The bed next to

Lazzaro flew off the floor as the Variant searched for another victim to devour. It was the end, and Lazzaro knew it.

At the far end of the room, the sick bay door opened just as the malformed feet of the creature came to his bunk. The Variant sprung away. Muted cries came from the end of the room, and the sound of both human and Variant screams echoed back to Lazzaro. A brief struggle ensued, and the Variant got out of sick bay and into the open passageway. The creature was loose, and Lazzaro felt a pang of guilt. He'd prayed for just such a miracle and it had come true. But now, the rest of the ship was at risk. Lazzaro began to regret his selfishness just as the adrenaline that had been coursing through his veins began to make him shake. He began to hyperventilate and quiver. He couldn't control his body. Lazzaro lay several minutes, listening to the newly wounded man whimper.

The door to the sick bay opened.

"Where is it?" a man screamed out.

"I don't know!" the injured sailor answered. "Just help me. Please."

Several sailors could be heard in the waiting room. They were searching for the creature, and the quicker it was found, the less chance there was that they would lose the ship.

Lazzaro had begun to pull himself out from under the bunk, when the conversation in the adjoining room became more frantic. He froze and listened.

"Damn it, sailor. Where did it go?"

"Oh God. It bit me," the injured man cried. "Just get the doc. Please help me."

"I will. Just tell me which way it went."

"It ran out and went to the left," he cried.

The second man began to bark out orders, sending the armed sailors to try to contain the emergency. Infection in these tight quarters meant certain death.

"Get the doctor," the injured man pled. "I need a doctor."

"He's on his way. Do you know who it was? Who changed?"

"It was the Marine. The one with the wound to the abdomen. He must have gotten infected by the shrapnel. It probably went through a Variant before it hit him. Please. Get the doc. I need help."

"Yes, son. You do need help but Doc's dead. His body is in the passageway outside. That thing got him. There's nothing we can do. I'm sorry."

"NO!"

A single gunshot echoed.

"That's all the help I can give you," the first man said soberly.

Lazzaro remained frozen as he heard the sound of footsteps. He saw a pair of combat boots walking slowly toward him. He dared not even breathe.

A yell came from the hall. "LT! It's gotten into engineering!"

The boots turned and sprinted away, leaving Lazzaro alive, but very much afraid.

What if I'm infected then, as well? What if that shrapnel had passed through one of those creatures and put its blood inside me?

Lazzaro crawled out from under the bed. Miraculously, the IV was still attached to him. He ripped the needle from his arm and was rewarded with a steady trickle of blood. He staunched the wound with a piece of

4x4 gauze that was on a nearby stand.

Confused, he sat down on the bed and put his head down in his hands. *What to do? Where to go? I can't risk the others if I'm infected.*

Lazzaro was having trouble forming coherent thoughts. He didn't want to report to his superiors and risk being summarily shot, but he also didn't want to turn into another rampaging monster. He couldn't do that to his brothers.

He thought about committing suicide. He got up from the bed, convinced that this was his only option. He moved toward the door and saw the remains of the dead corpsman. The Variant had eaten away half his upper torso. The heart was missing, along with most of the lobes of his lungs. The liver was also partially devoured.

Lazzaro staggered past. The next room wasn't much better. The sailor who had been shot after being bitten lay back on the floor, a bullet between his eyes. Lazzaro stared at the corpse, knowing that this was his fate if he turned himself in.

He spun around, looking for something to end his miserable life. He looked on the dead man's waist. There was a holstered sidearm. He grabbed the M9 from the corpse and found the waiting room's head. He staggered over to it, convinced that ending his own life was the only option.

Lazzaro opened the bathroom door. It was a small, private head with a single sink and lone toilet. There was a small metal door in the wall. It was a pass-through for urine samples. Under it was a bank of shelves with towels and plastic cups.

He bolted the door and sat on the floor then began to

cry. He racked the M9's slide, chambering a 9mm round. He clicked the safety to the fire position and rolled the pistol around with his hand. He mindlessly inspected the firearm, looking it over like he'd never seen one before. He was on autopilot. His brain couldn't focus on a conscious level, so he stopped thinking and let his subconscious mind take over.

He put the end of the barrel to his forehead and massaged the trigger guard. He kept attempting to put his thumb into the trigger well and press, but no matter how much he tried to end his life, he couldn't do it.

Lazzaro finally dropped his hand to his side and sobbed. He couldn't kill himself. So, he did the next best thing. He got up, left the bathroom, and found a pen and some paper. He wrote a note and taped it to the bathroom door, then he went inside the head and locked himself in.

If he couldn't kill himself, then at least, he could warn others. He'd have to leave his death up to his brother Marines. He'd warned them, and that should be enough.

Lazzaro lay down on the cold, white tile and closed his eyes. He was exhausted. He'd been awakened while his body still had opioids coursing through it. Now that the immediate threat was gone, the drugs began to take over. He grabbed some hand towels from the nearby shelf and lay his head on them, then passed out. He could only pray that he didn't wake up as he turned. That would suck.

Outside, as Lazzaro lay in a drug-induced sleep, the USS *Boxer* had a slow and horrible death. The infection spread and within hours, most of the sailors and Marines had either been infected or consumed. Meanwhile, Lazzaro slept behind a door that had a note taped to it.

Caution: Infected Inside

Lazzaro had done the best he could. But like many important and momentous events, it was something small that had been overlooked which doomed the large vessel. Infected blood within a piece of metal shrapnel had made its way into a man, without anyone recognizing this risk. For the want of a horseshoe nail, the kingdom was lost. Small mistakes can lead to big consequences, and the *Boxer* had been doomed because of one tiny error.

— 23 —

High Mountain Dessert
Ranchita, California
John Eric Carver

"You always have two choices: your commitment versus your fear."
-SAMMY DAVIS, JR.

Carver reflected on the turn his life had taken over the last twenty-four hours. The change had complicated his future life. The transformation was both frightening and wonderful at the same time. He wasn't alone anymore. He had Hope.

Suddenly, risks took on a whole new meaning because there were other people to consider. When he and Hope had physically committed themselves to each other, it was unlike any other intimate encounter he'd had before. It wasn't just a merging of their bodies. It had been a fusion of their souls. He wasn't ready for that change, but it happened. He was in new territory and had no map or guide to help him understand. For the first time in a long while, Carver was confused. That frightened him.

He wasn't frightened by the thought of suffering. He'd become familiar with plenty of physical pain over his military career. It wasn't even the idea of his own death and the unknown afterwards.

It was about living up to his new responsibilities. Hope had committed herself to him, and Carver now had two people relying on him in a whole new way. He feared falling short of his duty to protect them.

He'd learned quickly, during his BUDs training, that failure was inevitable when you were pushing the boundaries and living on the edge. Being a SEAL wasn't about falling short of your goal. It was pushing yourself to the limit, giving every last ounce of effort, and learning from the experience. Regardless of the outcome.

BUDs training was treading water with your hands and feet tied together and willingness to keep going until you were literally drowning. It was showing your commitment to risk your life then so you wouldn't fail your brothers later.

Now, there were no more SEALs to live and die for. It was about Hope being hurt. It was about Kyle losing another father. Before yesterday, protecting those two was an abstract idea. It was like fighting for the flag or guarding the walls. Now, it was about failing two innocent and vulnerable people who had become his family.

Carver's mind began to wander as memories of his two intimate encounters with Hope washed over him. The first time they had sex in Beckham Hall's back office, it had been animalistic, neither of them having had a partner in over a year. But this morning, after Harold had announced that he was going to work on the pickup truck in preparation for their trip, Hope had unexpectedly shown up.

She was beautiful. Her combed, silky hair hung loosely on her shoulders. She had put on a bit of makeup, and she smelled of scented soap and a hint of perfume. She'd worn a black lace bra and thongs that highlighted every part of what made her a woman. It had been an encounter by choice, rather than need. They made love accordingly, with thought and patience, rather than need and lust. They used a bed instead of a desk. It was the opposite of their first time, and it was just as wonderful. Just as fulfilling. Just as right.

"Hey, Cowboy. Think you can stay between the lines?" Harold Kinney said.

Carver had been drifting on the road, his mind wandering. "Sorry, brother."

"You need to get right," Kinney replied.

Harold stared out the passenger window, watching the desert roll by. Several minutes passed and he sat silently, his mind fighting to control his irritation. He'd been against this mission from the start. His job was to protect the camp and the people in it. His responsibilities ended at the borders of the 3000-acre facility and not a foot beyond. Risking them all for someone who was likely dead made no sense, other than to placate Hope. But Harold was a good Marine. Once the plan had been formulated, he would do it to the best of his ability.

Harold glanced at Carver, who continued to stare blankly onto the road. He suspected that his buddy had recently gotten lucky with the boy's mother. He'd known about her since he'd met Carver over two years ago. He'd never met Hope until recently. She was the proverbial girlfriend back home, just like the ones he'd heard about from so many of his fellow Marines. Amorphous people who were part of a life that was in the rearview mirror.

But that changed yesterday. Harold suspected something had happened between the two of them. His suspicions had been raised during dinner last night. They were a little too coy and a bit too cautious around each other. Furtive glances and conscious efforts to avoid drawing attention to themselves, all while finding a way to brush up against each other when they were close, was the main clue.

If his buddy finally got some, then good for him. Kinney had no problem with that. But when Hope had asked him to give the two of them a bit of alone time this morning, it got serious. Carver's mind had been taken over, and Kinney wasn't going into battle with a buddy who wasn't one hundred percent into it.

"You all right?" Kinney asked as they sat in silence.

Shrek was lying across the center console, his butt snuggled against Carver's side and his head in Kinney's lap. The Malinois turned and stared back at his master so that when Carver took his eyes off the road to look at the two passengers, they were already staring back at him.

The sight was comical. Shrek and Kinney both had the same, questioning look. Carver began to laugh.

"Okay," Kinney replied, as Carver chuckled on. "I didn't know that was so funny."

"I wish I had a camera. You two had the same stupid look on your faces."

Shrek gave Carver a snide squint and turned back to lay his head on Kinney's lap.

"Dude, you need to get your mind into the game."

"I'm fine," Carver said.

Kinney didn't know how far to take it, but both of their lives were on the line. There were now no boundaries, especially on a mission he had no heart to take part of.

"Was it that good?" Kinney said absently as he stared out the window.

"Excuse me?" Carver feigned, with a little indignation thrown in.

"Come on. You don't think I wanted to crawl out of bed that early this morning just to work on your damn truck?"

Carver hadn't thought of that. Kinney loved his sleep, almost as much as he loved his Modelo beer.

"Shit. Did she…"

"Duh. Of course, she asked me to leave. And I thought Marines were dense," Kinney shot back.

Carver blushed, bringing a smile to Kinney's face.

"No. Not big John Carver. Don't tell me the famous SEAL has been whipped. I never thought I'd see the day."

Carver smiled, the color fading. Kinney was right. He was whipped and it felt right.

"What can I say. I'm now a taken man."

Kinney stared at his friend and tried to decide if he was joking. Carver raised his eyebrows and smiled. Kinney laughed so hard that Shrek had to sit up.

"I won't ask for details," Kinney finally said.

"You sure?" Carver joked. "I can give you the highlights."

Kinney looked at his friend sideways, but the smirk on Carver's face told him that he was joking.

"All right. I get it. You're in love. But that makes it even more important that you focus. You're not in the zone, and I need you there, with me."

"Copy that. You're right. I'm not focusing."

"Thank you. Now, let's go over this one more time. I want to know we're on the same page."

The pickup truck continued forward, barreling past the

small crossroad that marked the town of Ranchita. Inside one of the homes nearby, a mutated creature and several of his minions feasted on a recent kill. The sound of the truck's engine made its head snap up. It ran to the door just as the vehicle sped past.

— 24 —

Ranchita California
Former Home of Manual and Teresa de Chiara.
Deceased
Cyclops

That sound. I know that sound. I rush out of the house. I look down to where I can hear the growl of the metal beasts that the humans ride within. It passes by.

I see them. The human and his partner, a coyote traitor named Shrek. I've heard his master calling him from afar.

Shrek. He smells me. He is dangerous. I remember, from the memory of before the burn. Before the change, when I became what I am now. I vaguely remember killing the animals they were keeping. The humans used other animals for their own food. Now, I am using the humans as my food.

I turn back to my clan. We must return to the cave. The cave where our master now lives. The master that burns within, just like we now do. The master that brought other burning humans to join us. We are a team. We are strong. We are one.

He will be happy when I tell him about this. The weakening of the human clan in the mountains because Shrek has left along with his warrior master.

I yelp at my clan. They are not happy that we have to leave such a wonderful meal of two fresh kills. Human meat is becoming more difficult to find. But if I know my master, he will be happy that Shrek has left. We will pay them a visit tonight. There is a lot more flesh at the human camp for us to eat.

It's bright out, and it hurts our eyes. But we can do it. The burning humans don't like the light either, and their eyes are even more sensitive than ours. But this is important, so we travel back to the cave. Our master demands that of us.

We slink through the desert, finding cover from the bright light above. It is traveling across the sky, like it always does. It is moving down to the ground and will be gone by the time we get back home. Then, our master and the rest of his clan will come out. We will attack and kill the humans, feasting on their flesh. It will be a good night.

We move quickly and quietly. The light in the sky has started to change colors. The bright, white light is now turning red. We turn a corner and stare at the giant hole in the side of the mountain. Inside, the rest of the clan is waiting. Burning humans and coyotes live together, each relying on the other. My loyalty to the master is instinctive. I don't know why we came together. It just seemed right.

He is a big male. Fierce and strong. He was leading a large pack when we met. I saw him and he saw me. We immediately knew our place and I told my clan to join his. We moved together until we found our new home.

I yip, letting my clan know that we have returned. I trot inside and wander about until I smell the master. As always, he is sitting in the middle of the clan. Females groom his head, seeking his attention. The males stay nearby, frozen in a sleep that would disappear if food was brought in or the master called out. My clan's job is to stand guard, protecting all of us.

I run up to him and wait for him to give me attention. It doesn't take long, his hand finding my head, rubbing it. He recognizes my leadership and I recognize his.

I tell him about Shrek and his master. He is pleased. We both walk out of the mouth of the cave. The darkness will soon be complete. My master stands next to a human sign and looks up at the points of light that show up after the bright light goes below the ground. He screams loudly in excitement.

I look up at him. Like humans, his body is covered by a coat of smooth, removable skin. His legs are thick, ripping through a blue fabric through their sheer size. His upper body has a sky-blue cover that is tearing away as well. He moves as quickly as I do, his joints popping and clicking with each stride.

The wood he leans against has human markings on it, as does a shiny plate that is attached to the frayed covering on his chest.

"CHARLIE" gleams back at me from the polished shield.

Then, the master rips the wooden piece from the ground and hurls it straight up into the night air. It lands nearby, and the symbols stare back at me.

ANZA-BORREGO STATE PARK
SATAN'S GATE ARCHAEOLOGICAL SITE
DO NOT ENTER

The master screams. We all reply and begin running toward the mountains and the human flesh that awaits us.

— 25 —

Jennifer Blevins
Coronado Beach Resort, Coronado Island
Dusk

*"It must be, I thought, one of the race's most persistent and
comforting hallucinations to trust that 'it can't happen here' — that
one's own time and place is beyond cataclysm."*
JOHN WYNDHAM
The Day of the Triffids

Jennifer squealed with delight. She had hit the motherlode.

She'd been searching the south side of the island for hours. It was nearly dark, and she'd already missed her flight out, but there were plenty of people willing to take her place. She'd grown tired of looking through the private homes. The ones that were open yielded very little on her list. A partially filled box of tampons that were not the size she used. A couple of Ziploc bags with Band-Aids and one small jar of instant coffee.

There were plenty of homes she hadn't tried, primarily because they were locked, and she had no idea how to open them. Smashing glass was not an option because that could draw attention to her. Patrols still roamed the streets, and it would be her luck that Garrett's HUMVEE would not be the one to respond to the sound. Looting was a serious crime, one punishable by death under martial law.

Jen wandered down toward the harbor in the hopes of finding a trawler or sailboat that had supplies for an extended voyage. Some folks lived on them as well. They were floating apartments.

A few blocks from the water, she spotted the Coronado Beach Resort. A place she had always fantasized about. Its art deco façade reeked of old-world opulence, even with a month's neglect. It had to have something for her.

She stood in the lobby's gift shop. It was an overpriced convenience store whose shelves had been cleared. But in the back, behind the cash register, a supply room was filled with all the product that had once filled the shelves. Every item she needed was all contained in that one, beautiful room.

Jen thanked God and flung her navy-blue duffel open and began to load it up. She used a penlight to work by, holding it in between her teeth. Feminine products, basic first aid, soaps and shampoos, and oral care products. She shoveled it all into one of the two bags and dragged it out the door.

She went back in and gazed at the remaining products. Batteries! How had she forgotten those? They went in along with boxes of energy bars, candies, and crackers. She spotted a box of small bottles of wine. They weren't supposed to bring alcohol on board, which she regretted. They'd have made excellent trading stock.

She spotted a box of Coronado Beach Resort shirts and socks. She took one of each in her size. Just for the memories. She dug into her pocket and left a twenty-dollar bill in the emptied register. She smiled at the thought that some employee thought to take the daily till.

Money was worthless now.

Most everything else was garbage. Knick-knacks and fake jewelry. Little of substance and certainly nothing worth hauling back. Jen had enough to fill out her list, and then some. She abandoned the second duffel and slung the filled on over her shoulders. It was heavy, but nothing she couldn't handle.

She glanced at her watch. It was a little after seven. She'd left a note on Garrett's backpack that she was still here. Her pack sat next to his, so he should have figured that out without the reminder. But he was a man, and they could stare you in the eyes and say they heard what you just said, then swear that you never said a word about the topic an hour later. How the world survived with men in charge was beyond her.

Garrett's flight out wasn't scheduled until after midnight. Her note told him that she'd be back to the room by eleven. She had about a thirty-minute walk back to their place. There was plenty of time to enjoy the night and this wonderful hotel.

Jen became fascinated by the resort. She had dreamt of places like this. She used to fantasize about staying there, lounging at the rooftop restaurant that overlooked the Pacific Ocean. She used to go on the Internet and gazed longingly at the pictures of the old building. She'd dropped several not-too-subtle hints on Garrett that this was a good place to take her if he wanted a weekend he wouldn't forget. But that had fallen on deaf ears.

Jen lugged her bag to the nearby stairwell. She opened the door and dropped the duffel on the ground within. The door hinges squealed in protest. They hadn't been used in weeks or longer. She turned to go up the steps and was struck with a near panic attack. The bottom of the stairs reminded her of the Hyatt Manchester, where she'd escaped just a few weeks back. She'd killed one of the Variants and eluded many more, escaping that day. But, at one point, she'd been trapped in a stairwell similar to this. Caught between the creatures that were running down the steps from above and the infected creatures that were in the hotel lobby, she'd been close to becoming a meal for those horrid things.

Jen stopped and forced herself to slow down. Her breathing began to return to normal, and she was able to assess her surroundings. There were no sounds in the dark vertical shaft. She was alone.

She propped the bag against the outside door and slowly climbed to the first landing. One more flight up and she came to the second-floor exit. She gently opened the metal panel and shone her penlight down the hall.

She went to the first room and found it locked. They used magnetic card readers, and with no power, she couldn't open it. In fact, she wouldn't be able to open any of them.

Disappointed, she made her way directly to the top floor. A doorway led her through to the rooftop deck. She remembered this from her many cyber visits as she web-stalked the hotel. She moved about carefully, the furniture having been shuffled around by winds and storms long past. The dipping pool was cluttered with debris and the bar area was shuttered. Jen didn't care. It was a piece of romantic history, and she'd finally made it.

She reached into her front pocket and pulled out a small bottle of red wine she'd taken from the supply room. She brushed off a chair and brought it to the outer wall. She leaned out and took in the abandoned city. The bluish light from an overhead half-moon bathed the buildings, creating black shadows between the moonlit manmade towers. In the distance, she could see a vehicle driving back and forth, likely a HUMVEE on its last patrol. By tomorrow, everyone should be safely offshore and steaming toward their new home. Wherever that may be.

Jen didn't waste any time looking for a wine glass. It would have been filthy anyway. She sat down and unscrewed the top. Toasting the town, she drank half the bottle in one large swig. It wasn't half bad.

She was transfixed by the city. The deck was on the north side of the hotel, giving her a view of the naval air station over a mile up the island. Various aircraft were ferrying people out to sea. Their landing lights blinked red and green as they approached the naval station's airstrip. She could see a line of Ospreys and helicopters going from east to west, forming a flashing line in the sky. With no light pollution to wash out the aircrafts' beacons, it looked like someone had hung flickering red and green Christmas lights from the clouds. The trail ended over the horizon. It was magnificent and gave her hope that they'd all make it out.

Jen found a brochure for the resort and used her flashlight to read it. There were boats to be rented at the nearby marina and bicycles in the parking garage available for the guests. She fantasized about the facility and the nearby fancy restaurants. She finished the bottle and checked her watch once again. It was almost nine. She decided to head back to the room and wait for Garrett.

"Why not?" she said to herself. She'd take a bike.

Jen found the bike rack a few minutes later. Several were unlocked. They were all identical, so she grabbed one and balanced the duffel on her back. After several adjustments, she finally felt stable enough to ride.

Jen swerved and struggled to get going, the canvas duffel swinging to her side every time she started to pedal. She was about to let out a curse, when an explosion crackled in the distance. She looked over the nearby buildings and saw another orange flash, immediately followed by another boom. Automatic fire assaulted her ears. The bridge was under attack.

Jen brought her duffel around and laid it across the handlebars. She got up on the pedals and pushed. A third explosion ruptured the air, echoing between the tightly spaced buildings.

She panicked. This was more gunfire than she'd ever heard before.

Behind her, the skies lit up. A momentary flashbulb popped at her back, and she turned in time to see an orange cloud billowing up into the night sky. More machine gun fire came from the thin southern isthmus followed by another explosion. Jen froze. It was happening. The Variants were attacking, and she was stuck on an abandoned street with no weapon, riding a bicycle. If it hadn't been so tragic, it would have been funny.

She started pedaling up Ocean Boulevard. The four-lane-wide road was lined on both sides by abandoned cars that had been parked and left during the evacuation.

She nearly dropped her duffel as she accelerated, but she managed to hold on. She was moving as fast as she could, given that she was riding a beach bike with oversized wheels. Leaving her duffel wouldn't help.

She'd only gone a few hundred feet when the lights of multiple vehicles careened toward her. The sounds of a pitched battle continued to come from the bridge while, to the south, more explosions erupted.

Jen slid to a stop and pulled onto Loma Avenue. She watched as dozens of HUMVEEs approached. Five of the vehicles shot by, but the sixth slammed on its brakes and cut hard to its left. The driver barely missed her as they came to a stop just a few yards from where she stood.

"JEN!" she heard.

Garrett popped out of the driver's side door and gave her a smothering hug.

"Come on!" Gardner yelled. "Get in the fucking vehicle."

Garrett grabbed Jen and pulled her to the rear door. She was shoved in and her duffel dumped on her lap. Garrett bounded into the driver's seat. He circled back, using the front yards of two homes to make his 180° turn. By the time they'd returned to Ocean Boulevard, the other vehicles were receding red dots on the horizon. Garrett slapped the steering wheel and began to drive.

"Hold it!" Gonzalez said. "Did you hear that?"

Garrett canted his head, listening to the radio in his earpiece. All three men gasped and turned to each other.

"What is it?" Jen asked in a panic. All three had gone quiet. In the dim light from the dashboard, Jen could tell that something bad had happened.

"What is it?"

"They're gone," Gonzalez stammered.

"Who's gone? WHO'S GONE?" Jen screamed.

"Echo Company, 2nd Battalion, 4th Marines. They were holding the southern isthmus but were overrun."

"There's nothing between them and us," Garrett added.

"Hold on," Gonzalez said, holding his fingers over his headset, pressing it into his ears. "Shit!"

"We're fucked," Gardner added.

"What is it?" Jen asked, afraid of the answer.

"We're to evacuate the island," Garrett said quietly.

"I know that," Jen replied.

"No. We're to evacuate the island right now. Any way we can get off, we have to do it now."

"I don't understand," Jen said.

"Babe. The Variants are moving up from the south. A helicopter reported that they are moving rapidly and there are too many to count."

"How are we supposed to get off the island?" Gonzalez asked. "What the hell are we supposed to do? Go out into the surf and swim to the T.R.?"

"Can we go back to the base? We can get on one of the Ospreys," Jen said.

"You kidding? There were still a few thousand people to pull out. We haven't gotten any boats from the *Boxer* yet, and each Osprey can only hold a few dozen."

Another explosion rocked the ground. This one was less than a mile away. A fast mover streaked overhead and dropped its payload on the advancing horde. No one thought that would do much, given the reported size of the attack.

Garrett turned the wheel of the HUMVEE to the right, and Jen grabbed his shoulder from the back seat.

"No—turn left," she said.

"What?" Gardner shouted. "Go toward the Variants?"

"Go to the marina," Jen said. "There has to be a boat we can get. It's our only hope."

The three Marines looked at each other and nodded. She was right. If they could get a boat going, they could make it to the middle of the harbor and maybe, just maybe, get out to sea.

Water, food, and a final destination were the last thing on their minds. Their first job was to live. They could worry about surviving afterward.

Garrett turned south on Ocean and shot forward. The harbor was just ahead, but from the explosions erupting to their front, the Variants weren't much further down the road. It was a race, and the odds were not looking good.

— 26 —

Outside Borrego Springs
Steele/Burnand Anza-Borrego Desert Research
Center
John Eric Carver

"Insanity is doing the same thing over and over again but expecting different results."
-ALBERT EINSTEIN

"Damn it!" Carver yelled.

The front wheels of the Ford were stuck in a creek bed. It wasn't quite quicksand, but the locals called it "jelly sand." Carver had no idea what the difference was, but it had the same effect on his 4x4. Even with the rear wheels spinning, the vehicle wasn't moving.

"I'm so sorry!" Kinney said for the umpteenth time. "This shouldn't have happened."

They were less than a half mile from the resort. The drive in had been remarkably uneventful. Not a single creature had been seen.

Kinney had the bright idea of searching the Desert Research Center. He'd been to the facility in the past and noted that they had a supply of communication electronics they could use back at the camp. With three families having joined their group, they had run out of portable radios. Backups were needed as well, so Harold talked Carver into the detour. It seemed like a good idea until they pulled around behind the main building and

184

tried to cross a creek that dribbled down the side of the mountain. That's when the front of the truck sank to the axle, entrapping their only ride home in several feet of sand.

They'd tried shoving boards under the sand to engage the front tires of the truck. They used chains that Carver had in his bed-mounted toolbox and pulled and pushed with all their might. All to no avail. They'd been trying for the better part of three hours and the F-150 was still entombed by the desert mountain.

"We need a tow truck," Kinney sarcastically said after their last try failed.

Carver was about to finally let loose on his friend. But he held back. They'd just get angrier and solve nothing. Any argument would also risk attracting the infected. So far, Carver had been surprised at the lack of response from the nearby homes.

The facility sat on top of a ridge that overlooked Borrego Springs. Houses peppered the road up to the buildings. Most looked abandoned, with front doors open or garages vacant. But statistically, Carver knew there should be at least a few creatures lingering about. They had kept their weapons nearby for that reason. But nothing had shown, even with the roar of the pickup's engine as they tried to extricate themselves from the sandy trap. Even Shrek had remained calm, which was the ultimate sign that there were no infected in the area.

Carver took a deep breath and let the anger subside. After all, he'd agreed with Harold's idea. He should have had them focus on retrieving Hope's friend rather than going on a scavenger hunt. He was as mad at himself as much as he was at their situation.

"You're not far off," Carver replied. "We need something to pull the truck out."

"Where the hell are we going to get a tow truck?"

"We don't need a tow truck. We just need something with a strong rear axle that can pull us out."

"I didn't see a single car or truck that could help us," Kinney said as he nodded down the hill toward the abandoned homes.

"I know. But we have to try," Carver shot back. "We aren't going anywhere like this, and I sure as hell ain't leaving my truck."

"We can find a car and drive back to the camp and get some help," Kinney said. "If we have enough people pulling, we could get your truck out of there."

Carver didn't like that idea. It would take most of the adults back at Schoepe to even attempt such a thing. He couldn't leave the kids unguarded like that.

Carver was beginning to think they'd have to leave his beloved pickup and abandon it for good, when he noticed the resort in the distance. If he wasn't mistaken, there was a large delivery truck there that could pull his pickup out of the sand without a problem.

The sun was nearing the western horizon. They had less than an hour left before the night claimed the desert.

"Come on," Carver said. "Grab your gear. We're going to the resort."

"What? We can't go in there without a vehicle! We'll be swamped."

"You're right. We'll find a car and take it. If the place is swarming, we'll keep going and leave my truck behind."

"What about Randy?"

"We'll make that call when we get there," Carver said.

"We're going nowhere doing what we've been doing. Insanity is repeating the same thing and expecting a different result. We've been beating our heads against the wall for hours. We should have done something different a long time ago."

They gathered their gear and let Shrek lead the way. The war dog had an incredible nose. With him in front and Carver directing him with his Dutch commands, they finally found a functional sedan in the seventh house they'd searched. Two of the garages they had searched contained cars but no keys. One home had cars and keys but a near-empty gas tank. Then they found the 240 sedan.

"A Volvo. Now we're safe," Kinney joked.

The older sedan was boxy, but reliable.

The tank-like car started after three attempts. It was a hideous yellow color and had an underpowered four-cylinder engine in it. No way they could use it to pull the truck out, but its longevity was a testament to its simple design. The car was over thirty years old, and it still ran.

Kinney rolled down the window to get a clear line of fire. They had thrown their assault packs in the back seat but kept their chest rigs on. The MOLLE vests had their spare magazines stuffed into five pouches on the front, which made going prone difficult. But the back held a three-liter CamelBak water reservoir as well. Between the front pouches and rear bladder, Carver had no room to move. The seat wouldn't push back far enough from the steering wheel.

So, with arms extended to the side as he was stuffed into the front seat, Carver and Kinney drove the small-motored Volvo out of the garage and down the hill.

Kinney glanced at his friend as he scanned the road ahead. Carver looked like a tactical carnival worker, stuffed into a little clown car. He cracked a smile but dared not laugh. Carver might go ballistic if he did.

Carver knew how he looked and saw Kinney's reaction in the corner of his eye. He felt the same way. But with no mobility as he was jammed into the seat, he'd be nearly worthless if they were attacked. There was no way he could maneuver his rifle, let alone reload the damn thing.

They stopped at the bottom of the hill. A right turn and a quarter mile away lay the resort. Carver managed to roll his window down a bit to let the air and sounds find Shrek's nose and ears. They gave the dog a full minute to sense his surroundings. There was no reaction.

Carver pulled slowly up to the gate and stopped.

"Should we go in on foot?" Kinney asked.

"I vote we run and gun," Carver said. "I'd rather find out that the infected are around at thirty miles an hour instead of on foot. I'm done screwing around with our safety. This is a fool's errand, and I'm not going to take any more risks."

Kinney nodded. "I like the way you think."

Carver gunned the underpowered engine and brought it up to speed. The winding asphalt drive sped by, and he noticed that the manicured landscape had kept its pristine beauty. It had been over a month since the infection, but the beds were covered by lava rock and had kept their tailored look. The ornamental plants were native to the area and were still thriving, even with a lack of human care. Sprigs of grass and weeds had popped up here and there, but for the most part, you wouldn't have known there had been an apocalypse. Carver took this as a good sign.

He flew under the main entrance's portico and swept back out the other side. He kept up his speed and circled back to the front entrance. He stopped, and they waited for something to react to their presence. Nothing happened.

Carver shrugged and repeated the stunt, this time beeping the horn as he went through by the front doors. Again, nothing.

"Maybe there's something out back," Carver said, remembering the side entrance where he and Hope had escaped from.

Carver returned through the roofed overhang and drove by the paved path down to delivery. He backed in so that he could quickly escape any infected horde.

They wound down the asphalt lane and found themselves back where he and Hope had made their escape.

There was a single, eviscerated body still lying on the pavement. It was the one that Carver had shot in the face with the recovered riot shotgun. Even though it had been loaded with rubber pellets, the creature had been so close, it punched through its skull. It was almost a decapitation from the sheer force of the blast. The corpse had been stripped bare by either the infected or by scavenging animals, leaving only a pile of scattered bones to bleach in the desert sun.

The door to the building had been left propped open. Nothing had changed since Randy had drawn the horde to him, allowing Carver and Hope to escape.

Carver stared into the dark hallway. The day was

nearly spent. The sun was tickling the nearby mountain range as it closed in on the end of the day.

"There's the delivery truck," Kinney said.

The ten-thousand-pound P30 was more of an oversized step van. But it had a large diesel engine and a chassis that had been made for school busses. It would be able to pull his F150 free.

"Let's take it back and get your pickup. Then we can come back for Randy. If he's alive," Kinney said.

Carver looked at the setting sun. They had less than thirty minutes of light left. He prioritized. If push came to shove, Randy was more important than the pickup. They needed to find out if he survived.

"No. Randy has to come first. We can always retrieve the Ford later."

"You sure?"

"Yeah. There doesn't seem to be any infected in the area. That may be pure luck, or it could be that Randy is one of them and they've left the area to look for more victims. Either way, I don't think we'll get a better chance than right now."

"Where do we even begin?" Kinney asked, staring at the large building. "They've got over a hundred hotel rooms and God knows how many other places he could hide. How do we find him?"

Carver had been thinking about that. He and Hope had brainstormed just that question, and she'd narrowed it down to three places.

"Hope thinks he would have survived in one of three locations. The most likely one is in the main kitchen. There's a reinforced door protecting their liquor and fine foods."

"If not there, then where else?"

"The maintenance shed is all metal. That would be number two, and the security office has a metal door and that would be number three. But these last two locations don't have any supplies. If he did get stuck in one of those, he would have died of thirst or starvation by now."

Carver thought for a moment, then decided their best course of action.

"We check the kitchen. If he's not there, he's dead. Either he ran out of water or he's infected and roaming about Borrego Springs looking for his next meal."

"Makes sense. But let's see if we can start the van."

"Good idea."

Carver opened his driver's side door and commanded Shrek. "Los!"

Shrek bolted out of the car and sat facing Carver. His eyes pled for an order.

Kinney pulled himself out of the other side and scanned their surroundings through his M4's optics. Carver did as well and after a full minute, they retrieved their assault packs, one person at a time while the other stood watch.

The pair tactically advanced to the delivery vehicle. They paused at the back doors, allowing Shrek to assess the area. The dog remained stoic, his nape hair normal and eyes scanning the surrounding gardens.

They flung the rear doors open and found an empty vehicle.

Kinney slid the driver's side door open and, after verifying it was safe, found the keys to the delivery truck still in the ignition.

"Go on," Carver said, prodding the camp ranger into the driver's side seat.

Kinney shook his head and moved past some black-speckled goo that was caking the floor of the truck. He turned the key and started the van on the second try.

All the while, Shrek and Carver maintained watch. After ten or fifteen seconds gently revving the motor, Kinney shut the vehicle down.

"It's got over half a tank."

"Perfect. Now, let's get Randy and get the fuck out of here," Carver replied.

They turned and made their way back to the open side entrance.

Shrek stayed on Carver's right hip, never straying more than a few feet. His eyes darted back and forth, but it was his nose that warned him of the asps within. Shrek's hair stood up on the back of his neck, and he froze. It was his "tell" that he'd smelled something wrong.

Carver took note as he looked into the blackened hallway. "Use your tubes once we're inside."

Both men reached around to the back of their packs and retrieved their ballistic helmets. There was a square plastic frame attached to the head protector's front grill. They each snapped their night vision monocular onto the helmet using a retractable J-arm that clipped into the NV bracket. As long as they left the arm up, the monocular was inactive. Once the arm was swiveled down, it activated the intensifier tube, giving them a green-hued image. They donned their helmets and clipped the chin strap.

Carver stopped at the open door and listened. There was no sound.

"Revieren!" he commanded, telling Shrek to enter and search.

Shrek shot forward, moving quickly with a slight stoop. He smelled the asps, their odor like a flood pouring out of the dark hallway.

Shrek's speed concerned Kinney. He didn't understand how the dog could bypass so many rooms without stopping to check each one. But each door they passed revealed an empty room, providing more proof of the Malinois's near-magical nose. The dog moved like a wire-guided torpedo, weaving around corners and bypassing rooms and hallways like it knew the way. He and John lost sight of Shrek at one turn, giving Kinney pause. But Carver didn't seem to mind. He just kept moving at a fast walk.

At every corner, Kinney expected to see an infected waiting for them. Instead, they always found an empty hallway. Kinney finally realized that Carver didn't even have his rifle up at low ready. He trusted Shrek completely, so Kinney decided to do the same. They moved rapidly, deep into the underside of the giant facility. By their fourth turn, Kinney had become comfortable. They were, as his Southern Marine brothers used to say, running knee deep in high cotton.

At the fifth turn, things changed.

Shrek froze. His body stiffened as he pointed to an open doorway where a pair of swinging doors had been torn from their hinges. Kinney struggled to hear, trying to glean any sound he could. He held his breath.

There! A shuffling sound trickled out from the black room.

Carver gave Shrek a hand signal. Shrek reluctantly sat

down, his body still stiff and angry. The SEAL waved Kinney up to his side and, with hands and silent lip movement, directed Kinney to follow behind and break to the left.

Kinney nodded and put his hand on Carver's left shoulder. Carver held up his left, reaction hand, and raised three fingers. Then he dropped his ring finger.

Two, Kinney said to himself as he tightened his hand on the rifle's foregrip.

Carver dropped his middle finger, leaving the index up.

One.

A moment later, although it seemed much longer to Kinney, Carver brought his whole hand up and pointed it forward. They moved swiftly.

They were in.

27

Corporal Antonio Lazzaro
U.S.S. *Boxer*
Sick Bay

"Cowards die many times before their deaths; The valiant never
taste of death but once."
WILLIAM SHAKESPEARE
Julius Caesar

Lazzaro woke cold and sore. It took him a moment to recognize his surroundings. He tried to move, but the pain from his leg seared his nerves, shooting into his spine. It was the kind of pain that made you want to stay unconscious.

He tried to move his head, but a cramp seized his neck.

Is this what it's like to be a Variant?

He opened his eyes and looked at his hand. It was normal. No black lines tracing his blood vessels. He touched his mouth, expecting to feel razor-sharp teeth but found normal incisors instead. He scratched them and found that he'd taken off a thin, white layer of plaque. It was stuck under his fingernail. He remembered that he hadn't brushed his teeth since before they entered the Forum. He was still human.

How long does it take to change?

He checked his watch. The analog dial showed that it was almost seven.

Seven at night, or seven in the morning? He had no clue.

The other man had been injured about the same time he had been, both of them hit by shrapnel. But how long ago was that?

He remembered that a corpsman had mentioned the time when his hospital records were being updated. The man entered his blood pressure, oxygen saturation, and heart rate into the bedside computer. That was just before the Variant mutation took hold of his fellow Marine. That was at 1530. If it was 1900 hours now, then he'd been out for over three hours.

Three hours, and he hadn't turned. Maybe he hadn't become infected. If that was the case, then he needed to get help. He had to move.

Lazzaro struggled to his feet, but the pain in his leg exploded. He doubled over and caught himself on the room's sink. After a few seconds, the pain subsided to a dull throb. He pulled back his gown to check the bandaging. There was no leakage from the wounded leg. He needed a splint, or at least some crutches, to assist him. Until then, he'd need to keep his right knee straight to avoid tugging on the sutures.

Lazzaro hobbled to the door and turned off the overhead fluorescent lights, casting the room into an inky darkness. He slowly unbolted the door and eased it back. The waiting room was empty, and the door out to the main passageway was closed.

He moved slowly back to the treatment area, dragging his leg behind him. He searched the drawers and cabinets for anything that could help him walk. Minutes went by as his leg became more and more painful. He quickly realized that he wasn't going to be able to walk if this continued.

Lazzaro gave up finding crutches. He sat down heavily on one of the beds and sank into a deep depression. He was of no use here while the rest of the ship was fighting for its life.

He had to do something. He stood then buckled over. It felt like a knife had been shoved into his thigh. It reminded him of when he had developed an abscess around an impacted third molar. The shooting pain from that oral infection went back toward his ear and was the closest thing he could compare this to.

That gave him an idea. Lazzaro limped to the medical supply bay. He checked the door but found it locked. He limped back to the desk where the corpsman lay. He steeled himself and bent down, searching the eviscerated body for keys that might open the supply room's door.

"Bingo!" he exclaimed, pulling out a set of keys that were all hooked onto a carabiner. There was also a ring with a magnetic plastic card attached. Lazzaro limped back to the door and scanned the card. He was rewarded with the click of an opening lock. A minute later, he came out of the room with a bottle of naproxen and a syringe. He carried a vial of lidocaine and iodine wipes, as well.

The pain was becoming unbearable, affecting his ability to think logically. He chewed two of the giant blue pills, putting the medicine into his system as quickly as possible. He then pushed the needle of the syringe through the vial's rubber stopper. He sat down and wiped his thigh with the iodine pads, just above the sterile bandage that covered his fresh wound.

Jabbing himself with the needle was something he thought he would never be able to do. But the burning and pain, combined with the need to escape, overrode his natural fears. After drawing four milliliters of lidocaine into the syringe, he slowly pushed the needle into his thigh. His eyes exploded with an intense flash of light, and he lost his breath. He let go of the needle and continued to bounce around inside his flesh. After a minute, he was finally able to take hold of the syringe.

The needle was about an inch into his thigh when he slowly pushed the clear liquid into the muscle. The numbness started to spread but soon stopped, leaving the bottom half of his wound in continued pain. The tissue was too thick to allow the medicine to spread properly. He would have to do another injection.

Five minutes later, he was numb. The top of his leg no longer hurt, but he was physically and mentally exhausted by the effort. He had no idea how long the numbness would last, but for now, he could move freely.

Amazingly, his wound had yet to start bleeding again. Lazzaro grabbed an ace bandage and firmly wrapped his upper thigh. He drew another four milliliters of lidocaine into the syringe and put the cap back on. He stuck it in his pocket, knowing he would likely have to use it again before the night was done.

Lazzaro found his dirty BDUs and boots. They were intact, other than the tear that Shader had made in the pants to access his wound. He used some sutures to stitch the slit closed then stood, feeling good once again. Having his camo back on was empowering, but he needed more.

Lazzaro went to the waiting room and retrieved the

corpsman's belt, which had a thigh rig holster with two spare magazines attached to it. Lazzaro put the belt around his waist and holstered his weapon. He bounced up and down on his toes, confirming that the throbbing was gone and his mobility had not been impaired. Satisfied he would be able to move without pain, Lazzaro walked to the door that led to the outside passageway. He slowly opened it.

The hallway outside reflected the chaos brought by the infection. What usually was a clean and well-maintained space was covered by splotches of blood and human detritus. Far off, Lazzaro could hear the cries and screeches of the infected. He shuddered, remembering the horrific night he had spent in the bowels of the Forum.

He had no idea where he was on the large craft.

He returned to the room and found a phone. He dug through the desk, looking for a directory that would tell him what extensions to punch. He couldn't find one, so he hit the "0" button and listened. No one picked up.

With nothing to lose, he began to punch in numbers, hoping to connect with anyone who could help. On the third try, he got through to someone, somewhere on the ship.

"Where are my reinforcements?" a man screamed in the phone.

"Who is this?" Lazzaro replied. In the background, he heard sporadic gunfire and confused calls for help.

"It's Lieutenant Raymond. We called for you guys an hour ago! Where the hell are you?"

"Where are you?" Lazzaro asked back.

"What the fuck do you mean, 'where are you'! You

don't know? Jesus. You fucking Marines are as dumb as bricks. We're in Primary Flight Control. We need help, now!"

"I'm not the reinforcements," Lazzaro admitted. "I'm in sick bay. I just need to know what's happening."

"Get off the fucking line."

The phone disconnected.

Jesus, Lazzaro thought, *it's already spread.* He couldn't believe it had only taken a few hours to get that far. Primary Flight Deck was above the bridge at the top of the *Boxer's* superstructure. If the Variants were outside that station, they had overrun the brains of the ship.

With the *Boxer* seemingly lost and the pain in his leg temporarily under control, he knew he had to do something to get off the ship while he still could.

Lazzaro began punching more numbers but nothing connected. Either he had been unlucky at his number combination, or there was no one left to answer.

He decided to contact the PFD one more time. He connected.

"It's you."

Lazzaro recognized Lt. Raymond's voice. He was remarkably calm.

"Yeah. I'm Corporal Lazzaro. I just want to know what's happening."

"How can you not know what's happening?" Raymond asked suspiciously.

"I've been out. I had surgery this morning. The drugs have finally worn off."

"Christ. You really are out of the loop."

"I saw how it started," he quietly replied. "It was a fellow Marine. He was wounded at the Forum. He took

200

some shrapnel that had Variant blood on it. He turned and got out of the sick bay. That was about three hours ago."

"Hold your position. That's all I can recommend. We've sealed ourselves up. I've called for help."

"Where am I on the ship? I need to know how to get to the flight deck."

"You're on the main deck, forward of the hangar bay," Raymond said. "Just hold your position for now. I don't know how long it will take for your brothers to get here. But let me give you directions, just in case."

Lazzaro listened, memorizing the path up to the *Boxer's* main flight deck. He'd have to move quickly and without a misstep if he wanted to get out of there in one piece. He unconsciously rubbed his right leg above the wounded thigh. He knew his injury could hinder him when the lidocaine wore off. Until then, he'd wait patiently for the lieutenant to call, informing him of the evac plan.

After he hung up, Lazzaro realized he was going to have to make a major decision. The Variants were strong. He had doubts that a counterattack would work. He'd either have to stay in sick bay and wait for rescue or leave the compartment and rescue himself.

Either way, he would be ready.

28

Borrego Springs Spa, Golf Resort, and Country Club
Shrek

"War does not determine who is right – only who is left."
BERTRAND RUSSEL

The smell of asp is strong. The rancid breeze coming from the dark building is thick with their scent. To me, it is as obvious as a flare in the night. But the humans don't have my nose. To them, the smell is just a background noise like the drone of insects or the cries of the birds in the nearby trees. They know it is there, but it means nothing to them, other than the knowledge that a bird or insect is nearby. To me, it is a roadmap, as reliable and accurate as anything the humans could use.

My eyes see in the dark. And when they fail to detect something, my nose fills in the gaps. They work with my feet without conscious thought. I only need to concentrate on what I will do when I find the infected creatures. I know that my master won't want me to attack. He fears I will become sick if I latch onto them. Their skin crawls with the acid of their blood. But I am Shrek. I am the ghost that rules the night, and I am now in the darkness that makes me so feared. I am the hunter of the asp. I will kill them all.

Carver

Shrek was on a mission. Carver could sense when his battle buddy had gone into "wild mode," a term he had coined when describing the Malinois's attitude after acquiring the scent of its prey.

Turn after turn flew by. The dog seemed especially focused. By the fourth turn, Shrek was so far ahead of Carver that he disappeared around the bend. Carver pushed down a moment of panic, worried the dog would attack without command. But as the SEAL took the bend, he was gratified to see his war dog companion standing motionless.

Carver slowed down and brought his rifle up to low ready. Shrek stayed frozen, staring up to the next hallway. Carver felt Kinney's hand on his shoulder, letting him know that his friend was there. They advanced slowly and turned. The hallway was empty.

A set of swinging doors stood open, their hinges bent, the panels canted back into the room beyond. The men moved forward and stood in the hallway, just outside the room where Shrek had pointed them to.

Carver gestured with his hands, positioning Kinney on his left side. They lined themselves in front of the door. Carver clicked on his infrared intensifier that was attached to the NV monocular. After a moment, Kinney did the same. Their beams cut into the room beyond, revealing an industrial kitchen. There was no movement.

Carver held up his hand and counted down from three. At zero, he aimed his open hand forward into the room and moved. They were in.

Carver swept right, while Kinney went left. The room

was in shambles. Cast-iron pans and pots were strewn across the floor while cutlery was scattered across the room from overturned tables. Three steps in and Carver accidentally kicked a pot or pan, sending it clattering across the tile. Screams erupted from the back of the room. A lot of screams.

Carver's brain went into combat mode. Time slowed as his hands and feet instinctively reacted to the threat. The infected began to stream at them, their clicking joints and snapping teeth creating a cacophony of cracks and pops.

He watched the horde as his body responded. He was mentally detached, floating above the morass, an observer of his own deadly actions.

He saw his rifle spit bullets at the oncoming rush. His uncovered, right eye was blinded by the muzzle flashes, but his left eye, covered by the monocular, was unaffected. The green image created by his night vision remained strong, giving him a clear picture of the advancing monsters.

The laser attached to the rail of his rifle created a green line that he used to aim the weapon. He squeezed the trigger every time the emerald beam touched a target. With Kinney adding his rounds to the fray, there were dozens of lead pills pouring out at the infected creatures.

"MAGAZINE!" Kinney cried out, letting Carver know his friend had run dry and was inserting a fresh mag into his rifle.

Carver slowed down his rate of fire. The last thing they needed was for both of them to run dry at the same time, allowing the creatures to advance without consequence.

Shrek barked. Carver knew his dog didn't break silence if it wasn't for a good reason. Carver looked down at Shrek, who was looking to their right.

The SEAL heard Kinney's rifle once again join the battle. He took the opportunity to look where Shrek was staring. He didn't see a thing, but Shrek barked again.

Before he could register what the dog was looking at, Shrek bounded forward and jumped. An infected had scaled the ceiling and was leaping right at him.

Carver brought his rifle up, holding the plastic-and-metal firearm out and across his body.

A piercing scream shook Carver's soul. All he could see was a maw of razors rushing at him, just inches from his own face. He felt the infected man hit his rifle, sending them both to the ground. The last thing Carver remembered before his back slammed into the tile was the stench of the thing's breath. It was acid and rotting flesh, all rolled into a putrid wave of hot air.

It's the smell of death, Carver thought as his head smashed into the unforgiving floor.

Kinney

Kinney continued to fire at the oncoming creatures. A prep table stood between him and the infected. Open metal shelves, which used to hold finished plates for the waitstaff to grab, made accurate shots impossible. One of the monsters lurched into the table, sending it crashing to the floor. Kinney put his laser on its head and let loose a round. The bullet exploded in its skull, ending its miserable life. Pots still hung above the downed table, swinging about as either a bullet or an infected creature hit them. It was surreal as he took shot after shot at the advancing horde.

Kinney heard a crash to his right. He took his eyes off the front for a moment, spinning to find Carver. Kinney was surprised to see his friend on his back, lying at the retired Marine's feet. Even more startling was what was on the floor, just beyond the downed SEAL. It was an infected, and it was battling Shrek.

Shrek

Carver doesn't see it. The asp is crawling at us, up on the ceiling. It is quick, but I am quicker. It is getting ready to spring at us, and I must take it out.

The asp jumps at Carver the same time I leap, and the three of us collide.

I am the fastest of the three. I latch onto the infected man's shoulder, pulling it away from Carver.

The asp howls. It spins, grasping at me. It can't reach me as I bend it down to the ground. It lets out a primal scream, a cry of anger and frustration. I keep my grip on the angry asp, hanging from its back like a giant leech, refusing to let go.

Bending back to try to grab me, it forgets about Carver. But my master doesn't forget about me. Carver brings his rifle and shoots it in the face, sending us both to the ground.

I jump back, keeping myself from being trapped under its caustic, infected body. But I don't let go of its tattered shirt. It is dead, but it still reeks of acid and infection. I drag it back a few feet further, pulling it away from my master.

Kinney

Harold Kinney had never seen Shrek in action before—at least, not in battle. Sure, he'd seen the dog follow a scent, its strides quick and sure. But he'd never seen it attack a foe. He'd never witnessed such unrestrained, raw power. It was stunning.

The clattering of metal on tile reminded him there were more infected to deal with. He turned to face the back of the kitchen, where three of the creatures remained. Each had been wounded in some way. There were over a dozen infected down on the ground, their diseased blood pooling on the slick floor. The remaining three were slipping and fumbling forward, either from the goo at their feet or from non-fatal wounds.

Kinney took his time and placed three pills into their brain boxes. They dropped motionless to the floor. The silence was complete.

Carver

Carver rushed to Shrek's side. The war dog continued to hold onto his prize, like he'd been trained to do, refusing to let go of the dead creature.

"Los!" Carver barked, commanding the dog to release the creature.

Shrek refused, even pulling the body further away from his master.

"LOS LOSLOTEN!" he yelled.

Shrek finally let go.

Carver scanned the room, including the ceiling. The threat had been neutralized. There was nothing left moving except the three of them.

"Flashlights!" Carver commanded.

Both he and Kinney produced their SureFire tactical lights and lifted the night vision monoculars up on their hinges. Then, once the intensifier tubes had shut down, they turned on their bright tactical lights.

Carver inspected his dog. He opened its mouth and looked closely for blood or sputum. He checked for cuts and abrasions. He inspected its ears and eyes, making sure no diseased liquid had entered Shrek's body. The dog appeared clean.

"God, that was close," Carver finally sighed as he stroked his faithful dog's coat.

Shrek simply let his tongue loll out of his mouth and sat motionless, letting Carver praise him for another job done well.

Shrek deserved Carver's attention, so Kinney let them bond. He would take the time later to treat the Malinois to some jerky he'd saved. The damn animal was smart and had saved their lives once again.

A faint cry came from the back of the room. "Hello?"

Both Carver and Kinney stared at each other. The rush of the battle had made them forget about their mission.

"Is anybody out there?"

"Jesus, he's alive!" Kinney blurted.

Carver smiled. Despite his misgivings and the way everything had gone sideways, the mission had turned out well after all.

"Hello!" Carver yelled. "Stay there. We're coming to you!"

Carver looked down at Shrek and pointed his finger. "Blijf!" he said, which meant "stay" in Dutch.

Shrek froze, telling Carver the animal understood. He didn't want Shrek exposed to all the blood and gore between them and the back of the kitchen.

Carver and Kinney picked their way through the mess. Using their flashlights, they were able to weave their way around most of the black-speckled goo and get to the back of the room.

"Hello!" Carver called.

"Oh, God. Are you human?"

Kinney chuckled. He looked at Carver, who had a grin of his own. It wasn't often that they were able to do something positive since the infection took hold.

"Yeah. We're human. Is that you, Randy?"

"Yes! Yes! Yes!"

The snap of a lock and the sound of a bolt being retracted announced the opening of a metal door that sat at the end of the short hallway. It cracked open, revealing a very tired, dirty and grateful man.

"Ouch!" Randy said. "I haven't seen light in weeks."

"Sorry," they both replied.

Kinney shut his light off, while Carver put his flush to his vest, dimming it significantly.

Randy pulled the door back and stepped into the hall. He stared around like a child who had just been woken early from his afternoon nap. His hair was greasy and matted. His face carried a light beard from weeks of inattention. His clothing was filthy and disheveled. But he was smiling from ear to ear. The biggest grin either man had ever seen.

"Is that you, Carver? It is you. I knew you wouldn't leave me! I knew it! I told Hope you were a real man! I told her you would never leave her. Now, you came for me!"

"Hold on there, cowboy," Kinney said. "Let's have our reunion back at the camp. We need to get out of here."

"Oh!" Randy said. "You're right! What am I thinking?"

He turned and went back into the room.

"Come on!" Kinney barked. "We don't have time for this."

"No, please. Come in here. I need some light."

Kinney strode angrily into the room and was hit with the stench of a room continually occupied for many weeks. It was stale and musty, like a locker room after a full day of summer football practice. A slightly fouler odor came from an attached bathroom.

"What are you looking for?" Kinney complained as Randy pushed clutter aside.

"There!" Randy exclaimed, picking up a religious necklace that lay in the corner of the room. "I lost this over a week ago. I figured that meant I was done for. I guess I was wrong."

Randy clutched the silver chain, a cross dangling down.

"Thank you!" he said quietly.

Kinney simply nodded and turned to leave. His light flashed over some blue boxes with black lettering. He suddenly stopped and shone his light on the chest-high stack.

He smiled.

Carver stood in the kitchen. Kinney had gone to retrieve

Hope's friend. He heard them talking and knew Randy had found something he lost. But that had been almost two minutes ago. Since then, he'd heard some mumbling and the scrape of boxes being moved about.

He was about to go retrieve the two men, when the door to the supply room opened and Randy stepped out, pushing a dolly stacked high with cases of Modelo beer.

"Are you shitting me?" Carver asked as Randy stopped in front of him. Kinney trailed behind, holding a long-handled broom. Each wore a large smile.

"Hi, Sailor," Kinney joked. "Wanna have a good time?"

Carver shook his head at the Marine who would risk their lives for a few cases of beer. "I should shoot you now."

"Why not?" Kinney asked. "With that dolly, we're just as mobile as before, and we might be able to salvage twelve cases of this liquid Mexican happiness."

"I can do this!" Randy added. "It's the least I can do for you two. You saved my life!"

"If we get into trouble…" Carver said.

"I know. Mr. Kinney said I was to dump the beer and stay with you. He told me."

"It had better be a real emergency," Kinney said, half-serious.

"I'm a wiz with the dolly. I've been doing this for a decade."

"I've got a broom," Kinney added. "Let me push the bodies out of the way."

"Like I have a choice," Carver complained. Although, looking at the stack of beer tempered a lot of the anger.

Kinney bolted forward and shoved infected carcasses

and fluid aside, creating a fairly clear path out of the kitchen. Randy pushed the two-wheeled buggy through the mess and stopped by the broken swinging doors.

Carver went to Shrek and led him to the door. They stood silently, listening for any sound of the infected. They heard nothing.

"Voruit!" Carver commanded, which sounded like he was saying "Fore At," sending Shrek out into the hallway.

The Malinois shot forward, retracing their steps. Carver followed close behind while Randy kept pace. Kinney followed in back, guarding the rear and making sure Randy kept up. The man was remarkably adept with the two-wheeler. He took the corners without slowing down and didn't hit the walls once. Within a minute, they were outside and in the fresh air.

Shrek stopped and sat down. The area was secure.

Loading the beer into the delivery van went smoothly, other than having to remove the bottom case from its cardboard tray. Being closest to the ground, the tray had infected blood on it from when they moved out of the kitchen.

Both vehicles fired right up, and within five minutes, they were back at Carver's pickup.

Twenty minutes after that, they were driving the F-150 back to the camp. Randy sat in the passenger's side seat, while Kinney and Shrek sat in the truck's bed. They put the cases of beer, along with some communications equipment they'd salvaged from the research facility, in the bed as well. Carver smiled when Kinney had volunteered to sit in the back. He really loved his Modelo.

— 29 —

SCPO Porky Shader
Raven 14
V-22 Osprey
Off the California Coast

"A leader is a man who can adapt principles to circumstances."
—General George Patton

Shader sat in the Osprey, hating every minute of the ride. They'd been ferrying survivors from the San Diego Naval Air Base all afternoon, dropping them off on the *Theodore Roosevelt* or the *Boxer*. It was nearly night, and the flow of air traffic had been, so far, steady and amazingly smooth. He'd moved four flights of people, getting over a hundred souls from the mainland. It was a miracle that Coronado hadn't been overrun by now. Those Variants must be terrified of the water, given their insatiable appetite and just half a mile of water between them and a zombie gourmet feast.

They were returning to the island for their fifth extraction, when his headset crackled to life.

"This is First Lieutenant Erin Donaldson," the Osprey's pilot announced. "We just got word that the naval base is under attack. Our mission has been aborted. We are to pause for further orders."

Not good, Shader thought. He looked up at Sergeant Potoski and received a knowing glance. They both had

213

enough experience to know the LZ must have been overrun for the Navy to abandon the remaining sailors and their families.

A few minutes dragged by while the craft flew slow loops, several thousand feet above the ocean.

"Shader. Get over here," Potoski said.

Porky stood and moved to the back. The rear ramp was down, and the big New Yorker stared out the window.

"Look at that!" Potoski said.

Shader leaned out and looked at the surrounding air. The sky was lit up with dozens of aircraft. Osprey, SuperCobra helicopters, and a few legacy C2A Greyhound twin-prop airplanes were in holding patterns. They all were turning slowly, their green and red flashing lights dancing around them. Shader hadn't seen so many aircraft in such close quarters before. The night sky took on an almost festive feel.

Shader was mesmerized. With all the shit things that had happened over the last two days, seeing the light show created by the military aircraft gave him some measure of peace. Both Potoski and Shader let the drone of the Osprey's engines lull them into a quiet place.

The pilot's voice shook them both from their mental slumber. "This is First Lieutenant Erin Donaldson. We've been given search and rescue orders. Coronado has been ordered to abandon the island by any means necessary. We are to search for survivors and bring them home. Donaldson, out."

"Here we go again," Potoski said with a grunt.

Shader returned to his seat as the V-22 banked slightly and headed straight toward the island. Potoski held onto his SAW, swinging on his feet with every dip and lunge the aircraft made. He was dancing with the Osprey, his knees bending and swaying with every turn.

"Big guy's got game," Shader said softly as he watched the Marine move with the aircraft. Since he was the only other person in the hold, no one heard his remarks.

Just as well, he thought. No one would guess that a man Potoski's size could move like that. It would remain a secret for as long as both of them lived. However long that would be.

Shader quickly lost track of their direction and became hopelessly lost as the pilot weaved back and forth. With nothing to look out toward, no horizon to give his brain a frame of reference, he was becoming nauseated.

With about two seconds to go before he lost his dinner, the craft leveled off.

"This is Donaldson. Variants moving in from the south. You are clear to engage."

Shader repeated their actions at the Forum. He unbuckled himself from the hull and moved to the open backdoor.

Potoski pulled on the SAW's charging handle, sending a round into the machine gun's chamber.

"Grab the spare ammo," Potoski said.

Shader got a second box of belt-fed ammunition and set it down at the big grunt's side. The Osprey was hovering a few hundred feet above the surf. The pilot knew her aircraft and had provided them with a level platform to shoot from.

Shader knelt and turned on an NV scope he'd attached to his rifle. It was sitting in front of his ACOG. It gave him a magnified green image through his battle rifle's optics. He held it up to his right eye and scanned the island out to the south. His four-power Trijicon danced as the Osprey tried to maintain a steady altitude. The magnification of his optic exaggerated the motion of the craft. His emerald-colored image slowly moved up and down as the rotorcraft pitched. The mass of creatures was advancing less than a mile away, yet the slight pitch of the Osprey made them disappear in the 4x scope.

The SAW began to bark. Potoski was using his own Trijicon ACOG and was timing the shots as the craft rose and dropped. The movement of the V-22 was constant, and soon, they had coordinated fire on the thousands of Variants that were moving up the Coronado isthmus.

"Hold on!" the pilot suddenly shouted.

The Osprey banked hard to port. The sudden move slammed Shader against the starboard hull. He saw stars, followed by a throbbing pain in his left temple.

He was about to berate the pilot over the craft's radio, when three Super Hornets blasted by, not fifty yards from where they had been hovering. If Lieutenant Donaldson hadn't moved them, they'd be dead from a very massive and fatal collision with one or more of the jets.

Multiple explosions erupted at the head of the advancing Variants. The concussion from almost ten tons of bombs destroyed the Variants' front line and sent the surviving leading edge of the advancing creatures scurrying back where they'd come from. Shader almost believed they had stopped the creatures, but moments later, the Variants that were retreating ran into the unaffected ones moving north. Like a ripple being crushed by a wave, the flight of those from the front was washed away by the larger advancing group. In the end, they'd bought the people on the ground just a little more time.

The Osprey settled back down, and Potoski began his rhythmic fire once again. And as before, Shader joined the big Marine. At best, they'd buy the island a few minutes. Whether that little time would mean anything wouldn't be known for a while. Maybe Shader would hear about it from some lucky sailor or family member when he returned to the *Roosevelt*. Until then, he'd continue sending .556 rounds down into the infected mob and hope it makes a difference.

Jennifer Blevins
Just north of Glorietta Bay
Coronado Island

"Where the battle rages, there the loyalty of the soldier is proved."
—MARTIN LUTHER

Explosions ripped the road, sending the HUMVEE careening to the left. Garrett slammed on the brakes as the asphalt four-lane street erupted less than half a mile in front of them. Several jets streaked overhead as dozens of fiery clouds fused into a single maelstrom. The light from the combined explosions momentarily blinded them all.

"That's close," Jen said, her eyes adjusting back to a normal level.

"They're dropping ordinance on the front of the horde," Gardner said. "We don't have much time. How far to the marina?"

"Just up there and to the left." Jen pointed at an intersection about two hundred yards ahead.

"Move it!" Polodare yelled, pointing down the road. "We're running out of time."

Garret pushed the accelerator, slowly speeding up the sidewalk and back onto the street.

The marina came into view, boats occupying most of the hundred-or-so slips. Garrett swung left and ran parallel to the water. The billowing cloud from the bombing run was still glowing slightly in the dark sky, its clouds illuminated by the fires ignited by the detonations.

The flyboys caught the Variant mob on the isthmus, leaving the infected horde blocked by water on both sides and a fire to their front. The ensuing flames should buy them some time to find a boat and cast off.

"Cut right!" Gardner yelled. Garrett saw a parking lot and swung into it, sideswiping a few cars in the process. Several curses came from the passengers, but Garrett ignored them as he jammed the brake pedal to the floor. They screeched to a stop, and all four flung their doors open and ran to the harbor.

The wooden dock was dimly illuminated by the nearby fire. Jen was grateful she didn't need to rely on one of the guys to lead her along. Their night vision goggles were great for them, but she would have needed their help if it was any darker.

They stepped across a ramp that hung over the water and walked onto the dock. It was in a "Z" shape. The boats were on the upside and top legs of the zig-zag.

They scurried down the base and turned right, moving further away from land and into the mass of schooners, offshore fishing boats, and trawlers that were parked along the way.

"Everyone! Take a boat. Look for a key and make sure there's fuel."

"I have no idea how to check on that," Jen said. "And it's pitch black in there. I can't see a thing."

"Dude," Manny said. "I have no clue either."

"How don't you know?" Garrett shouted. "You were raised on an island."

"Yo soy del jibaro!"

"English!" Gardner barked.

"I'm from the countryside! Dumbass."

Gardner snorted. "A damn hick. Now it all makes sense."

"Sure, Mr. Flo-ri-duh! Like your state is so fancy. You know how to run one of these things? You practically live on an island, you know!"

Gardner flipped Manny a one-finger salute and shook his head. "It's not that hard. The gauges are marked."

"Uh. Guys," Jen said.

"Screw you," Manny shot back at Gardner. "You don't have a clue either."

"Uh. GUYS!" Jen repeated.

"Let's do this together," Garrett finally said. "We can figure this out…"

"GUYS!" Jen shouted, grabbing Garrett by the arm. She twisted him around and pointed out to the isthmus.

"What?" Garrett yelled back.

The fires were still burning, the buildings and even asphalt smoldering from the bombardment. There was still a wall of protection between the rest of the island and the infected horde coming up the isthmus. At least, that's what they all thought.

But they were wrong.

First a few small groups, then finally a large mass of the creatures broke through the flames. The Variants sprinted forward, the heat and fire failing to stop their advance.

Thousands poured through the inferno, their bodies and clothing alit with patches of fire. The jerky motion of their disjointed limbs had them bouncing up and down while the orange and yellow flames slowly consumed their skin and hair. Their shrieks and moans cut through the crackle of the fire. Their cries reeked of anger and starvation.

"Holy mother of God," Jen gasped.

"Come on," Garrett whispered. "We don't have much time."

The four stayed together. They scampered on adjacent boats, trying craft after craft. Each one proved fruitless. Either there was no key, or the larger boats were locked.

Jen jumped onto the back of a trawler. The forty-four-foot boat swayed after she landed, knocking a patio table and its two chairs across the rear deck. The entrance to the lower helm station and sleeping berths was behind a smoked glass entrance. There was a handle with a key lock. After trying over a dozen craft, she perfunctorily tugged on the ship's sliding glass door, expecting it to be locked like all the others. It opened!

"Garrett!" she yelled.

She rushed into the dark compartment and was hit by a wall of odors from rotting food and mildewed linens. She covered her nose and gagged.

She heard the thump from one of the guys landing on the back of the boat. She was about to turn and call them in, when something groaned from in front of her. Jen froze, terror immobilizing her limbs. A groan, this one louder and more frightening, shook her to her soul.

Jen searched but couldn't see anything moving. It was like staring into a pool of black ink. She heard shuffling from her left. She held her breath, daring not to make a sound.

Another creak on the wooden floors! It felt like someone or something was lurking just ahead. She searched futilely for anything that would tell her where it was. Nothing but a curtain of darkness stared back at her.

Jen took a small step back and hit a weak spot in the floorboards. It loudly creaked.

A primal screech echoed from the left. Jen screamed. She looked into the inky blackness and saw two glowing embers staring back at her from below.

It was a Variant moving at her from the lower berth. It bellowed a horrifying cry, freezing Jen. Her legs refused to respond. The creature leapt, its eyes wide in anticipation of a fleshy fresh meal.

Jen closed her eyes and let out a final cry. She was dead, and she knew it.

Garrett

It was getting difficult to swallow the terror growing inside. They'd checked fourteen boats so far and were just starting on the docks at the furthest end of the marina. They'd come up dry.

The owners had locked their crafts as they normally did when they weren't in use. The infection had spread rapidly, and the likelihood that any one of these had their keys was slim to none. They were on a fool's mission, and Garrett was likely the only one who knew it.

The others had no boating experience. That surprised him. Both Manny and John had come from boat-rich areas. Manny from Puerto Rico and Gardner from Florida. How they hadn't set foot on anything larger than a Jon boat was beyond him.

It was up to him to find their salvation. Garrett knew it was unlikely they'd find something other than a dinghy or a smaller tender. But even those would be locked to their boat's cranes. It wasn't looking good.

Garrett had just landed on the back of a super sport fishing boat. Its fishing tower swung lazily above him as he tried to open the back door. It was locked.

He was about to smash through the glass, hoping the keys had been left inside. He knew it was a fool's errand. If someone had locked the access door, they'd taken all the keys with them. It was the natural thing to do.

"Garrett!" he heard Jen yell.

She sounded excited. It probably meant she'd found an open boat.

He turned and leapt onto the dock and sprinted around to the adjacent dock, where Jen had just gone. He saw the back door slide open on an old Thompson trawler. Garrett smiled. He'd spent time on a similar boat a few years back.

Garrett dropped onto the back of the Thompson. He was about to call Jen's name when he heard her scream. He flipped his NV monocular down over his eye and brought his rifle up just as Jen screamed again. This one, however, held as much despair as it did fear. Garrett knew his fiancé was about to die.

He spun into the doorway just as a Variant leapt at Jen from the lower berth.

There was no time to stop the attack. Garrett futilely brought his rifle up to bear, but the creature was already airborne and would be latched onto Jen before he could do anything about it.

Jennifer

The eyes! That's what she would remember. Not the heart-stopping scream, nor the rancid, pustulant odor. It would be the eyes, radiating a hate and hunger that bore into her soul. She watched, almost in slow motion, as the two burning orbs flew at her through the air. She waited for its hands to clamp down on her with a pincer-like grasp. Would she feel the shark-like, razor-edged teeth slice through her flesh, or were they so sharp that her nerves would fail to register her death? She would soon find out.

Then something incredible happened. The eyes stopped their ascent and suddenly plunged out of sight. The Variant lunged for her but hit the overhang above the lower berth's door. Then, just as she thought she would escape death, a hand grasped her from behind and pulled her back. She never saw the other creature as it flung her onto her back. *How fitting*, she thought. *I'm going to die, and I never saw it coming.*

Jen closed her eyes once again. She'd lost the ability to care anymore.

"Jen!" Garrett screamed.

She opened her eyes and saw Garrett standing over her. He held his slung rifle in his right hand and was reaching down with his left to pull her up. It had been him that flung her back out of the hold. She was lying on the back deck, staring up at the torn, canvas Bimini above.

A scream bellowed out of the boat. Garrett spun just as a Variant flung itself out of the darkened interior, its deformed arms extended and round maw snapping and spitting.

Garrett just had time to put his rifle up and shove it into the creature's chest. He dropped as the creature was pushed away and over him, slamming into the aft gunwale. It bounced onto the deck and twisted itself up before rearing its head back with a shriek.

It squatted down to leap at them both, Garrett having landed next to Jen on the deck of the craft. Just as it started its final jump, two rifles erupted nearby. The Variant was rocked by automatic fire from twin M4s, shredding its upper body with .556 rounds. Its torso and head disappeared in a cloud of infected chunks of flesh. The force of the strikes sent the rest of the corpse over the back and into the water. Jen looked up and saw both Gardner and Polodare standing on the dock, their rifle muzzles billowing smoke from the sustained gunfire.

A moment of quiet had them all feeling like they'd dodged a bullet themselves. They had just enough time to crack smiles at each other before an answering scream came at them from the shore. Jen and Garrett stood and looked to the parking lot where they'd left the HUMVEE. It was thick with the infected, and the creature's scream had alerted them all to the fleshy meal it had found. As one, the mob rushed to the nearby shoreline.

The four stood, transfixed. The horde wouldn't push into the water. It was as before. Back at the bridge, the creatures refused to go anywhere near the ocean, making the bridge a fatal choke point and perfect funnel to prevent the base from being overrun. Now, the water was providing them a barrier as well.

Their newfound sense of security was short-lived. A few found the ramp to the dock and began leaping from boat to boat. Almost a dozen advanced on them. They had less than a minute.

"Jacobs! Clear that craft and get us the hell out of here!" Gardner yelled.

"Cut the lines and push us off," Garrett answered.

He pushed Jen to the side and strode into the craft as Manny took his KA-BAR and began cutting the lines holding them to the dock.

The Variant horde trying to get at them from the land was growing in size. In just a minute, what had been a few hundred was now in the thousands, as many of the creatures coming up the isthmus had directed their attention at them. The back of the horde was pushing hard to get to the front. The seawall was lined with the infected, all screaming at the meal that lay just beyond their grasp.

Gardner opened fire. Nine of the Variants were jumping from craft to craft, and they were closing in on the four survivors. Gardner's suppressed rifle spat lead at the lead creature. With it leaping and bouncing from deck to deck, John's shots failed to find their mark. Five more creatures were not far behind with three of them having disappeared, slipping into the surrounding ocean.

Gardner swapped magazines just as Manny cut the last line tethering them to the dock. He brought his rifle to bear. The two guns now erupted together, cutting down the lead creature.

"JACOBS!" Gardner shouted.

Garrett reappeared from inside, adding his rifle to the other two. Within seconds, the three men put the remaining five advancing Variants down.

"Get in there and start this damned thing!" Gardner screamed.

"Battery's dead," Garrett said glumly. "We're not going anywhere."

As if they could hear Garrett declare that they were stranded, the horde of creatures back on shore let out a scream that shook the very decks of the nearby boats. The four looked back to the mass of infected and watched as the front creatures were pushed into the water by those in the back. It almost looked comical as the infected lost their purchase and fell forward into the murky ocean. The next in line were pushed into the water as well, followed by even more. The back of the horde had grown. They were too numerous to count. Tens of thousands were pouring through the dying flames at the mouth of the isthmus, many of them turning toward the sound of the wails and cries from the shore.

Then, a strange thing happened. The leading edge of the infected stopped falling into the ocean. They seemed to be getting closer. They were still being pushed, but it was like the land was reaching out toward the group.

It took Gardner just a moment to understand what was happening.

"They're stepping on the ones that've already dropped into the water. We have to get the hell out of here. NOW!"

"Push us off," Jen pled. "At least, let's get us away from the dock."

The three men leapt out of the boat and began to push the forty-four-foot trawler out and away from the mooring. At the last minute, they jumped onto the back of the boat.

The craft slowly drifted towards the center of the harbor, as more and more of the Variants were pushed into the sea. The line of creatures was never ending. They all realized that, given enough time, the Variants would create a mass at the bottom of the harbor that would eventually reach them.

Jen looked up at Garrett and saw, for the first time, fear in his eyes.

She clutched his chest, hugging him tightly as the boat slowly drifted. Its momentum would eventually be overcome by the tide. At some point, they'd be moving back into the clutches of the infected.

"Can we use the dinghy?" Gardner asked as he stared at the Variants being pushed into the water.

"The crane runs on electricity," Garrett replied. "It won't lower into the water."

"Can't we cut it loose?"

"No. It's bound by steel cables. I checked."

"What do we do?"

"Find life preservers and get ready to abandon ship. The only thing we can do is swim for it. Maybe if we go in the water, they'll lose track of us."

Jen pulled herself from Garrett's chest and looked up at him. "You think that will work?"

"Yeah. I think so."

He kissed her forehead.

She smiled but held her thoughts. Garrett may have said it would work, but his eyes betrayed his true beliefs. He was still frightened. His uncertain gaze told her he didn't think they would make it. She could see that as he looked down.

Jen grabbed him tightly. It was all she could do.

— 31 —

Porky Shader
Raven 14
V-22 Osprey

Shader had emptied most of his magazines into the advancing horde. The fires that had been lit by the F-18 bombing run were now starting to dissipate.

Watching the creatures push through the flames was probably the most amazing and horrifying thing he'd seen to date. The leading edge of the monsters had been engulfed in fire, running forward like human torches. They'd lasted almost a hundred yards before they started to lose their direction. Hundreds began to wander aimlessly as the ones behind pushed past. The best he could tell, Shader figured that their eyes had been burned through, leaving them blind. Yet, they continued to haphazardly advance, searching for their next meal.

Potoski was loading his last of the belt-fed ammunition. His barrel glowed red from sustained fire. It might even warp with their last 800 bullets, but they didn't have a spare barrel to swap out. He ripped the empty drum magazine from under the weapon and dropped it to the floor. It joined over a dozen other empties. He slid one of the four remaining 200-round drums under the weapon, locking it in place. He pulled a belt of ammunition from the oversized drum and laid it on the top of the machine gun's open chamber. He dropped the cover back over the belt and pulled and pushed the charging handle, putting the first round into position. He was ready to rock and roll.

"You dry?" Poloski asked.

"Nah. I've got two more mags."

The two men watched the creatures continue to pour onto the main part of the island. Most of them were heading directly under their hovering craft, moving north toward the naval air station and the remaining survivors. But some of them weren't. In fact, a lot of them were moving to the east and massing at the local marina.

"That's strange," Shader commented. "There's a shitload of them over by the marina."

"I noticed. You think something attracted them over there?"

Both men strained to see the harbor area. They weren't far from the mass of boats, but with the Osprey pitching slightly, it wasn't easy to see into the dark harbor. It all looked like a mass of ships and more Variants than he could count.

"I think we should take a look," Potoski finally said. "We ain't doing shit here. Just wasting ammunition."

"Copy that," Shader said. "Let's see if our pilot can swing over there and have a look."

Jennifer

On Board the Trawler, *Finally*
Glorietta Bay Marina

"That didn't last too long," Manny commented. "We're already moving back toward land."

Garrett had realized the tide was working against them. They'd made it about two or three hundred feet from the dock before the tide and the drag of the salt water stopped their momentum. They were now slowly drifting back toward the dock.

"Do we jump?" Jen asked.

"Has anyone found life preservers?" Garrett asked.

"What do you think?" Gardner angrily replied.

They had all been searching the boat for anything they could use to paddle them out further. They hadn't found a thing. What was worse, there were no life-preservers. From the look of things below deck, the Variant they'd killed had likely been using the craft as a floating home before becoming infected. It was possible he hadn't left the dock for the open seas in months or years. Without the need to navigate the ocean, life-preservers were not necessary. At least, that's what Manny had predicted.

The other three would like to have ignored his pessimistic predictions, but Manny's negative outlook had been remarkably accurate. They hadn't found a single thing that would help them float, other than an ice chest that might act like a small buoy that they could hold onto.

Garrett looked at the shore. More infected were pouring into the water, and the line of creatures was getting closer by the minute as the ones under the surf provided those above with a platform to stand on. Between the advancing infected horde and the push of the relentless tide, they had less than five minutes before the two forces brought them together.

"I think it's time," Gardner finally said.

They grabbed the empty ice chest and tossed it into the water.

"Ready?" Garrett asked Jen.

She nodded and stood up on the gunwale.

"Wait!" Manny said, freezing Jennifer on the edge of the craft.

"What is it?" Garrett asked.

"Don't you hear it?"

"No! The only thing I can hear is those things on shore," Gardner replied.

The sound from the horde was deafening. Screams and barks echoed around them. It was like being at the primate enclosure of the San Diego Zoo. If you could take the screeches and barking from the chimpanzees and run it through a stadium loudspeaker system, you might come close to the sound of tens of thousands of Variants trying to get to their next meal.

"No," Manny said. "It sounds like…"

"A plane!" Jen shouted, pointing into the sky.

The four stared up above the Variants and watched as an Osprey slowly hovered over the crowd. The Variants, intent on eating the four of them, suddenly turned their attention to the military craft that was dogging them from above.

The V-22 moved slowly back and forth as if searching the area around the infected.

"You think they're looking for us?" Gardner asked.

"I don't know. But I have an idea," Jen said.

She ran into the boat and came out a few seconds later with a flare gun. She loaded a round into the gun's chamber and snapped it closed.

"I hope this works," she said quietly to herself. She raised the gun and pointed it out and over the open water. She pressed the trigger. A small explosion erupted from the barrel and sent a large red burning ball into the air. It arced over the harbor and landed in the bay.

Jen watched as the Osprey stopped its lateral movements and froze over the creatures. For what seemed like an eternity, it hovered unmoving. Jen loaded another flare into the gun. She broke it open, took the remaining flare, and dropped it into the back. She shut the chamber and began to raise it up once again.

"They saw us!" Manny screamed.

Sure enough, the Osprey began to move in their direction.

"They saw us!" Garrett repeated.

"Yeah. But, so did they!" Gardner said, pointing at the Variants on shore.

What had been a slow but steady push into the ocean became a rush. When Gardner first looked at the horde through his NV goggle, they glowed brightly, dropping creatures into the water at a slow and steady rate. It looked like a Hawaiian volcano oozing lava into the ocean. Now, it was like a flood rushing down a mountain stream. Thousands were being pushed into the bay water, pushing the horde toward them at an even greater rate.

"Jesus. They'll be on us in no time!" Manny cried.

With the horde filling the bay with the Variants and the ones behind using them as infected stepping-stones, their time to stay alive was rapidly dwindling.

"Maybe ninety seconds," Gardner said, estimating how long it would be before the creatures got to them.

The Osprey hovered overhead then began to descend. Its rear ramp was down, and Jen could see two soldiers leaning out, staring down at them from above.

Garrett looked up and saw the same thing, but he

expected a rope to drop so they could be hauled up. Instead, the transport continued to descend. If it didn't stop soon, the aircraft would be floating in the bay, marooning that crew along with the four of them.

"What the hell are they doing?" Garrett commented.

"Shit. It looks like they're gonna land on the water."

"Do they float?" Jen innocently asked.

"Nope," Garrett replied as the air around them shuddered from the downdraft. "If they hit the water, they ain't coming back up."

Jen watched in horror. The Osprey looked like it was going in. The rescue was quickly turning into a fiasco. She closed her eyes as the rotors of the twin-engine craft pushed over them. She didn't want to watch.

Shader
Raven 14

The flare had been unexpected, but once Lt. Donaldson saw the red ball arc into the air, she decided to initiate a hot extraction.

"Sergeant. Do you have any rope back there?" Donaldson asked after seeing the SOS signal shoot into the sky.

Shader and Potoski searched the craft for anything they could use to rope down or at least, pull the survivors up with. They found nothing.

"That's a negative," Shader replied into his headphone.

The Osprey continued to hover, then slowly began to drop.

"I'm going to go down and get them. We'll use the ramp. I'll need some help with the last few meters."

"I've got your back," Potoski replied. "Let's bring them home."

"I sure hope she knows what she's doing," Shader commented as they slowly descended toward the trawler.

Potoski leaned out over the edge of the ramp, calling out directions to the pilot. The giant twin-engine craft was pushing massive amounts of air down onto the trawler, forcing the four survivors to duck for cover. About ten meters above the water, the boat's Bimini ripped and flew towards shore.

That's when Shader noticed that the rotor wash was pushing the trawler toward the advancing horde.

Porky froze as the canvas cover shot away. And he never froze. He had been so intent on helping Potoski guide the pilot, he hadn't noticed the Variant horde pushing into the harbor. The interior lights of the Osprey, combined with the noise from the engines, had masked the wall of flesh that was rolling at the ship.

"Pull up!" Shader yelled into his mic.

The Osprey suddenly shot up as Donaldson shoved the throttle forward, lifting the craft into the air.

"What was it?" the lieutenant barked in his headphone.

"You're pushing the ship into the shore."

Donaldson tilted the craft to the left, giving her a view of the shoreline. She gasped.

Thousands were pouring into the water, shoved forward by tens of thousands from behind. The harbor was only so deep, and it was filling up fast.

Donaldson pushed her fears aside. The Variants would be close enough to the ship within a minute and pushing them toward the horde wasn't the best idea. Then she had an idea.

"Let's do this again," she said over the craft's internal coms. "Give me some help back there."

Shader and Potoski looked at each other as the Osprey swung around and came at the boat from the shoreline. As she began to settle lower, Shader recognized her plan.

If coming down on the harbor side pushed them closer, then doing the same from the shore side would push them out.

At ten meters, her plan was working. The boat began to slow its movement inland. Unfortunately, the size of the infected horde was exponentially increasing. There were hundreds thousands of Variants pushing up the island, and many of them were turning in the their direction.

Donaldson settled down to five meters above the ship. Having angled the Osprey toward the land, she was staring at a rising mound of infected flesh. It looked like a pile of ants crawling over each other, attempting to get to their next meal. They were less than a hundred meters away and as high in the Osprey.

"Down three meters," Potoski said.

Donaldson eased the throttle back and lowered them just a little more.

"Down one more meter," Potoski said.

"For Christ's sake," she muttered. "Do they think I'm running a crane?"

Cranes don't have downdrafts to worry about. There's no wind shear operating a winch. One-meter increments were for hand tools and home builders, not a sixteen-ton flying steel tube.

Donaldson did her best not to look forward. She

concentrated on maintaining a stable platform.

"Back one meter," Potoski said. "They're drifting away."

Donaldson shook her head and adjusted her controls.

Another minute went by. Potoski hadn't said a word since their last correction. She assumed they were bringing the survivors on board.

Her co-pilot wasn't really involved with these maneuvers. He was staring out the front glass, watching in horror as the mound of Variants grew. They were now towering over the Osprey and less than fifty yards to their front. He could see the infected creatures near the bottom smashed as the top of the pile grew. Even with tons of flesh crushing them from above, the Variants near the bottom of the heap reached out at the Osprey, snapping their jaws and whipping their tongues about. Their primal instinct remained, even as their bodies were pulverized by the weight of the growing mountain of flesh.

He estimated the advance of the Variant growth. They had just a few moments remaining before the pile would overwhelm them.

"GO!" Potoski screamed. "We've got them."

Donaldson instantly pivoted in the sky and pointed the craft away from the Variants. She had begun to accelerate with a sigh of relief, when several heavy thuds echoed through the craft. Her controls became a bit mushy, but she quickly compensated with a bit more juice to the throttle.

"How are we doing back there?" she said into her mic.

There was no response.

"Sergeant, reply."

Again, nothing.

She turned to the co-pilot, who had a look of dread on his face. Something had happened and neither of them wanted to find out.

Porky Shader

Shader and Potoski gripped the harness, leaning out over the harbor water. They were able to concentrate on the survivors with the aircraft now facing away from shore and with the wash of the rotors and drone of the engines blocking out the screams from the Variants.

The people on the trawler had a rough ride, though. Porky wasn't sure they'd make it when he saw the wall of creatures rising above them, the wind from the Osprey's blades pushing them into the oncoming horde.

But that damned pilot knew what she was doing. Repositioning the bird put the engine's backwash in just the right position to move the ship away from the threat. Donaldson was slowly dropping them down to the deck, just a few inches at a time.

Shader turned and motioned to the pilot's ramp camera, giving Donaldson hand signals on direction and height. She was a magician.

Porky looked over the edge and watched the four huddled in a clutch, heads bowed from the tornadic winds whipping around them.

It was three soldiers in camo and a woman.

With just three meters remaining, porky gave Donaldson a "slow down" signal and held up three fingers. The tilt-rotor slowed down even more, dropping at a snail's pace.

Shader saw one of the men break free from the huddle and bring his rifle up. He was pointing it toward the Osprey!

Before Shader could react, the man began firing.

The shots rifled to the side as the man dumped his 30-round magazine at a threat unknown.

Shader realized he was concentrating so intently on directing the aircraft that he'd momentarily forgotten about the Variants massing on the shore. Less than a minute ago, he was staring at a growing mountain of infected monsters. How he'd forgotten that terrifying scene was beyond belief.

The ramp settled down, and the survivors were hauled up one by one. The last man on was pulled in and Potoski yelled into his mic.

"GO! We've got them."

Shader held onto his harness as the tilt-rotor craft spun on its axis, turning out to the water. The view suddenly changed as the shoreline came into view. Porky was stunned. The mountain of flesh had grown exponentially. In less than a minute, it had swelled almost a hundred feet in height, untold numbers of creatures boiling over the edge. He had to lean out to see the top of the pile.

The Osprey began to move, slowly accelerating and lifting at the same time.

Then Porky watched as hundreds of the Variants flung themselves out at them. Just like at the Forum, bodies began tumbling from the sky as the creatures dove at the craft. The Variants screamed as they hurled themselves just past the open ramp, plummeting into the water by the dozens.

Shader and Potoski both backed up away from the rain of death and heard the thump of several bodies landing on the aircraft's frame.

As the Osprey began to move forward, the nose of the craft lifted, dropping the rear into the air. As they banked to port, two Variants fell onto the ramp with a thud, having lost their hold on the aircraft's frame.

The woman screamed as she and the others gripped anything they could hold onto while the pilot sought speed and altitude with her severe angle of attack. The creatures crouched on the ramp as they sought their prey.

One of the rescued soldiers brought his rifle up and pulled the trigger. It clicked on an empty chamber.

A Variant leapt into the narrow compartment and came down on one of the men. His rifle came up butt-first. He dropped and rolled as the Variant was flung over top of his body. The creature tumbled against the closed cockpit door and sprung back with amazing speed. It was met by Potoski wielding a fire extinguisher he'd pulled from the wall. He smashed the thing in the head with a roundhouse swing, and it fell back against the bulkhead. Potoski used the metal canister as a pile driver and crushed its head, leaving the extinguisher partially buried in its skull. Potoski watched as the creature's tongue continued to instinctively whip about its mouth as the rest of the body died.

Shader was a little less barbaric with the second Variant. He drew his M9 and placed two bullets in its head as the creature readied itself for an attack. It staggered back and off the ramp, falling into the harbor below.

"DON'T TOUCH THAT BLOOD!" Shader yelled

over the screams of the twin Rolls Royce engines. Both he and Potoski wore a flight helmet with ear protection and a boom mic, while the survivors were struggling with the high-pitched whine of the rotors. They all nodded back.

Shader moved around the dead Variant and pounded on the cockpit door.

"It's Shader," he said into his mic. "We're clear back here. Four more souls on board."

"Copy that," Donaldson said. "We're heading back to the *Roosevelt*."

— 32 —

Antonio Lazzaro
U.S.S. *Boxer*

"A hero is no braver than an ordinary man, but he is brave five
minutes longer."
–RALPH WALDO EMERSON

It was becoming abundantly clear to Lazzaro that he was going to have to save himself. He'd communicated with primary flight control several times over the last few hours. They'd managed to let fleet know that the *Boxer* was overrun, stopping any further flights onto the ship. But by the sound of the lieutenant's voice, it wasn't looking like anyone was coming anytime soon. Raymond had admitted that Coronado was being evacuated and all air assets were tied up for the foreseeable future.

But his last attempt to contact the LT had proved fruitless. He'd let the connection ring and ring. No one picked up. Chances were they had finally been overrun.

Lazzaro had to move. He'd given himself another round of lidocaine injections after noticing that the pain was returning to his leg. He refilled two more syringes and stuffed them into his pocket.

He called the primary flight deck one more time. No answer.

"No time like the present," he said to the empty room.

Lazzaro moved to the passageway door and listened. After a minute of silence, he slowly opened the door and

243

moved outside. He crept forward, following the mental path he'd memorized to move up and out of the ship.

He came to a ladder and quietly ascended. He spun the handle on the hatch and pushed it open. This second deck was littered with bodies, its bulkhead sprayed with human and Variant blood.

He secured the hatch behind him, dogging the door so he didn't have to worry about something following him.

He picked his way around several dead Variants and found a Marine who had been nearly decapitated. Lazzaro picked through the corpse and retrieved any clean item he could use.

An M4 lay on the deck and, with several other corpses nearby, he kitted himself out.

His prized find was several flash-bang grenades. They'd been effective back at the Forum, disorienting the Variants and pushing them back.

With a squad headset, full loadout of ammunition, weapons, and full body armor, he was ready to roll. He pulled back on his rifle's charging handle, ensuring there was a loaded round. Then he moved.

As he made his way through the ship, he realized he had found the QRF the primary flight deck had called for. Over a hundred Marines and many more Variants were lying dead, their bodies riddled with bullets or their corpses eviscerated.

Twice, the sound of Variants slurping and grunting as they fed drifted down the passageway, warning him to change course well before he could stumble on them. But he was becoming disoriented. He'd memorized the way with specific instructions. Once he varied from that path, it became a crapshoot. Several placards seemed to give him some direction, but after two more hallways and another ladder and hatch, he knew he was lost.

Lazzaro found himself moving down a passageway when he heard the clicking and popping of dozens of Variants moving toward him.

He had to find a place to hide. He tried several doors but found them locked.

"Damn it!" he said in a low voice as he heard the creatures just around the next bend. He brought his rifle up and stared down its red dot optics.

"Fuck!" he said to himself.

The door next to him opened, revealing a dark room beyond. A frightened sailor stood back as Lazzaro rushed the door. He closed it and within seconds, the sound of a pack of Variants rumbled past.

After the last of the creatures had moved on, Lazzaro finally turned around and looked at his savior. It was a young female sailor, barely a teenager by her looks.

"Thanks," he whispered.

She just nodded, a fearful look on her face.

Lazzaro took off the helmet he'd recovered and put out his hand. She held her arm back, refusing to shake his hand.

"Corporal Antonio Lazzaro. United States Marines."

"Are you here to rescue us?" she asked hopefully.

"Afraid not. I was in sick bay when it all went down. I'm just trying to get out of here."

The young girl assessed him for a moment then finally replied. "Seaman Janet Gruber. Communications technician."

"How long have you been in here?" Lazzaro asked.

The E-3 turned away and refused his stare. "A while," she cryptically replied.

"A while?" Lazzaro replied. "What does that mean?"

"Nothing!" She had started to yell before catching herself so she didn't alert the creatures outside. "Just a while," she whispered.

Something wasn't right. She seemed to shrink into the corner of the room.

"Hey. It's all right. I can get us out of here."

"That's okay. I'm fine here."

"You're what?" Lazzaro replied. "You do know what's going on out there, don't you?"

"Sure. That's why I have the door locked."

"You can't survive in this room for long. You'll die of thirst or worse."

"No. I'll be all right. If you want to go, I'm good with that."

Lazzaro was dumbfounded. The frail sailor stood in the far corner, holding her left arm over her right.

"Well, I'm lost. I'll need your help to get to the flight deck."

"I can tell you how."

"Why don't you show me? We can go together."

"No," she quietly replied. "But here's how to get up there."

She gave him instructions. It wasn't far.

He was confused at her reluctance to move. He understood her fear of leaving the safety of the room, but she'd be dead in a few days. Dying of thirst was a horrible way to go.

He approached her slowly.

"Hey. I know it's scary. But we have to do this. No

one's coming for us."

She looked back at him with terrified eyes, shaking her head side to side.

"No. No, I can't," she sobbed.

Lazzaro tried to take her hand to console her, but she twisted away from him. Her left arm came down, exposing a wound on her right hand.

"Let me see that!" Lazzaro commanded.

After a momentary struggle, the girl relented.

Lazzaro examined the bite mark. Black lines were already spreading up her arm. She'd been bitten by a Variant.

She sobbed as he traced the infection up the limb and onto her neck where he noticed that her jugular vein was beginning to distend and turn dark. She didn't have long.

"Please, just leave."

Lazzaro stood quietly. They both knew what was coming.

"Hey," he said with a smile. "I can fix that!"

The girl stopped crying and gave him a doubtful stare. "How?"

"I have medicine. Here. Let me show you."

Lazzaro pulled out one of his syringes and held it up for her to see.

"It's from sick bay. They found a cure."

The girl continued to look doubtful.

"Seriously," Lazzaro said. "Look. I had a wound, and it fixed me."

He pointed to his sutured pants where Shader's knife had cut through the fabric to access the shrapnel wound that he'd received at the Forum.

"I can pull down my pants if you don't believe me," Lazzaro joked as the girl continued to assess him.

"No," she finally replied. "I believe you."

"Let me give it to you. Sit down over there."

The sailor seemed to relax. She moved to a chair and sat down.

Lazzaro grabbed a large towel from a nearby bench and handed it to her.

"This is going to hurt. I know, because I got one. You need to cover your face and bite on this, so you don't yell. We don't want to die because the Variants heard you scream."

She smiled and nodded, covering her face with the folded, thick towel.

"I'm ready," she said.

The gunshot from Lazzaro's M9, muffled by the thick cotton-blended towel, barely echoed in the small room. The sailor fell back to the floor. The towel dropped to the side, revealing the young girl's face. She was grinning, a bright smile of hope frozen on her face.

Lazzaro squatted down next to the girl and brushed back some hair that had fallen over her cheeks. She looked so young. So innocent.

Lazzaro wiped a tear from his eye and took a deep breath. He'd given her a good death. In this new world, that was all any of them could ask for.

Shader
Over the Pacific Ocean

The noise inside the Osprey limited conversation. The four survivors, Potoski, and Shader moved to the rear of the craft, putting as much space between them and the dead Variant as they could.

Shader approached the four they had rescued, who had settled into bulkhead seats. Two of them stared at the bulkhead, lost in thought. The other two, a soldier and woman, sat next to each other. They were holding hands.

Shader bent over and yelled to the couple. "My name's Shader," he yelled.

"Jacobs!" the man yelled back. "Master-at-arms."

"My name's Jennifer," the woman answered loudly. "I'm his fiancé."

"That's Gardner, and the other guy is Polodare," Jacobs shouted. "They're also B640."

Shader nodded. At least these guys had some training with a rifle. Not many sailors spent time behind a trigger.

Shader went back and sat down by Potoski. "Shore Patrol," he told the big Pole.

"Hrrumph," he said. "Never liked those assholes."

Shader smiled. He was sure the Marine had been rung up more than once by the Navy's police.

Potoski continued to have a sour look on his face as Shader closed his eyes to wait out the short trip to the T.R. His rest didn't last long.

"Attention. This is Lieutenant Donaldson. We've been tasked to check on the *Boxer*. They were fighting an infection, but fleet lost contact with the ship a few minutes ago. We'll be over her in about five minutes. All crew members, weapons hot."

Shader gave Potoski a tired look. They both sighed, got up from their bulkhead seats, and stood at the ramp. They had closed it after the rescue. Potoski hit a switch, and it began to open once again.

Potoski flipped open the top of the SAW and verified that a round was waiting. The open-bolt weapon was ready, the first bullet in the string sitting next to the chamber and firing pin retracted. A full belt of .556 rounds snaked back into the attached box. If need be, they had plenty of lead to share with the Variants.

Jacobs moved to ramp and leaned over next to Shader's ear. "Do you need another rifle?"

Shader looked at the young man. He was half his age. He even had a few small pimples showing from under his helmet. He was just a kid.

"Don't know!" he screamed back over the howling wind and engines. "We're doing recon on the *Boxer*. They lost contact with the ship, and we're going to find out why."

Jacobs gave him a knowing look. He checked his M4 and verified that a round was chambered. He made sure it was on safe and nodded to Shader.

"We can probably handle this," Shader said to the kid. "Why don't you take a seat."

"I'll stay."

"Why?" Shader yelled back.

He looked back at his fiancé. "I have a lot to protect."

Shader understood. A man had to do what he could to keep the ones he loved safe. For some, it was as instinctive as breathing.

"Keep to my left and try not to spray us with your brass."

"I'll do my best!" Jacobs replied with a smile.

There were no promises in war. Shader grunted his approval.

The Osprey began to slow down. Soon, Shader could

see the deck of the amphibious assault ship pass below them. Donaldson was slowly moving a few hundred feet over the craft as they searched back and forth, looking for survivors.

She ran the length of the ship, the deck peppered with abandoned machinery and a few corpses. She made a wide turn over the ocean, preparing for a second run. This gave Shader a view of the entire craft. He gasped when he saw the island covered by Variants. The infected creatures were scurrying up and down the ship's superstructure. The windows of the multi-level bridge had been broken open, with infected sailors scurrying in and out like an ant infestation. No matter how secure the hatches, the bridge had been doomed. That explained the loss in communications.

"One more pass," Donaldson said over the craft's internal radio.

Shader sighed. It was another failed mission.

As they glided down the flight deck on a final run, Potoski slapped Shader on the shoulder and pointed to the ship.

"There!" he yelled. "I see something."

Shader looked where the Marine was pointing and saw a single soldier sprinting across the deck. Behind him were dozens of Variants leaping after him.

"We have someone," Shader said to Donaldson.

A moment later, the craft slowed down and began to settle on the deck. As they descended, Potoski opened up with his machine gun while Shader and Jacobs fired their M4s. They took down the leading edge of the Variants, before they descended too low to shoot above the running soldier.

The man was churning his legs and arms, but he seemed to be running with a slight limp. A couple of the Variants were beginning to catch up. One, in particular, was practically flying up the deck. Shader estimated the distances between the survivor and the Variant. The man wasn't going to make it.

Shader started to move out of the craft but was shoved aside by Jacobs. He ran out onto the deck and moved slightly to his left, creating a clear lane of fire. He took three shots, the last one punching through the advancing creature's neck. The wound sent it tumbling to the deck.

The survivor and Jacobs sprinted onto the Osprey.

"GO! GO! GO!" Shader yelled into the boom mic.

Donaldson pushed the throttle and lifted the bird into the air. They were over the water in moments as hundreds of Variants swarmed the spot they'd just left.

Shader turned to see who they'd taken on. He couldn't believe his eyes.

"Hey! PORKY!" Lazzaro said.

Shader was stunned. He didn't even want to think about the odds of finding the stupid Marine alive, let alone running across the deck of a doomed ship.

Shader went over to Lazzaro and gave him a hug. They took a seat on the bulkhead while Potoski raised the ramp. Within a minute, the V-22 was buttoned up and shooting toward the *Roosevelt*. Shader was satisfied. It had turned out to be a successful night, after all.

— 33 —

U.S.S. *Theodore Roosevelt*
Galley

"If you believe you can accomplish everything by 'cramming' at the eleventh hour, by all means, don't lift a finger now. But you may think twice about beginning to build your ark once it has already started raining."
MAX BROOKS
The Zombie Survival Guide

The survivors and their saviors, minus the pilots, gathered in the ship's galley as they had planned. Lazzaro's reunion with Keele and Gonzalez was nothing short of epic. The three men hugged and then wrestled each other until one of them grabbed Lazzaro's injured leg. The transformation from alpha males to mother hens was sudden and comical. Keele picked Lazzaro up off the ground and deposited him in a chair, while Gonzalez grabbed Lazzaro's pants and pulled them down to the knees, exposing the wound.

Shader didn't want to admit it, but he looked closely at the Marine's thigh above the dressing. He was relieved that Lazzaro's wound wasn't sprouting black veins. It would have sucked to have to put him down after such and ordeal.

"Dude. How come you aren't limping?" Keele asked.

Shader had thought the same thing, but it went to the

backburner. The Osprey was far too loud to have a conversation and, besides, Lazzaro needed to rest. They all did.

Lazzaro reached into his BDU pants and pulled out a syringe.

"Novocaine!" he said proudly.

"You gave yourself a shot?" Gonzalez said almost reverently.

"You do what you gotta do," Lazzaro stated confidently.

"You're not such a pussy after all," Shader said. "I seem to remember a certain Marine puking his guts out because of some bad smells."

"It toughened me up," Lazzaro replied. Then he lost his smile, got quiet, and looked away.

Shader recognized the man's mental situation. He'd seen some really bad shit that night but wasn't ready to talk about it.

"It can wait," Shader assured him. "Why don't we rest on it and pick it up again tomorrow?"

Lazzaro continued to tap his finger. He put his other hand under the table and gripped his injured leg, which was bouncing up and down along with the tapping.

"I'm worried," he finally said. He looked around at the large eating area. Over half the tables were full of sailors and quite a few of the rescued from Coronado. "I saw how it started. I'm afraid it may happen here too."

They all stared at the injured Marine, their eyes begging for more.

Lazzaro told his story. He described the infected Marine, his conversations with Lieutenant Raymond and the poor sailor he had to kill.

"It's fucking quick," he concluded. "That Marine turned in late morning, just a few hours from when he was infected. The ship was lost three hours later. The whole damn ship!"

The *Boxer* was nearly as large as the *Roosevelt*. For something that size to fall in such a short period of time gave them all pause.

The mood suddenly changed. It seemed their refuge wasn't so safe anymore.

"What do we do?" Jennifer asked.

Potoski folded his arms across his chest and leaned back in his chair. "It's not like we can swim ashore. We're thirty miles out."

The group became somber, each person trying to assimilate the new situation. After a couple minutes of silence, Shader stood and addressed the small group. "Tell you what, why don't you all get some sleep. Potoski and I have someone we need to see."

Potoski frowned. "We do?"

Without replying to the Marine's question, Shader turned and strode toward the exit. Potoski stood with a sigh and followed the SEAL.

Garrett watched the two men leave then stood, addressing the others. "I'm going to the armory. We need to top off our magazines."

"You think they'll let us do that?" Gonzalez said. "They find out we have our rifles, and they'll make us turn them in."

Garrett was stumped. Gonzalez was correct. They'd snuck the M4s onto the ship by separating the upper receiver from the lower. Then Potoski used a ruck he'd brought on board the Osprey to store them under Donaldson's bunk.

With so many extra people on board, there was no privacy. There were only so many beds and they were all hot bunking. Stacked three high, they had no privacy in their sleeping quarters. Further, their assigned lockers were shared as well. The only people with their own rooms were the officers. When Garrett asked Potoski if Donaldson approved of the subterfuge, he just shrugged his shoulders. Donaldson had no clue.

"Don't go," Jennifer pled. "I don't want you to leave me."

"Yeah. Wait for Shader to get back. Then we can decide what to do," Gonzalez added.

Garrett reluctantly took a seat and quietly simmered. He knew that bad things were going to happen. It was not a matter of *if*, but *when*. He wanted to do something to prepare. Anything to give them an advantage once the shit hit the fan.

— 34 —

Hope Torrence
Schoepe Boy Scout Camp

*"While I thought that I was learning how to live, I have been
learning how to die."*

LEONARDO DA VINCI

Hope was standing over the industrial stove in Beckham
Hall. She could hear hundreds of campers in the main
dining hall, all crying out for food. Hope had all six
burners going. Large pots of boiling water bubbled,
spilling out over their brims. Hot water splashed onto the
metal burners. She opened the double oven to check on
the trays of cookies she was baking. She'd put them in
over an hour ago, but they hadn't even melted down into
their final shape. The chunky chocolate chip dough still
had not begun to cook. She adjusted the temperature up
to 500. She just hoped they'd cook soon.

Hope looked down and began to grab live lobsters
from a large, wooden box. She had to use outdoor grill
tongs to pick them up. They dropped into the boiling
water but kept crawling back out. At one point, she had
almost a half a dozen red crustaceans crawling around on
the stove top. She couldn't understand why they hadn't
died.

The cacophony from the Boy Scouts was becoming
deafening. She heard them chanting for food.

She kept trying to put the lobsters into the pot, and

they kept crawling back out. It was a strange game of whack-a-mole. The lobsters were unrelenting.

Smoke began to pour out of the oven. She jumped back and flung the door open. All of her cookies had burned and several of them were on fire.

The kids were screaming. She panicked. She grabbed one of the boiling pots and threw it on the oven fire, burning her hands in the process.

The screams from the hungry boys became louder. She heard them pounding on their tables. *Pop. Pop. Pop.* They were using their forks to drum out a tune. She was frantic. Nothing was right. She finally threw her hands up and began to run away.

Hope bolted upright. She'd fallen asleep in John's bed. She was waiting for him. She wouldn't be able to rust until she knew that he'd gotten home safely.

"What a horrible dream," she sighed. She squinted and checked her watch. It was nearly eleven. She lay her head back on his pillow and smelled his musky scent. She allowed herself to drift back and relax. She began to think.

Hope couldn't stand having John gone. After they confessed their love for each other, the dam of emotions burst, and her feelings flooded out. She felt like a teenager again. Only this time, it was better. Teens had crushes. Infatuations without responsibilities. What she'd felt with John was so much deeper. Appreciation for his physical and mental strength as well as the maternal gratification of finding a father for her precious son. This was so much more powerful than the innocent lust of a teenager. John was a protector. He'd shown his honor over the last years helping Kyle become a responsible adult without pressuring her for more. John was a real man. Someone who took responsibility for her and Kyle along with the rest of the group. He was a leader who gave orders but respected her in all ways. The perfect man had lived a quarter mile down a dirt road from her for almost two years, and it took an apocalypse to bring her out of her shell.

But now the reality of the situation struck home. Before, she didn't want to risk a relationship for fear of abandonment. She couldn't get hurt if she didn't let anyone in. She also justified her decision to avoid dating because she had a son who needed her full attention. Having had a horrific divorce stripped her of the ability to trust. It created a wall around her soul.

Now, her fears were far graver. With John, it was now about life and death. He had been gone all afternoon and now several hours into the night. She wasn't worried about him cheating on her, like her first husband did. She feared that he'd be killed, or worse, turn into one of those monsters.

Her eyes began to droop even more. She hadn't completely woken from the daze you get when a dream or nightmare keeps dancing on the edges of your consciousness. She kept seeing fragmentary images of the macabre fantasy. The lobsters crawling and leaping out of the boiling water and hearing the kids slamming their spoon handles on the Formica tables. It had almost sounded like someone had set off firecrackers.

She began to drift off again, when the beating of the tables started back up. She forced herself awake. She didn't want to repeat that nightmare. It was all too unsettling.

She pushed herself out of John's bed and stumbled outside to the porch.

She sat on the plastic couch that John was fond of using for his naps. She leaned back and looked out at the night sky.

Pop! Pop!

She sat up, adrenaline coursing through her bloodstream. She caught her breath as more of the tiny explosions echoed from the distance. She hadn't dreamed the sounds after all. She'd just incorporated them into her nightmare.

It was gunfire. And it was coming from the campsite where the new families had temporarily taken shelter.

Bra-ta-ta-tat.

Kyle! She had to find him.

Boom! Boom-baboom! Several shotguns fired.

Hope sprinted off the porch and ran to the camp's administrative building. She and Kyle shared space with the rest of the original group, creating bedrooms out of the camp's offices.

She flung the door open to the business office, frantically searching for her son.

No one was there. It was abandoned.

She ran out and cut under a copse of trees that stood between her building and Beckham hall. She ran with abandon. The only thought was of her son.

The gunfire was creeping closer but dissipating in intensity. Hope exploded through the door to the cafeteria. The eating hall was empty. She turned and checked the kitchen along with the loading dock area. No one was around.

"Kyle!" she screamed. "KYLE! ANSWER ME!"

"In here!" she heard from the business office.

Hope tried turning the locked door. "Open it!"

She heard a deadbolt sliding back and the twist of a knob lock. She pushed herself into the room as soon as the door started to move.

"Hope!" It was Laura Reedy, the San Diego detective who, along with her EMT husband, had been invited to stay at the camp by Jennifer Blevins. She was there with her daughter, Lisa. There was no one else.

"Where's my boy?" Hope begged.

"He's out there. He went with the rest of them. Someone had to stay with Lisa, but everyone else grabbed a shotgun and ran south."

"I've got to find him," Hope said, a tinge of panic in her voice.

"No, Hope. Let me go," Laura said. "You stay with Lisa, and I'll bring him back."

"There is no way I'm leaving my son out there."

"My husband and son are out there too!" Laura replied. "Besides, you don't even have a gun. What are you going to—hey!"

Hope had no time for logic. She spun and sprinted out of the office, leaving a very angry woman behind. She pushed through the outside door and followed her son south.

Shotguns were firing from just beyond the next stand of trees. She raced through ankle-high mountain grass, straight toward the battle ahead. She heard a boy's scream, and her mind went blind with anger. She sprinted forward, into an unknown maelstrom. A mother protecting her young. She never gave it a thought that she had no weapon, and deep down, she knew there were infected out there. And by the sounds of the battle, there were a lot of them.

Hope rushed through the small stand of trees and found herself in the middle of a pitched battle. The sound of gunfire was deafening and coming from different places.

She saw muzzle flashes to her right. The mini-explosions sent flames almost a yard out of the tubes. She ran to them, desperate to find her boy.

She was almost to a small group of people and began yelling her son's name.

"Kyle!"

A shadow spun toward her and raised a shotgun right at her. She froze and threw her hands up.

Click, was all she heard.

"NO! It's me. Kyle's mother."

Chris Reedy grabbed the shotgun from Gavin Gringleman.

"Hold it, boy!"

Chris waved her into their defenses. The Gringleman boys were his only companions.

"Where's Kyle?" Hope asked.

"I don't know," Chris said. He turned to Gavin and reprimanded him. "Reload. I told you to reload whenever there's a break in the action. Don't wait until it's empty."

Gavin began to slide shells into the underbelly of the shotgun, shaking his head with fear and frustration.

"Where is he?" Hope said forcefully.

"He was with the Darden twins. They were holding our left flank. I called for them to pull back, but I lost track of them," he said regretfully.

Gary Gringleman seemed detached from the

conversation, distracted by his own thoughts. "The infected... they've got dogs. At least, they acted like dogs."

"What do you mean?" Hope asked.

"One of the infected was the leader. All of them did what he told them to, including the dogs."

"How is that possible?" Hope asked, looking at Chris for confirmation.

"He's right. They had one male that seemed to be in charge. I don't know what kind of creatures they were running with, but they were armored, nearly hairless, and about the size of a large dog or small wolf."

"They're fast, too," Gavin added. "I saw..." His voice trailed off as an unwanted memory thrust itself to the forefront.

"Things are really screwed up," Chris said. "Without Carver and Kinney here, we're undermanned. I mean, John was supposed to lead a squad and my wife, the other one. Neither one is here."

"What about the Yuma families?" Hope asked. "Can't they help?"

"They're dead," Chris said somberly. "That's why we were pulling back. We need to get to the office or even Beckham. At least they're block construction and not canvas tents."

"All of them?" Hope quietly asked. There were seventeen men, women, and children who had come up from Arizona.

"Yeah. We tried to help but by the time we got to their encampment, the infected were all over the place. Every tent was ripped apart and the infected were..." Chris's voice trailed off.

"They were eating them all." Gary finished Chris's sentence.

Shotguns erupted from their left and Hope spun toward the battle.

"Wait. We'll all go," Chris said.

The four began to jog toward the noise. With only a partial moon in the sky, they trotted slowly. Several times, Hope nearly wrenched her ankle on the ground's uneven surface or the occasional rock.

Three more blasts revealed the other group's location. Hope sprinted ahead, determined to get to her child.

"Wait!" Chris called.

It was too late. Nothing was going to keep her from Kyle's side.

Kyle Torrence

When the first of the gunfire started. Kyle was in Beckham Hall with the other kids. Mrs. Reedy was the supervising adult and they were all playing a board game. Everyone, that is, except the Lisa Reedy. Being much younger that the others, she was content to sit and watch the older kids interact.

They had all been trained to keep their shotguns at their sides, and tonight was no different. But by the sounds from the Yuma encampment, there was a major battle being fought. So rather than rushing right to the battle, Mrs. Reedy had a different plan.

"Back to the admin building!" Laura Reedy said. "Get my husband and bring all the spare ammo you can carry. You'll need more than what's in your tube."

The boys did as they were told. Mr. Reedy was already

armed and had a box of 12-gauge buckshot for each of them.

Kyle shoved spare shells into his front pocket as he looked about, trying to find his mom.

"Tuck in your shirts!" Mr. Reedy commanded.

They did as they were told and over a dozen more rounds were dumped down each one of their shirts.

Then they ran toward the sound of battle.

It was dark, but his young eyes quickly adapted to the dimly lit ground.

Mr. Reedy had to be pulled in the right direction. His older eyes didn't see as well as the boys could. Kyle took the lead. It was just over a quarter mile to the encampment. Darkness, the uneven ground and the disorientation caused by the gunfire all slowed them considerably. It took them a few minutes longer to reach the tents than it would have during the day.

The guns from the Yuma group went silent before they got to the battle, and Chris Reedy pulled Kyle back. Silence meant that either they'd killed all the infected, or the infected had killed them. Either way, there was no need to rush.

Chris took the lead and crept into the underbrush, just outside the encampment. Menily, Kyle, and the Gringleman boys did likewise. They eased forward and stared out at the scene.

A tent was on fire. Its sides had collapsed and the wooden framed furniture inside was cooking off. It gave them enough light to see that there were no more people left alive. Dozens of infected and several four-legged animals were feasting on the corpses of the seventeen.

"Those are the things that bit my dad," Menily whispered to Mr. Reedy.

The Darden twins pushed their way forward and looked out as well. Brett Darden hadn't seen the infected before this, nor what they could do. His brother had fought them when they'd gone to the hospital to retrieve insulin. When the young man got a look at the carnage, he let out a gasp.

One of the four-legged creatures took notice of Brett's tiny cry, and it let out a screech, getting the attention of a number of its brethren. One, in particular, seemed to clue in. It screeched and barked in reply. Dozens of the infected looked up from their feast and turned toward them as one. They let out a primal scream and began running right at the group.

"RUN!" Chris Reedy hissed. "Back to the camp!"

They all turned and sprinted away. Except, Chris Reedy became disoriented and ran in the wrong direction.

Kyle sprinted forward, followed by Menily and the Darden twins. They hadn't gotten more than a hundred yards out of the underbrush when the yips and cries of the infected dogs bellowed out from the trees they'd just left.

Kyle looked for Mr. Reedy, but he and the Gringleman brothers were nowhere to be seen.

"Hasty ambush!" Kyle said, pointing at a small cluster of trees just ahead.

The four ran to the trees and spun around.

Kyle and Menily stepped forward and brought their shotguns up. Five dog-like creatures sprinted forward. Over a dozen infected people were not far behind.

"Wait for me to shoot," Kyle said.

Menily shook her head. "No, you wait for me."

Kyle had to smile. She was feisty and didn't take orders well.

The popping and cracking of the creatures' joints was barely audible over their primeval cries. Kyle recognized the canine sound beneath the infected creatures' screams. But the night masked the rest of their features.

There was a swale just in front of them, about twenty yards away.

"When they get to the dip, shoot low. That worked back at the hospital. We shot out their legs. It's hard to hit their heads when they run."

"Gotcha," Menily replied.

The lead animal tried to jump over the depression. Kyle pulled the trigger just as it left the ground. The pellets caught it in mid-air and pushed its lower jaw out of the back of its neck. It died instantly.

Menily let loose as well, taking the legs out from under the next creature. The thing howled and cartwheeled end over end. It slid to a stop ten yards in front of them. One of its partners stumbled over its body and it too tumbled on the ground. Kyle put two blasts into its back. It stopped moving.

Both Kyle and Menily emptied their weapons, all five of the animals were on the ground either unable to walk or dead. The pair stepped back and began shoving shells into the underside of their Mossberg shotguns as the Darden twins stepped forward and took their place.

Trey and Brett were ready, although the flash from so many shots reduced their night vision. The teens squinted into the dark, catching glimpses of shadows bouncing up and down on the high-desert pasture.

"I can't see them," Trey complained.

A malevolent scream blasted out of one of the creatures.

"I can see their eyes!" Brett yelled.

Kyle looked up. Yellow, burning slits were bouncing up and down on the dark grassy field.

"Aim just below the eyes," Kyle shouted.

The twins let loose with shot after shot. Each boy fired, pumped another round into the chamber, then fired again. Screams of pain followed almost every blast, but the eyes were getting closer. The twins hadn't finished emptying their guns when Kyle joined them. A wall of lead stopped three of the closest creatures, but still more came.

The twins ran out of ammo, leaving Kyle alone. There were two creatures left and they were within yards. He pulled his trigger and got a click. He was dry. A screech came from the closest one. It dipped to the ground and exploded toward him with an impossible leap. Kyle brought his shotgun up, trying to block the infected attack. The hungry eyes flew at him. There wasn't time to defend himself. He braced for an impact that would likely kill him. Suddenly, he was hit from his side, sending him toppling to the ground.

He felt wind from the leaping creature as it flew over top of him. He could smell its foul, decaying odor.

Kyle was shocked. Did another one of the infected just take him down?

He heard three shotgun blasts, then silence.

Whatever had tackled him was lying on the grass nearby. The young man scrambled to his feet. He spun about, searching for his attacker.

"Kyle!" he heard from the ground.

It was his mother! She'd tackled him, saving him from the creature that was going to kill him.

Menily stepped forward and helped Hope up, just as Mr. Reedy, Gavin, and Gary Gringleman joined them.

Chris Reedy looked down at the twins. Trey Darden was just getting up, a dead infected human at his feet. His brother had blown out the creature's spine, but its tongue continued to involuntary flick and teeth continued to snap while the rest of its body died.

"You boys all right?" Chris asked.

"Yeah. I think so," Brett said. "What about you, Trey?"

"Fine," he said in a flat voice.

The sound of more infected howled from the tree line. They all turned to look. They were almost halfway to the safety of the camp's buildings when dozens of creatures exploded out of the brush.

"RUN!" Chris yelled. "Get your asses moving!"

The group began to sprint.

"HURRY!" Hope yelled as she flung her son back toward the camp.

The group was moving fast. Hope glanced over her shoulder and saw an uncountable number of amber points of light chasing them.

They were still about a hundred yards from safety, but they were far enough ahead that they should be able to make it. Then she saw the Darden twins falling back. One of them was injured, and the other wouldn't leave him.

"Chris!" she yelled.

He didn't respond. They were running for their lives and hearing was one of the first things to be ignored by a brain in fight or flight.

Hope saw Kyle keeping pace with the rest of them. He would make it to safety.

She couldn't leave the Darden boys out there; the mother inside of her refused to abandon them. She did the only thing her instinct would let her do. She stopped and went back to help the injured boy.

The twins were moving, but a brisk walk was the best they could manage. The snapping jaws and cracking joints of the infected were bearing down on them.

"Who's hurt?" she screamed.

"I am," Trey said. "It's my foot."

Hope slung his arm over her shoulder while his brother Brett did likewise on the other side. They began to move. It was considerably faster than before, but Hope could tell the creatures were getting close. She risked a look back and saw an infected human and one of the armored creatures sprinting ahead of the rest of the group. She looked ahead—the lights of the camp buildings were just beyond the next copse of trees. She urged the boys to go faster.

The sounds of heavy feet slamming into the earth were right behind them. The hair on the back of her head stood stiffly, and she could feel the rancid odor of death breathing down her neck.

She glanced back again and almost froze. It was a one-eyed armored creature and an infected human. They were going to be caught.

Hope let go of Trey and turned to face her death. The infected human slammed into her, knocking her to the ground. Its animal companion sprinted forward, the twins in its sights. They were all going to die.

Bright beams of light pierced the darkness. They flashed over the scene, illuminating the two creatures that were going to be her demise.

Hope caught her breath. She couldn't believe what stood over her. It was the infected security guard she'd known back at the resort. He had nearly killed them once, and now he'd returned to finish the job.

"Hope!" she heard from the distance.

It was John. He'd come to save her, but he was too late.

It scooped her up and turned into the darkness, carrying her on its shoulders. They sprinted away at an incredible pace.

"No! Charlie, don't!" she screamed as rifle shots echoed from behind the twin beams of light. In a flash, they were moving away and out the glare.

Moments later, the animal companion joined them.

They bounded through some trees, where her head caught a low-hanging branch. As she faded into darkness from the blow, she felt relieved that she'd saved her son and the Darden twins. Her last thoughts were of John. She hoped he'd be proud of her. Then, the world went black.

— 35 —

Porky Shader
U.S.S. *Theodore Roosevelt*

"If something can go wrong, it will."
—EDWARD MURPHY, JR. (American Aerospace Engineer)
"Murphy's Law"

The only surprise Shader felt when the emergency claxons went off was how quickly it had happened. He glanced at his watch. It was only three in the morning. He'd gotten exactly ninety minutes of sleep.

"Well, I've had worse nights," he grunted.

Porky bolted off the floor and stood over his people. A quick count of the tired and confused bodies let him know all were present and accounted for.

With a large influx of refugees onto the T.R., people were scattered throughout the massive ship. Porky had chosen a room just one level below the flight deck, within yards of the ladder topside. He knew this time would come, and he just prayed the few hours of prep time would be enough to save them.

A few hours before, he and Potoski tracked down Lieutenant Donaldson. Shader wanted them to prepare for the worst. Ultimately, the meeting went well, but it hadn't started that way.

Donaldson had to be clued in on how virulent the virus was. They met another pilot, a SuperCobra air jockey named Everly, and grabbed some coffee in one of the officers' wardrooms. From their greeting, Shader knew that Donaldson and Everly had more than just a professional relationship.

The sight of a Marine sergeant and a Navy SEAL in the wardroom didn't faze the other officers in the least. In fact, several lieutenants insisted they tell their story. It took almost an hour to narrate their participation in the battle of the Forum. From the REMF's reaction to the story, Shader and Potoski were walking gods.

When the four of them finally got some privacy, Shader and Potoski explained their concerns to the two pilots.

"The virus will eventually infect the ship," Shader said. "It's just a matter of time. There are too many variables to control."

Both Donaldson and Everly remained skeptical.

Shader gave the pilots a condensed version of Lazzaro's experience. "He watched the *Boxer* die, all from one infected Marine. What do you think is going to happen with thousands of people flooding the ship? How many of them had some incidental exposure to the infection? How much virus is on the ship now? No one knows."

Donaldson glanced at Everly then met Shader's eyes. "I hate to say it, but you might be right. I had a chance to talk with some of the other pilots. They were doing hot extractions at the base, sometimes landing in the middle of a pile of dead Variants. The rotors had to have been putting infected blood into the air. How many of them are carrying the virus now?"

There was a moment of silence as each of the group

considered the implications of the lieutenant's report.

"One thing I can tell you," Potoski said. "Is that there ain't anything wrong with preparing."

"We can't just do what we want," Everly replied. "This is the Navy. We do what we are told. All this belongs to Uncle Sam."

Shader looked at both pilots. "Let me ask you something… what are your orders? What's the game plan?"

The pilots looked at each other, then shrugged.

"Your birds aren't tasked for anything right now, are they?"

"No. But that can and will change," Everly replied.

"I doubt that. Even if we miraculously avoid an infection, our next port of call won't be for a while. Have you heard of anything on the continent that isn't overrun by Variants?"

Everly shook his head. "No. Our last briefing was that the virus was everywhere."

"Exactly. Now, where has it not spread?"

The pilot had no answer.

"That's my point. We're going to start searching. Probably an island somewhere far away. It will be weeks before your birds will be needed."

"I'll give you that," Everly said. "So, what do you want?"

Shader pulled out a folded piece of paper and handed it to the two pilots. Everly looked at it and groaned.

"You're kidding, right?"

"Nope. We could use all of that."

"We'll be court marshalled. If we steal all this, they'll hang us from the yardarm."

"You're not stealing. Just, reallocating," Shader replied. Donaldson shook her head. "You're crazy. I wouldn't even know where to look for this stuff."

"I've got that covered," Potoski replied. "If you give this your blessing, I'll make all the arrangements."

Donaldson looked at Everly and nodded.

"What do I know if someone uses my bird for a storage unit?" she said.

"Okay. I'm in too. If Erin's good with this, so am I."

"Stay close, especially for the next twenty-four hours. I have a feeling, that if the virus is going to happen, it will be in the next day."

As it turned out, it was much sooner.

"That was fast," Potoski said as he wiped the sleep from his eyes. The claxon's shrill scream was something he'd never get used to.

"I hope your buddy got what we asked for," Shader added as he watched the group they'd rescued crawl up from their blankets on the deck.

"What's the plan?" Garrett asked.

"We give it five minutes, then make our way to the Osprey."

"And if the pilot isn't there?" Garrett asked.

"Just worry about what you can control," Shader said. "Make sure your people are squared away."

"We're squared away and ready to rock!" Gonzalez replied.

Lazzaro was slow to get up with his unattended wound beginning to throb. He produced his last syringe of lidocaine and pushed it into his leg, right through the thick fabric of his BDU.

"Damn. That's just wrong!" Gonzalez said, cringing as Lazzaro shoved the needle into his thigh.

"I just might take up dentistry after we get out of here," Lazzaro replied with a grim smile. "I think I'm getting good at this."

He pulled the needle out and held it up to the flashing, red alarm light. "Half left." Then he recapped the syringe, shoved it back into his pants pocket, and buttoned it up.

Shader did another headcount and nodded. He checked his watch one more time.

"All right. Everyone line up. Stay with the person in front of you. Don't space out. Keep moving. Call out if you see anything. My squad will handle it."

Lazzaro wiggled his injured leg and gave a thumbs up. Shader nodded.

"Gonzalez. You're on point. You know where to go."

"Aye, Chief."

"Keele, you have the rear. Keep 'em moving."

"Aye aye."

"Lazzaro, you're in the middle. Keep up and head on a swivel."

"Got your back."

"The rest of you, once we start, keep moving."

Shader moved to the front, just as there was a pounding on the door. He spun his finger in the air, rallying the three Marines to him. They encircled the door and brought their rifles up, covering the entrance.

Shader pulled the door open and four rifles stared out into the passageway.

A small girl screamed.

It was the young girl from the Forum. She clutched a teddy bear as Morales held her in his arms. She buried her face in the big man's neck at the sight of the armed men.

Morales looked at Shader. "I heard the siren. We didn't know where else to go."

"We?" Shader asked.

Morales moved back and Shader stepped into the passageway. There were nearly a dozen survivors huddled against the bulkhead. Naval personnel were running by, some with a purpose while others in panic. It had already turned into a clusterfuck.

Shader did the math. He tried to calculate if the Osprey could handle all the additional weight of a dozen more people. After some quick math he decided that it would probably still work, depending on how much of the supply list Potoski's scrounger had acquired.

There was no doubt the people were more important than some cases of MREs. If push came to shove, the survivors would take precedence over supplies, but he hoped they could do both. Shader really would hate having to dump any of the ill-gotten treasures since he'd sacrificed his last bottle of Tennessee whiskey to acquire them.

Shader waved the survivors into the room. They arranged the unarmed civilians into an organized line, scattering the armed sailors and Marines amongst them. He gave them all instructions once again, stressing that they keep moving. When they were ready, Shader flung the door open, and Gonzalez moved forward.

The chain of refugees he was leading had grown to over double in size. All told, there were twenty-one souls he was responsible for. The four they'd rescued from the harbor along with the thirteen in Morales's group. Add in his fireteam and Potoski, and he was pushing the limits of the Osprey's weight capacity.

Gonzalez moved steadily. He had full battle rattle on and was walking with rifle up at low ready. Most of the panicked sailors in the passageway rushed by before they recognized the armed Marine. Some froze and spun away, assuming danger lay behind the advancing group.

Gonzalez reached the ladder and began to move up. He was halfway up the stairs when screams came from down the passageway. Shader and Garrett stepped forward.

"Move!" Shader commanded to Lazzaro. "Lay topside and find Donaldson."

"Everyone, move it!" Lazzaro yelled.

The group began to run.

"I don't need to tell you what to do," Shader said to Garrett.

Garrett performed a chamber check. "I can handle myself."

Shader nodded and did likewise. He'd seen the kid step out of the Osprey, put himself in harm's way, then take down a Variant back on the deck of the *Boxer*. He'd saved Lazzaro's life. That was all the proof Shader needed to stand beside the man instead of in front of him.

Most of the group had gotten to the ladder, when the rush of sailors coming at them suddenly disappeared. With the passageway beyond finally clear, Shader spotted the cause of the commotion. The noise from the disturbance down the passageway was drowned out by the blare from the alarm, so the first indication of the Variant horde was from flashes of several guns in the distance as they were discharged.

Shader felt Keele slap him on the shoulder as he

passed by. Their people were clear, and it was time to move.

"Up top with you!" Shader barked.

But Jacobs didn't move. Shader was about to grab him when the young man pressed down on his trigger and began to fire.

Shader looked back down the passageway, but it was several seconds more before he saw Garrett's target.

"SHIT!" Shader yelled.

It was a horde of infected. They crawled over and above each other. Like a tube that was being flooded, they filled the passageway. The younger sailor had seen them before he had. He silently cursed his aging eyes.

"GO!" Shader commanded. Then he began to open fire, as well.

Garrett emptied his magazine and sprinted up the ladder. Shader did the same, buying them a few seconds.

Shader felt, as much as heard, the creatures on his heels. It was eerily reminiscent of his escape from the underground garage.

He broke out on the landing above and shoved the hatch closed. The slamming of bodies into the metal door sounded like sacks of wet cement landing on the pavement. He dogged the lever, securing the creatures on the other side.

Shader ran up the next ladder to the flight deck. He'd worried they would have trouble finding Donaldson and the Osprey, but his concerns were unfounded.

The nearly two dozen people wound through piles of supplies, right to an idling V-22. Its blades were pointing up and spinning slowly. Donaldson had already arrived and prepared the craft. She was ready to lift off.

Shader followed Keele and Jacobs, looking over his shoulders. Nothing approached.

They all entered the back of the Osprey, jogging up the ramp and settling into one of the bulkhead seats. Gonzalez and Keele were moving up and down the line, one on each side, making sure the civilians were properly strapped in. Potoski stood at the back and rotated the aircraft's mounted SAW into position.

The craft's engines began to spin up and within a few seconds, they lifted off the flight deck. The bird felt sluggish as it accelerated into the sky, but they managed to get airborne, just as a swarm of Variants exploded onto the deck.

Shader gripped Potoski's shoulder and shook his head.

"Don't waste the ammo," Shader yelled, as the big Pole was lining up his machine gun to fire on the infected sailors below. "We'll need it later."

Potoski nodded. The ship was being overrun, and killing a few hundred wouldn't solve anything.

Shader wormed his way to the front of the craft and knocked loudly on the cockpit door. Someone unlocked the hatch and he looked in on the two pilots.

Donaldson flew the craft while Everly sat in the co-pilot's seat. She was directing him to monitor systems and familiarizing him with the controls. This was not his SuperCobra, and flying the bird was more like a fixed-wing plane and not a rotor-craft.

"Thanks!" Shader yelled.

Donaldson just shook her head and handed him a helmet. Shader put the green ballistic helmet on and adjusted the boom mic.

"Can you hear me?" Donaldson asked.

"Affirmative," Shader replied.

"I want to stay here for a few mikes and see if we can help."

Shader knew that was a fool's errand, but he understood the thought. He leaned in between the two pilots and gave a thumbs up.

Donaldson began a slow turn to get eyes on the other ships in the fleet. There were a nearly twenty other crafts of varying size, from a couple of littoral combat ships to the three remaining Arleigh Burke destroyers. None of them were to be trusted, given the survivors who had been pulled from Coronado had been spread everywhere.

Donaldson got on the fleet radio and began communicating with the ships. All were battling infection.

A massive fireball erupted from one of the destroyers, followed by multiple secondary explosions. Someone or something had set off the ship's magazine. The giant craft immediately began to list. With no one available to help, it would just be a matter of time before it flooded and sank.

Shader joined Potoski at the back ramp, weaving his way around boxes of supplies and the survivors. He strapped himself to the bulkhead and watched the fleet die.

About twenty minutes later, Donaldson turned the Osprey to port and accelerated. Shader moved back up front and saw them approach the U.S.S. *Howard*, one of the two remaining Arleigh Burke destroyers. He watched as the ship's Seahawk helicopter rose from the deck and lifted into the air.

Donaldson spoke over the fleet network to their new companion, then they moved to the remaining destroyer, where its helicopter already hovered over the ship.

Donaldson and Everly hailed the other pilots as well.

"We just picked up more survivors," Donaldson said to Shader over the craft's radio. "Looks like some of them made it off."

"What did they say?" Shader asked in his mic.

"Both ships are battling Variants. The *Howard* is lost, and their pilots abandoned ship. But the other Seahawk has four more sailors from the *Spruance* crammed into the back. I hope you have a plan because we have a lot of people to care for."

Shader hadn't told them where he wanted to go. He hesitated, because there was no guarantee this place was safe from the Variants. But it was their best hope.

He was about to tell them their destination, when someone pulled on his sleeve from behind. Shader turned back into the cargo hold and saw Jennifer standing there, holding onto one of the Osprey's many pipes that ran across to the bulkhead.

Shader lifted his helmet and shouted over the drone of the engines.

"What is it?"

"Where are you taking us?"

"Don't worry about it. I've got a safe place."

"So do I," she screamed.

Shader ignored the woman. He doubted seriously that she had a clue about what constituted a safe place from the Variants. She had no tactical knowledge and certainly didn't have the military chops to make an informed decision.

He waved her off and stuck his head back into the cockpit. Donaldson gasped and tilted the craft down, giving them a better view of the ship. Shader could see the U.S.S. *Spruance* and its helicopter hovering over it.

It took him a moment to understand what was happening. Shader was concentrating on the destroyer, looking for an explosion or a horde of Variants.

"They're going down," Everly said somberly.

Shader noticed the Seahawk now. It was listing and dropping toward the ocean. It kept up its slow descent, wobbling back and forth as if someone was tugging on its tail. Then it hovered briefly over the water and slid into the choppy sea. It was like the pilot tried to land on the ocean, rather than having it auger in.

"What the hell happened?" Shader asked.

Donaldson held up her hand as she listened on the network.

"One of the passengers was infected," she said over the local network. "The pilot took the craft into the ocean. They'll try and swim for safety."

The other Seahawk got to the downed bird and began to hover over the site. Donaldson kept the Osprey nearby, waiting for word of the crew from the downed copter.

"There's nothing we can do, is there?" Shader asked.

"No. We aren't equipped for a water rescue."

It felt like he was a witness to a horrific car accident and EMS was on scene. One of the Seahawk's primary functions was search-and-rescue. The problem was the only two people on the remaining helicopter were the pilots. Donaldson wasn't sure if they would be able to help.

Everly tapped Donaldson on the arm and pointed to a gauge.

"We've used almost a quarter of our fuel."

"Well," Donaldson said to Shader. "What's your plan?"

"Hey, Chief. You need to take a minute and listen to this woman."

It was Potoski. He'd donned a helmet as well and had been listening in on the conversation.

"Stow it, Marine. She doesn't have a clue."

"I don't?" came a reply.

It was Jennifer. The stupid grunt had given her his helmet.

Shader heard scratching and pops in his headset as Jennifer adjusted the large ballistic pot on her head. Finally, the boom mic was put in front of her lips and her garbled voice became clear. She had been speaking the whole time but didn't realize that the others on the network couldn't hear her.

"… and it has plenty of water. I'm telling you. We need to go there." She said, finishing a sentence that had been lost in the noise.

"What are you talking about?" Donaldson asked. "We couldn't understand a thing you just said."

"I was telling you about a safe place to go," Jennifer replied.

"I've got this," Shader said.

"Don't dismiss me. Just because I'm a woman, doesn't mean I don't know things. I have a perfect spot to take refuge."

"I think I know what's best here."

"Why? Because I'm a girl?" Jennifer spat back.

"You better think hard before you answer her," Donaldson said, reminding Shader that a woman was controlling their aircraft. "Be really careful, Chief."

Shader bit his lip. He didn't have anything against women in the service, as long as they knew their place. They were terrific in the right jobs, like pilots and support. But he'd never met a woman who could come close to qualifying as a special operator. Sure, they had the drive and desire, but they didn't have the physical strength to do what he did. The endurance and bodily demands that were expected as a SEAL was unimaginable for most men. It was an impossible task for any woman to accomplish. And a team was only as strong as its weakest link. He would never go on a mission with someone who might not be up to snuff. No woman could ever measure up to that demand.

He'd grown up in that world, and truth be told, it jaded him when it came to decision making. He only trusted people who had his shared experiences. Too many battle plans that he'd been a part of either woefully underestimated what a SEAL team could do, or fatally believed that a team could perform miracles. He would never knowingly put himself in that position.

"Sorry, Lieutenant. But I don't trust anyone that hasn't walked in my shoes. That's just me talking with thirty years of run and gun."

The coms remained quiet. Shader wasn't sure if she was digesting his logic or planning on how to have him thrown out of the back of the aircraft.

"Sorry, Chief," Everly cut in. "Donaldson was having a seizure just now. I think she's finished."

"Chief," Donaldson said, "I'd like to hear both of you."

"LT, With all due respect. I think I know what's best. Not some civilian who got a ride because she's doing the mattress dance with one of our sailors."

Shader was leaning into the cockpit, watching the U.S.S. *Spruance* steam away. Even as the infection overwhelmed them, the entire fleet of ships was maintaining their westerly course. It appeared from a distance that all was normal and the strike group had set a course for Pearl or Okinawa.

"SHIT!" Shader gasped.

Someone had pulled his KA-BAR from its sheath and was pressing it against the back of his neck.

"You're off balance, Chief," Jennifer said in her mic. "I don't think you have any moves out of this without losing your head."

Donaldson glanced into the opening and saw Jennifer holding the SEAL's knife to his neck. She'd pushed him partially into the opening, his center of gravity now centered outside his feet, preventing him from finding his balance. She had him at her mercy.

"All right!" Donaldson said. "Everyone, back off."

The knife disappeared and Shader caught himself from falling forward into the instrument panel.

"Do not ever talk to me that way," Jennifer barked over the radio.

"Both of you, shut your mouths," Donaldson said. "I am the captain of this craft. I will make the decisions on where we go. No one else. Is that understood?"

Shader and Jennifer muttered a reply.

"I can't hear you. Do you understand me?"

"Aye aye, ma'am," Shader said.

"Yes. I understand," Jennifer replied.

"Now. I will decide on our destination. We have over eight hundred miles of fuel on board before we run dry.

I'd prefer not to burn every last ounce. So, I am open to suggestions."

Neither spoke.

"Damn it. Tell me where the hell you want us to go," Donaldson hissed into the mic.

Both of them yelled. "Lost Valley!"

They turned to each other, surprise on each face.

"WHAT?" they both said at once.

Donaldson and Everly both began to laugh. The craft momentarily jumped before Donaldson brought herself under control.

"Well, Chief. Seems the lady isn't so stupid after all. Now tell me, where the hell is Lost Valley?"

Shader gave Jennifer a glare. He was confused. How the hell did she know about Carver and that camp in the mountains.

"Well, Jennifer. Tell the lady," Shader said.

"I only know how to drive there," Jennifer admitted, still shocked that Shader knew about her camp.

Shader shook his head and leaned into the compartment. He gave them GPS coordinates that he'd previously memorized in case this very situation would arise. That information would put them directly over the center of the property.

"That's not bad," Donaldson said. "Should be there in no time."

Donaldson switched to the fleet network and called to the Seahawk. It was hovering only a few feet over the water. She gave coordinates to the pilot, telling them to get there once they'd recovered any survivors.

Shader and Jennifer both took a seat.

"I want a full report when we land. I want to know

how you picked Lost Valley," Shader said on the radio.

"I will," Jennifer said. "It's a good story."

"Can't wait to hear it," Donaldson said, hearing the two banter over the radio. "But, for now, just shut your mouths. I'm flying up here."

The Osprey banked to starboard and began to accelerate. The moon and starlight lit up the ocean, its blue hue sparkling off the choppy sea. Donaldson could make out the coastline in the distance. She kept the speed down to minimize fuel consumption and engaged the autopilot.

She allowed herself to relax just a bit and hoped they'd finally be safe because she was exhausted. She needed some downtime and Lost Valley sounded like the perfect name for their new sanctuary.

They were heading east. In the distance, she could see the sun starting to push back the night. They'd be arriving at dawn, the beginning of a new day. It all seemed so fitting.

"I'll bet there isn't a Variant within fifty miles," Everly said, a relaxed smile on his face.

Donaldson reached out to squeeze her lover's hand. "I'll bet you're right. The name sounds perfect."

— 36 —

Shrek
Lost Valley Boy Scout Camp

"The real man smiles in trouble, gathers strength from distress, and grows brave by reflection."
THOMAS PAINE

They have Hope. Cyclops and the asp have carried her away. We are following them, but they are too fast for Carver. I could keep up, but Carver cannot.

We stop at the edge of the grass, where the desert sand has taken over. The land drops down and in the dark of the night, we lose sight of the asp and its clan. Now, they are so far ahead, even I cannot hear them. The final sound of the popping joints and clicking teeth have faded in the inky blackness of the canyons and desert floor below.

The mountain drops down, facing where the sun will rise, and Carver finally gives up. Kinney is way behind us and it is only me and my master. We stare out over the lower desert, the far sky beginning to turn a light orange color. The sun is coming.

The mountain behind us blocks all light from the moon. It is near the end of its journey and will soon drop below the land. This makes the canyon ahead even more black.

Carver stares into the abyss below. He is unmoving. I

sense anger and pain. But mostly, I sense frustration. Hope is gone, and we couldn't stop it. I hang my head in shame. We have failed. I lean into his leg and let him know I understand. He does nothing. The grief must be unbearable, because I feel it too. I am not used to losing.

I smell the acrid odors of the asp. I can follow it anywhere. I look up and see John's face. It is a cold, seething anger that I've never seen in him before.

I now know I will be back to avenge Hope. We will make them pay. We will kill the asp.

I stare down into the black pool of darkness and make a promise. I will avenge Hope. I will kill the asp. I will destroy Cyclops and his kin. I am Shrek. I am the ghost that kills in the night, and I will have retribution.

John Eric Carver

John's mind was blank. He tried to push away any emotion for fear it would paralyze him, and it was not the time to be locked down.

But anger seethed just above the surface, while guilt bubbled just below the rage.

I should have killed Charlie back at the resort. If I had, Hope would be alive.

Carver stood motionless. Nothing penetrated his thoughts. He was already planning his revenge, putting together a list of people and things he'd need to kill Charlie and that cursed creature, Cyclops.

He had seen it running with Charlie, its lone eye burning back at him as it rushed toward Hope. He should have killed it as well when he had the chance. He should have tracked it down and eliminated it when the bastard first began to raid his farm. Now, Hope was gone and it all could have been prevented.

Carver felt the anguish rise, like bile in his throat. It was a specter that would consume him if he didn't get control of it now.

"NO!" John screamed, startling Shrek. He wasn't going to let his anger overwhelm him.

The deep guilt of inaction subsided. There would be time for that in the future. Now was the time to push forward. It was time for war.

Heavy footfalls sounded from behind. John continued to stare stoically into the distance as Kinney finally reached his friend.

"Where are they?" he gasped, trying to catch his breath.

"Gone."

"Come on. Let's track them. Shrek has to be able to follow their trail."

John turned to Kinney and stared blankly at him.

"She's already gone," he said. "But we'll be back. We need more guns. We need a plan. It's time we went back to camp and regrouped."

"John. We can't stop now. What if she's—"

"Don't!" John hissed. "I don't believe in false hope. She's either dead or she'll turn soon. Either way, there's nothing we can do."

Kinney held his head up and scanned the desert floor.

"You know I'd follow you to hell," Kinney finally said. "I've got your back."

Carver's demeanor softened for a moment and he put his hand on Kinney's shoulder.

"I know, my friend. I know. I'll take you up on that

real soon, but now is not the time."

John turned to retrace their steps back to camp. He went about ten yards and noticed Shrek stood still. He hadn't moved.

"Loslaten!" Carver said.

The Belgian didn't move.

"Let's go!" he repeated, more forcefully, in English.

Shrek remained pointed down the mountain slope. He wanted to pursue Cyclops and the other infected humans. He didn't want to give up.

Carver's anger quickly changed into understanding. He walked back to Shrek and for the first time in their relationship, he squatted down and hugged the Malinois.

"I know," Carver said. "I miss her too."

Carver stood back up and rubbed Shrek's snout. The dog lifted his head to accept the attention. "We'll come back soon, I promise."

Carver nodded to the animal and said quietly, "Loslaten."

Shrek turned and began to trot back to the camp. John and Kinney followed closely behind, reviewing the camp's assets and planning an assault on the infected creatures' stronghold. Wherever that might be.

When they arrived back at the camp, the lights in the compound blazed brightly. They'd kept the spots off until tonight, for fear of giving their location away. But that was a moot point now. They'd been found and lights at night were now their friend. You can't shoot what you can't see.

John called out, warning those inside of their arrival. No sense taking friendly fire, if it could be avoided.

Chris Reedy was the first to greet them. The optimistic

look on his face faded quickly when he saw they were alone. They hadn't rescued Hope.

Chris got a nod from Carver and a shake of the head from Kinney. That was all he needed to know that Hope was gone.

Carver went into the reinforced office building and found Kyle sitting apprehensively on the bed. He didn't need to say anything.

Kyle's eyes began to swell, and his breath came in choking stutters. He stood up and rushed into Carver's arms. He began to sob.

John let Kyle cry himself out. Carver could feel his own sadness pouring out of the young man. Every breath and each tear the young man shed for his mother became a sign of grief for them both. It was a cathartic relief that let him focus on revenge, rather than the pain he felt. He was now more focused than ever.

When Kyle had stopped crying, Carver pushed him back slightly. "I'm sorry," John said. "I couldn't save her."

Kyle looked at Carver, his face puffy and red.

"But I can make you this vow," John continued. "I'll get them all. I'll kill every last one of them. I promise."

Kyle nodded. He caught his breath and stepped back. "No. We will. I have even more rights to kill them than you do. She was my mother, and I will have my revenge."

John stared at the young man. He was right. Regardless of his age, he was entitled to this.

"I wouldn't have it any other way," John replied.

Kyle looked tentatively at Carver, unsure if he was being honest or just placating him.

He reached out his hand to John. "I believe you."

Carver took his hand and they shook. Man to man. Warrior to warrior. They were family.

"It is done," Carver said.

He took Kyle into his arm and gave him a man hug. With the attack and loss of his mother, the young man would never be the same. His childhood days were over.

"John!" Chris Reedy said from the hallway. "I need you."

Carver heard the concerned note in his tone.

"Get some rest. We'll be leaving at daybreak," John said to the young man.

Kyle nodded as Carver turned into the hallway. He shut the boy's door.

"Yeah?" Carver said dryly.

"It's Trey. I think you better check his injury."

Carver began to ask a question but was waved off by the EMT.

"Just follow me," he said.

They walked to the Dardens' room, where Brett and Trey were sitting on the injured boy's bed. They were smiling at some unknown joke. Nothing seemed to be amiss.

"Mr. Carver wants to see how you're feeling," Chris said. "He wants to know when you'll be ready to get some payback."

"I'm ready now!" the young man said confidently.

"You better let me look at the injury before I have you running around the camp killing zombies," John replied, understanding the duplicity of Chris's request. Reedy wanted John to see the kid's foot without raising any concerns.

Trey pulled his sheets back and revealed a bandaged

lower leg. The four-inch sterile gauze wrap had been pinned at the top with a paperclip. Reedy unwrapped the bandage and exposed the wound.

Two parallel gashes, both penetrating the muscle, went from above his ankle to the top of his foot. The wounds had clotted, but that wasn't what brought Carver into the young man's room. The veins near the cuts were beginning to turn black. Tray had been infected. He had less than a couple hours left before he turned, and there was nothing they could do to stop it.

John stepped back and looked at the boys. His gaze froze their jovial banter and within a few seconds, the gravity of the situation took hold. Carver didn't have to say a thing. Deep down, they must have known.

"No, Mr. Carver," Trey pled. "Please, tell me I'm all right."

Carver just shook his head.

"I'm sorry," Mr. Reedy said. "There's nothing we can do."

"NO!" Brett yelled. "I won't let you kill him!"

Reedy tried to take hold of the boy to console him, but Brett shoved him away.

"You will not let him die!"

"Son, we can't stop it."

"I don't believe you. You have to help him. We can go to the hospital. They had insulin for him. They've got to have something to stop this. There has to be something."

"Brett," Carver said. "There's nothing. No cure. Not a thing that will even slow this down. You know that."

Brett stood back, his mind churning as he tried to think of a way out of the situation.

Reedy sat down next to Trey. The boy was in a trance,

his life condemned by a single bite from an infected animal. He lifted up his exposed foot and looked at it.

"It's turning black," he said absently. "But I don't feel a thing,"

"That's good," Reedy said. "At least you don't have any pain." He reached around the young man's head and began to adjust the pillow.

"NO!" Brett shouted. "Leave him alone."

Brett pushed Chris away, sending the EMT tumbling to the floor.

Carver stepped forward but was met by a shotgun that Brett had grabbed. He aimed it at Carver's chest.

"Anyone touches him, and they're dead."

Carver and Reedy froze. The boy's finger danced inside the trigger well. Just a few pounds of pressure would remove most of Carver's heart and lungs.

"You will not touch him. I'll fix him. Just leave us alone."

Brett's steely eyes left no doubt that he meant every word.

"Son," Reedy said quietly. "Just put the gun down. No one will touch your brother."

"I don't believe you!" he hissed. "You'll kill him as soon as I do!"

"No, they won't," Trey said.

He reached over and gently lifted the shotgun up and away from Carver. Brett stared at his brother, unsure what to do.

"They can't kill you," Brett said. "You're my twin brother."

"I know. But it's not their fault."

"I can't lose you." Tears welled up in Brett's eyes. "I

can't lose you. I've never been alone."

"It's all right," Trey said, smiling. "It's going to happen, if we want it to or not."

Brett dropped the shotgun and flung himself on his dying brother. Trey held his head on top of his chest, stroking his sobbing brother's hair.

"It's all right," Trey whispered. "It's all right."

Carver slowly retrieved the gun and unchambered the buckshot shells. The safety was off. He'd be dead if the kid had panicked. Even though he hadn't been shot, he didn't feel all that lucky. With everything he'd been through so far that day, being killed wasn't exactly the worst thing that could have happened. He would have taken a full spread of lead, if it would bring Hope back.

"How long do I have?" Trey asked.

"I truly don't know," Reedy replied.

Shrek sat by the bed. He was alert but calm. He seemed to understand what was happening. Every so often, the Mal would look at Trey, and the hair on his nape would stiffen slightly. He sensed the change and would provide an alarm as the transformation neared its end. Carver commanded the dog to stay by the boys' side. Both he and Reedy left the room as Trey continued to console his brother.

"We need to check on him every ten minutes," Reedy said.

"Agreed," Carver said. "Between that and Shrek, we should have sufficient warning before he converts. I want to get Brett out of there before that happens."

The two men stood silently, deep in thought and sadness. It had been a hell of a day, and they still had more to do.

Not only did Carver want to attack the infected, there was the matter of the three families from Yuma that had apparently been slaughtered. They needed to verify they had been killed but wouldn't know for sure until the sun came up.

"All those people dead," Reedy said, sighing.

"Who? The Yuma families?"

"Yeah. It's like they never existed. We were just getting to know them and now…"

"You need to put that kind of thinking in a box and stow it. You can unpack it later, but for now, stay focused."

Carver glanced at his watch.

"It's an hour before sunrise. Let's organize a group to check on the Yuma camp. Then, we'll get together in Beckham and come up with a plan."

"What are you thinking, John?"

"We need to find those infected things and destroy them."

"John. I don't want you to get pissed off at me, but are you sure that's our best move? Revenge?"

Carver shot Reedy a steely look. The hatred in John's eyes left no doubt about his intentions. He'd never seen such anger in one person before, especially such a capable killer.

"This isn't about payback, although it will be sweet. This is about survival."

Carver stepped away and looked in on the Darden boys. Brett had stopped crying and they were talking quietly.

"We were attacked. The enemy took the fight to us and we got whooped. What do you think will happen in the future? We can't control when the fight happens if we wait for them to come to us."

Carver started pacing back and forth, his hands moving about as he spoke.

"When we were in Afghanistan, our firebases were under constant attack. A rocket here, an IED there. Sappers one night and nothing the next."

John stopped and squared up with Reedy.

"You know what that meant? We had to be ready for anything, twenty-four seven, three sixty-five. We never had a break because we never knew when things would go kinetic.

"So, we went back to the basics. After all, a firebase is just a fancy term for a patrol base, right? Do you know what's the best way to protect a patrol base?"

"Uh, no," Reedy replied.

"You patrol," John said. "You meet the enemy away from the wire and take the fight to them. After we started to do that, the base was secure, and our nerves weren't frazzled from constant worry. You fight the enemy on your terms, at your time, and at a place of your choosing. That's how you protect a patrol base, and that's how we're going to protect this camp."

Reedy could see that Carver's confidence was back. Before, with the loss of Hope, he was adrift. It was frightening to see their leader, the rock of the camp, unsure of himself. Now, the old John Eric Carver was asserting himself. He must have, as he said, put it in a box and stowed it. His emotions were suppressed, and if he heard the SEAL correctly, there would be time to grieve later.

"Let's get the rest of the group and start organizing," Carver said.

"I'll look in on Trey one more time."

"Good idea. I'll leave Shrek there too."

Chris Reedy went into the room. Trey and Brett stopped their conversation. Trey smiled.

"I'm so sorry, Trey," Chris said.

"That's all right," he replied. "I didn't think I had much more time, anyway."

"How so?"

"My insulin. Mr. Carver risked his life for maybe four more months' worth. Then what? I'm dead, anyway."

Chris nodded. It was an incredibly mature and truthful statement. There would be no more insulin now that the world had ended. Chris knew that back when they'd gone on the mission to Temecula Hospital.

"This will be quicker and not as painful," Reedy said. "I want you to know that."

Trey just nodded.

Reedy checked the wound. The infection had spread a few inches. They had some time.

"Keep an eye on your brother," Chris said. "We'll be back."

Brett nodded. "Yes, sir."

Shrek sat and watched it all. He'd stay till the end. It's what his master wanted him to do. Then he'd kill the boy. He'd kill the new asp. It was his job, and he was good at it.

37

Brett Darden
Lost Valley Administrative Office

"I have never in my life envied a human being who led an easy life. I have envied a great many people who led difficult lives and led them well."
—THEODORE ROOSEVELT

"I don't want you to die," Brett said softly.

Trey gave his brother a grim smile. "Like I want to."

The twins sat facing each other. Trey lay on his cot, foot elevated, a dark line of viral infection creeping up his leg.

They sat quietly for a few minutes, each lost in their own thoughts. Shrek sat nearby, his ears standing straight and his eyes glaring squarely at the dying boy.

Trey watched the Mal sizing him up. Its gaze relentless. He looked at his leg and saw a greyish pallor absorbing his pink skin. He was beginning to feel the change.

"I want to get up," Trey said. "I can't just lay here."

Brett helped his brother stand and let Trey use his shoulder to support his injured twin's weight.

"Let's move around."

"Is that a good idea?" Brett asked. "Won't that make the infection spread more quickly?"

Trey stopped. Maybe Brett was right. What if the infection was already affecting his mind, directing him into the open where his change would be the most dangerous for those around him? Maybe the virus was making him a predator.

"Yeah," Trey said. "That might not be a good idea."

They put him in a chair instead.

The twins spoke about past shared adventures. They laughed at themselves and cried about lost friends and parents. An hour went by quickly. Too fast for them both.

"Hey," Carver said as he returned to the room. "How are you doing?"

"Okay, I guess. It doesn't hurt too much. At least, it's no worse than the cuts in my ankle. It's more of a burn."

"Let's take a look," Carver said.

Trey held his leg up for inspection. Carver saw that the tissue changes had progressed up to his knee. The tissue had lost what little hair the kid had before, and the black venous mutations had spread. His thigh was now laced with ebony striations. Another hour and he'd be a risk to them all.

"You're holding on," Carver said, hoping to give the boys some solace. "It isn't advancing as fast as I thought it would."

"You're not good at lying," Trey said. "But, thanks anyway."

Carver smiled and rustled the kid's hair. Several patches of his wispy blonde locks fell off the back of his head. Trey hadn't noticed but Brett's eyes widened. He knew.

"Can I talk to you, Brett?" Carver asked.

"Sure, Mr. Carver."

They left the room and walked down the hall.

"I don't know how fast it's going to progress at this point. You saw his hair fall out when I ruffled it. The color changes in his skin and veins may not be a good indicator. That may not be a good warning on when he'll change."

"He's still normal. When we talk, he hasn't done anything crazy."

Carver stood silently. It would be prudent to move Brett to a different building and put Trey down. Like a dog that had advancing rabies, there was no cure and giving the creature more time was a danger to everyone around them.

"Not yet, Mr. Carver," Brett pled.

John looked down and took pity. He sighed. It was not the smart thing to do, but he'd remembered what Hope had told him just a day or two ago. Giving the brothers a little more time wouldn't be the smart thing to do, but it was the human thing to do.

"Okay," Carver said. "On one condition."

"Yes, sir."

"Shrek stays with you. And if he turns before I get back, you have to lock him up inside the room. Do you promise me that? I've got a little more to do back at Beckham, but I'll be back in less than an hour. You should be good until then."

Carver drew his M9 pistol and handed it to Brett.

"This is for your protection. If it goes south quickly, use it. But please lock him up, if you can. You don't need to be the one."

"Yes, sir."

"You know how to use this?"

"Yeah. That's the safety," Brett said, flicking the lever

on the left slide up and then down, back into its safe position.

"Good. Now, please get me when he changes. I'll make sure he doesn't suffer."

"Thank you, Mr. Carver. Miss Torrence was right."

"What did you say?" Carver asked.

"Miss Torrence told Kyle that you were a good man. Kyle told us that once. She was right. You're a good father."

Carver froze. The mention of Hope's name threw him. He'd suppressed those emotions a while back, but just the mention of her name brought a tidal volume of anger and pain.

Brett shoved the large handgun into the waistband at the small of his back and pulled his shirt out and over it. He returned to his brother, and they began talking once again, like there wasn't a care in the world.

Carver sank into a deep, emotional well. He walked slowly back to Beckham, where the adults stood over a map of the area, planning their defense of the camp.

About ten minutes later, Trey felt a ripple of pain shoot from his head, down his spine. It spasmed his abdomen, causing him to throw up on the floor. The vomit was dusted with black speckles.

"You need to get Mr. Carver," Trey said somberly.

"No," Brett said. "We still have more time."

Trey sighed. He didn't want to die, but he didn't want to hurt his brother, either.

Trey felt a burning rush through his blood. The room became hot, and he felt like a trapped animal.

"I need to get out of here," Trey said. "I'm burning up."

"We can't leave. You have to stay here."

"No, I can't breathe!" Trey pled.

Brett stepped up to the window and looked outside. The night was giving way to the morning. Filtered pink sunshine backlit the nearby trees, and the mountain tops radiated a warm hue from the pink morning sun.

"It's almost dawn," Brett said.

"I just want to watch the sun come up, one more time."

Brett understood.

He helped his brother up, and they hobbled outside. Shrek walked with them, his eyes never leaving the rapidly changing boy.

"Where are we going?" Trey asked.

"Our spot," Brett replied. They both knew where that was.

They hobbled to a side path that wound around a hill to the camp's east. A few hundred yards' walk, and they came to "their spot."

A petrified bristlecone pine tree stood sentinel over the high mountain desert. It had lost its needles and cones many centuries ago. Its bark had solidified and calcified into ribbons of mottled brown, ocher, and grey. The desert floor lay in the distance. The floor of the valley spanned miles to the northeast. The undulating land was peppered with green and brown growth while in the distance, an eagle drifted on heat thermals that swirled updrafts coming off the nearby mountains.

They sat down at the base of the tree. Brett leaned back on the petrified bark while Trey lay back against his chest. He'd lost almost all of his hair on the walk as his heart pumped the poison from his leg to the rest of his body. Black lines had started to form on his skull.

"I can feel it, Brett."

Trey faced away from him as they watched the eagle soar in the distance.

"I know," Brett said. He pointed out at the hovering raptor as it danced in the updrafts.

"See it?" Brett said. "It's beautiful."

"Yeah," Trey replied, pain in his muted reply. "It's like he's floating to heaven."

Brett brought his left hand around Trey's stomach and hugged his brother from behind. He reached around his back and brought the pistol out, setting it on the ground next to him.

"Brett. You have to find Mom," Trey said, his voice beginning to change. "You need to find her."

"I will," Brett said, tears welling up in his eyes. "I promise, I'll save her."

Trey relaxed in his arms. He dropped his head back onto Brett's chest and sighed.

"I love you, brother," Trey whispered.

"And I love you too."

Shrek began to growl.

Carver

Carver walked into the admin building. It was quiet. He expected to find Brett holding his brother, waiting for the end. But instead, he found an empty room.

"Kinney! Get over here and bring help," Carver barked into his walkie-talkie.

Carver ran out of the building toward Beckham Hall. He was met halfway by Kinney, Kyle, and both Chris and Laura Reedy. They all were armed.

"The twins are gone," he yelled. "I shouldn't have left them alone."

"Where would they go?" Laura asked in a panic.

"How would I know? Let's start with the maintenance garage, then we've got to search the perimeter. Trey was hurt pretty bad—I don't think he could have walked too far."

A single gunshot sounded from the east, followed by silence.

The group sprinted down the dirt path and found the twins under an old, dead pine. Brett sat with his back against the trunk, his arm around Shrek. Trey lay at their feet with the top of his forehead gone, and black-speckled cranial fluid sprayed on the desert floor in front of the body.

Carver walked up to the corpse and felt for a pulse. There was none.

Trey's face still held some normalcy, even though his eyebrows were gone, and his skin had turned a slightly pale grey. Everything else was still normal. He had a smile on his face and calmness in his open, blank eyes. Brett had killed his brother while he was still normal. He had died human.

Brett handed Carver his handgun and absently stroked the dog's head. He began to cry.

Carver picked the boy up and hugged him tightly. Kyle rushed up and grasped them both. They all began to sob. Their losses had finally bubbled up to the surface.

They stood together, letting their sorrow flow. The others turned away and gave them time to grieve. The sun was just peeking over the mountains, and a blanket of light moved slowly across the desert.

"Do you hear that?" Kinney said.

A far-off droning sound came from the west.

"Yeah. What is it?" Laura asked.

The rest of the adults started jogging back to camp, while Kyle, Brett, and Carver unclenched and slowly walked behind. They were halfway to camp when the sound became more distinct, and Shrek began to bark.

Carver urged the boys along as the sound of an approaching Osprey echoed throughout the Valley. Carver got to the parking lot of the camp just as the massive tiltrotor settled down onto the hard-packed dirt space.

Carver separated himself from the boys and started walking to the back of the craft. The ramp dropped down, and a ghost from the past stepped off.

"Goddam, Carver. It's great to see you," Porky Shader barked.

The big SEAL strode over and gave Carver a bear hug but received nothing in return.

"What's wrong, buddy? The cavalry is here."

"You're a day late," Carver shouted.

John spun around and walked back to Beckham Hall, leaving a stunned Shader standing in the parking lot, dust swirling around as the Osprey wound down its engines.

Potoski walked up next to Shader.

"What the fuck's gotten into him?" the big Marine asked.

"Welcome to Lost Valley?" Shader sarcastically replied. "Come on. Let's unload the gear. Then we can figure out why we're not welcome."

38

Beckham Hall
Lost Valley Scout Camp

"We shall defend our island, whatever the cost may be, we shall fight on the beaches, we shall fight on the landing grounds, we shall fight in the fields and in the streets, we shall fight in the hills; we shall never surrender."
WINSTON CHURCHILL

They gathered in Beckham Hall. One group devastated at their losses and the other elated at their salvation. It didn't make for a good start.

"I'm sorry, John," Shader said after listening to the recount of their prior day. "We were in the same boat."

"Yeah. And I'd like to know what happened to my house!" Jennifer said.

Kinney sighed.

"We'll talk later," Kinney said. It was a story he didn't want to tell her.

Carver sat at the table, his head in his hands. The irony and tragedy of the new group's arrival was not lost on him. Had they come just one day earlier, their firepower would have turned the tide of the battle. Hope and Trey would still be alive. But fate dealt them a shit hand, and they'd all played it to the best of their ability. Most had survived, but the ones who mattered most to John, Kyle, and Brett hadn't made it.

"We still need to patrol down to the Yuma

campground and do a body count," Kinney said. "Then we've got to come up with a defensive plan to protect this place."

"Let's go," Shader said, patting Carver on the shoulder. "You need to move, or you'll stay here all day. Put it…"

"I know," Carver said, interrupting his friend. "Put it in a box and put it away."

Shader nodded and rose.

"Let's go," Carver said.

They walked to the campground about half a mile from Beckham. Menily and Gardner walked together, quietly commenting on the surrounding desert floor. Menily pointed to different spots on the ground, and at one point, they both squatted over some footprints and examined the sandy dirt.

They got to the tent city, or at least, what was left of it. The canvas structures had been ripped apart, and disemboweled corpses lay scattered everywhere. Men, women, and a few small children had been eviscerated. Nothing left but scattered bones and strands of sinew.

No one turned away. They'd seen enough death to tolerate the sight. It had been a rapid and traumatic transformation from their former "civilized" lives. They all now carried the scars of witnessing nature's brutality. Like jaded cops at a fatal accident scene, they walked calmly through the camp. Their purposeful movements were clinical and precise.

They finished their assessment and returned to Beckham Hall.

"We're short three people," Laura Reedy said. "Where are they?"

"Should we search for them?" Shader asked. "Maybe they escaped."

"I doubt it, but I don't want to just abandon them," Carver replied. "Chances are, if they weren't eaten then they're infected and running with the pack."

"Yeah. About that," Shader said. "We call the infected Variants."

"Whatever," Carver replied. "Variants. Infected. They're all the enemy."

"Looks like there were several hundred or more," Menily said.

"I agree," Gardner replied. "I tracked at least four large groups of over a hundred each. How many people lived in the area?"

"Borrego Springs had over three thousand. That doesn't count the ones outside of town. Maybe five thousand or so. But that's just a guess," Kinney replied.

"Maybe they carried the bodies with them, like they did Miss Torrence," Brett said.

"What did you say?" Shader asked.

"Huh? That they killed Miss Torrence."

"Did you say that they carried her body off?"

"Well, not her body. She was alive when they grabbed her. She's a Variant now, or worse," Carver said quietly.

Porky began to quiver. *Could it be possible?*

"Hey, Chief," Gonzalez said, "are you thinking what I am?"

"Yeah, Gonzalez. She might still be alive," Porky said.

Both Kyle and Carver bolted upright.

"Don't fuck with me," Carver hissed, both anger and hope in his voice.

"Chief ain't fuckin' with you," Lazzaro said, his leg rebandaged by Chris Reedy. He sat at the next table, his injured limb elevated. "Chief saw the Variant nest. They keep a stable of live people for food. Sometimes they don't eat them for days."

"Saw it with my own eyes," Shader said.

"Me too," Morales added, holding the young girl he'd saved. "This one here, I rescued from their farm."

Carver looked hopefully at Kyle. *Could it be true? Could Hope still be alive?*

"She was captured by the Variants?" Carver asked, pointing to the small girl in Morales's lap.

"Sí! She was there for days before I got her out."

"We just need to know where they took her," Shader said. "Where's their nest?"

No one knew. The group deflated. Hope and possibly three other victims could be alive, but that they didn't know where.

They couldn't save anyone if they didn't know where they were.

Shrek stood up and nudged Carver with his snout. He stared up at his master.

Carver looked down and into his partner's eyes. They communicated like no two humans could. After a few moments, they both understood what needed to be done.

"Shrek can find her," he said confidently.

Shrek barked, as if telling them all that he was up for the job.

"Yeah!" Shader replied. "That dog can hunt. But we need a plan."

"Hard to plan when we don't know what we're up against, Chief," Gonzalez said.

"The Pig's right," Lazzaro said. "What the hell are we up against?"

"I don't know, and I don't care," Carver replied. "But we don't have the time to do a pre-operation con-fab. Hope and those others…"

Carver stopped and caught himself. He'd already put Hope in a box and pushed her memory down into his ever-expanding emotional rabbit hole. He had to stay focused.

"Well, at least let's put a basic battle plan together. I'd like to know who's doing what."

"Agreed."

Thirty minutes later, the group had their basic assignments. Carver and Shrek would take point while Shader would lead the main force. They'd give the war dog team a chance to blaze the trail, then make an assault plan based on their final destination.

"Now, as far as the point. I think it should be just me and Shrek," Carver began. "We've been a team for years and we can move quickly. The trail started out going east. That leads into the mountains. It'll be a tough slog."

"Sorry, Carver," Shader said. "You need a team around you. You know that. Fire support can't come from one gun."

"I can go," Gonzalez said. "I'm in good shape."

"Keele?" Shader asked. "You want to join?"

"Sure, Chief. Someone's got to keep the PIG in line."

"Who else?" Shader said. "I'm too old to do that shit."

"I'll go," a quiet voice said. It was Kyle.

"Sorry kid. You're too young." Shader quickly replied.

Kyle stood up and racked a shell into his shotgun.

"That's my mom out there. I have more of a right than

anyone here to be with you! Don't take that away from me!"

The room remained quiet as Shader and Kyle stared at each other.

"Hey. I wouldn't mind a street sweeper on the team," Gonzalez said, referring to Kyle's shotgun. "Kind makes an impression, if you know what I mean."

Carver looked at both Shader and Kyle. The boy stood defiantly.

"Okay, kid. You're in." Carver said.

Kyle sat down, but his demeanor remained the same. He felt no fear, just anger and a commitment to bring his mother home or perish with her.

"Lazzaro, you're here with the refugees. Keep them safe," Shader said.

Lazzaro wasn't happy about being left behind, but the refugees from the Forum needing to be protected, and the injured Marine was a natural choice to stay back.

"Copy that, Chief."

"Hey. Don't drink all the beer while we're gone," Keele joked.

"You touch my Modelo and I'll break your sorry ass," Kinney replied.

"You've got beer?" Keele asked. He hadn't known that.

"Yeah. And it's not for the likes of you. Don't fuck with my beer!"

Lazzaro nodded. "No problem, Kinney." The injured man smiled. He didn't look too sincere in his promise.

"No, I mean it. Stay away from my house."

"All right. That's enough!" Carver yelled. "Quit screwing around. Everyone, focus!"

They all nodded, but the smiles remained.

"What are you grinning about?" Carver barked at Kinney.

"I don't know, John. It's just nice to smile. I mean, think about how we felt just a few hours ago. It sucked. Hope was dead and we were on our last leg. We didn't stand a chance against those things and they'd just kicked our asses. Now…"

"Now, my mom may be alive, and we have enough people to wipe them off the face of the earth!" Kyle added. "I know why I'm smiling."

"Copy that, young man," Shader said appreciatively. "We were on a death ship, until Donaldson and Everly got us out of there."

The two pilots blushed and nodded.

"And we'd all be dead if it wasn't for Mr. Shader," the little girl in Morales's lap said quietly.

Morales hugged the girl, who he thought was sleeping during the meeting. "She's right, Shader. We can't thank you enough."

It was Porky's turn to blush.

"Then, let's finish the day as good as it started," Carver said confidently. He stood up and grabbed his rifle. "I'm ready when you all are."

Shrek barked and went to Carver's side. The SEAL reached down and rubbed the dog's coat, then looked into his eyes.

"Let's find Hope!" he said to the Mal.

Shrek

Carver is ready to go to war. I am ready to track the

Variants and bring Hope back home. Their acrid odor saturates the air. It won't be hard to do.

We will hunt them now and bring death to them all. They've attacked us, and they will pay. The warriors around me are now my people, and I will protect my family with my life. It is what I was bred for. It was what I live for, and with Carver at my side, it is something I am willing to die for. We are Carver and Shrek. We were the best. I am the ghost that kills in the night. I will win. I always do.

— 39 —

Satan's Gate
Anza-Borrego Desert State Park

"These are the times that try men's souls."
THOMAS PAINE

Shrek moved with swift confidence. His intensity hadn't varied since they'd begun tracking the horde over two hours ago. They'd moved off of the grassy high plain and into the mountains where the rocks left no sign of the pack's passing. If it hadn't been for the Mal's nose, they'd have lost the trail long ago.

The group kept pace with Shrek, but the elevation changes made travel difficult. There were many trails and washouts the Variants could have taken, but either their simple minds failed to register less physically stressful routes, or they weren't affected by the climbs. Either way, the path Shrek followed was linear. Once, the climb went nearly vertical and Carver forced the Malinois to circle around the peak. He picked up the scent on the other side.

They were moving downhill, following a ravine that had been cut into the side of the mountain. The path wound around small peaks where the Variants would climb up and over the edges of the shallow escarpments. Carver kept Shrek in the washout, and they never failed to find the trail further down.

"Okay. Let's stop and hydrate."

Gonzalez, Keele, and Carver each pulled their hydration hose to their mouths. The end was clipped to their shoulder strap and connected to the CamelBak water pouches that were in their assault packs. They pinched the bite valve with their front teeth and sucked down several gulps of water.

Kyle grabbed a bottle of water from his backpack and drained it.

"They're heading toward the desert floor," Carver said. "That doesn't make sense. I don't know any large structures out there and these things don't like the light."

Carver studied the topo map he'd brought and found nothing that would hold the hundreds of Variants they were following. It was perplexing.

Kyle stood back as the adults talked. He waited for them to finish before he spoke up.

"Mr. Carver. Can I look at the map?"

"Sure, Kyle. Maybe you have an idea." He handed the map to the young man.

Kyle studied the map briefly, then held it out to Carver and pointed to a spot a mile down the mountain. It was a dead end to a canyon called "Satan's Gate."

"I believe they went there."

"Why do you think that?" Carver said. "There are no buildings. It's just a dead end."

"No sir. There is something there. A cave. A big cave."

Carver studied the topographic lines and various marked points of interest. "It's not on the map."

"Well," Kyle began. "It's kind of a scout secret. At least, we don't talk to the counselors about it. Some of the older guys said that they'd been inside, although I've never gone myself. But I've heard there's a cave and it has Indian artifacts in it. One of the OA's told me that inside, there are even rooms cut out of the side of rock and that an ancient tribe probably lived there."

"Shit. Not another hole to go through," Gonzalez said.

Keele knew what the little Marine had endured, crawling through the access pipes in the Forum. He'd never say it to him directly, but Keele was impressed by Gonzalez's courage. Going through those access tunnels and slithering along the conduits wearing only skivvies and armed with nothing more than a handgun took some serious cajones.

"I hear you, brother," Keele said respectfully.

"I'm not thrilled about it either, but we've got to follow the white rabbit," Carver said.

"What the hell is the white rabbit?" Gonzalez asked.

"You don't know *Alice in Wonderland?*" Kyle asked incredulously. "Follow the white rabbit down the rabbit hole?"

"Hey. I'll show Alice my wonderland!" Keele said.

"I got a rabbit for her, too!" Gonzalez added, giving Keele a high-five.

Kyle began to giggle.

"Don't pay attention to those two. Someone sucked their brains out and put shit back in," Carver said to the young man.

"Semper Fi!" Keele grunted.

"Let's just follow Shrek," Carver said, looking up into the sky. "It's barely past noon. Those things won't be out in this light, and I haven't seen anywhere they could be hiding to watch their back trail."

"ZOEK!" he commanded to Shrek.

"What the hell language is *zook*?" Keele asked. He'd never worked with a war dog.

"Dutch. It's where Shrek is from," Carver said as the Malinois shot forward.

The four started walking quickly, attempting to keep up with Shrek's fast pace.

"Why don't they just buy American dogs?" Keele asked Gonzalez.

"No clue," the diminutive Marine replied. "I don't ask questions. They feed me and let me shoot shit. That's all I need to know."

A half mile more and it looked like Kyle was correct. The straight line they were following led them directly to the dead end of the canyon.

When they were about a quarter of a mile from the edge of the escarpment, Carver called a halt.

"I'm going forward and scout the area," Carver said. "Give me a radio check."

After verifying they were communicating, Carver pulled a HAM radio out of his pack and gave it to Kyle.

"When I report back, let the rest of them know where we are and our sit-rep."

"Yes, sir," Kyle replied.

Gonzalez nudged him and whispered in his ear.

"Sorry," Kyle said. "Aye aye, sir." Then the young man saluted.

Carver smiled and returned the salute.

"Maintain the salute until the senior officer salutes back. But you don't need to salute me. I'm not an officer, and I never have been," Carver said when Kyle dropped his arm before Carver had responded.

321

"So, the only people I need to salute are Lieutenants Donaldson and Everly?" Kyle asked.

"If you salute those two roto-heads, I'll kill you myself," Keele joked.

Kyle's confused look made the other three chuckle.

Carver reached out and hugged the young man. "Let's go get your mom."

"Yeah. I'm for that," Kyle replied.

Carver signaled Shrek to his side, and the pair disappeared over the top of the next escarpment.

Kyle turned on the HAM and sent a radio check back to base.

Shader answered. They were ready to airlift the rest of the adults to their spot, then the Osprey would provide overhead fire support with their rear-mounted SAW.

They were as prepared as they could be. Now, it was up to Carver. With some luck, they'd be able to get his mother back. It was a long-shot. But, as Mr. Carver had said before, at least a long-shot was a chance, and no matter what the odds were, it was better than no chance at all.

Carver crept along the edge of the canyon, staying a few yards back from the edge. He moved them away from the end of the deep gully and stopped when the drop-off started to edge in. He crawled to the ledge and looked back through his binoculars.

A path had been cut into the side of the mountain near the base. It led directly into the mouth of a massive hole at the base of the limestone wall.

Carver was about a half a mile away and several hundred feet above the cave. With the sun directly above, the entrance was a curtain of black since no light was able to angle into the opening. He brought up his binoculars and glassed the entrance.

"Holy shit," he whispered.

There were scores of Variants standing in a trance-like state just inside the shadow created by the cave's rocky overhang. They were lined up, only feet apart, from one end of the opening to the other. They were a wall of infected flesh, and there was no way around them.

Carver was crushed. He'd hoped that they would be within the cave and that they might have a chance to sneak in and out without detection. It was an unlikely scenario, but he could only hope. Now, the odds were overwhelmingly against them. If the cave had any volume to it, there could be thousands within.

Carver hurried back to the team and gave them the bad news.

"There are just too many of them to get by," Carver said dejectedly. "We can't sneak in and they're dug in like a tick. The only way to attack them is with a frontal assault, and we don't have the firepower to do that."

Carver sat down on a rock and buried his head in his hands. He was frustrated and out of options.

"Mr. Carver. I know it's a long-shot, but maybe there's another way in."

Carver looked up at the boy and shook his head.

"Why would you say that?"

"Well, if there had been people living in there, they would have had at least two entrances. There has to be a cross breeze to bring in fresh air and take out any fire smoke. It only makes sense."

Carver still looked doubtful.

"All I'm saying is that if humans had inhabited the

place, there had to be at least a vent or another opening. It may be a long-shot, but you told me even that is better than no shot at all."

"Are you throwing my words back at me?" Carver said with a grin.

"I learn fast," Kyle replied.

"Hey, this kid could make a good Marine," Gonzalez said.

"I wouldn't let you guys touch him with a ten-foot pole," Carver shot back with a smile.

He looked at the map and pointed to some promising spots that were on the other side of the cave. "Let's go cave hunting."

They gathered and moved, looking for a needle in a haystack. Carver needed to locate an undiscovered hole in the ground where, with a good deal of luck and the help from a smart, young man, they could find a way to save the woman they both loved.

Several hours of searching had left them frustrated. Every swale proved empty. Each depression in the side of the mountain gave them nothing. Finally, with the afternoon sun halfway to the horizon, they sat down to rest.

"We've been up and down this damn mountain," Keele said. "I don't think there's a back door."

"There had to be, at one time," Kyle replied.

"Maybe an earthquake closed it off. That would explain why it had been abandoned," Carver said.

"There are too may 'ifs' and not enough answers," Gonzalez said.

The little Marine unlaced his boots and put his feet into the shadows created by a rock at the base of the hill.

"Man. That feels good on my dogs," he said, moving his toes around in his socks.

Carver studied the map once again. They were at the northeastern edge of the low mountain range. He could see the flat desert further out, the glitter of the Salton Sea in the distance. It was a sparkling jewel in the middle of a sandy landscape. The sunlight danced off its surface, creating a lightshow on the desert floor. Carver had thought of visiting there when they first took refuge at the camp.

Carver's concentration began to drift as he thought of these things. He glanced around and saw that Keele had imitated Gonzalez. Both of them had their boots off and were enjoying the shade of the rocky escarpment.

Kyle became curious. He watched the two Marines enjoying the shade a little more than he thought was normal. The young scout knelt down next to the rock and put his hands into the shadow.

"You can rub them anytime!" Gonzalez said.

Kyle didn't respond. His face brightened and he spun to face Carver.

"It's here!" he exclaimed. "The opening is here!"

Carver ran over and knelt next to Kyle. He put his face down in the shade and felt a cool breeze blowing out from under the rock. "Get your feet out of there!"

The two Marines pulled their boots back on as Carver began to push and pull on the large slab of limestone.

Soon, the four of them were working on dislodging the small boulder. Carver used his entrenching tool and rock to create a lever and fulcrum. They lifted, rocked, and shoved for nearly ten minutes before the boulder began to move. With a Herculean push, they tumbled the limestone away from the embankment and exposed a narrow crevice. Cold air flowed out.

"You found it!" Carver said to Kyle.

"Hey. I found it!" Gonzalez replied.

"Whatever," Carver said absently.

He measured the opening. It was barely two feet in height. He flattened himself and began to push in, but the ceiling of the tube dropped down. His large frame made it a difficult fit.

He backed out in frustration. "It's small."

"What about me?" Gonzalez said.

Carver sized him up but shook his head.

"I don't think so."

"He's a lot smaller than he looks in his battle gear," Keele said.

"Thanks, compadre," Gonzalez said sarcastically.

The two Marines began to bicker, when Kyle cut off them off.

"I'll go!" he said. "It's my mom and besides, I'm the smallest so I'm the one that should go."

Carver didn't like it. The kid didn't have the training to pull it off. But when there was no alternative short of a direct attack, it came down to the simple fact that it was their only option.

"Take your radio and this." Carver pulled out his handgun and flashlight. He had a rubber band holding green cellophane over the objective. It reduced the light to a dim, emerald glow.

"Watch your light discipline. If those things see you, any chance of getting your mom will be gone. Do you understand?"

"Aye aye," he replied without saluting.

"You're learning," Carver said approvingly. "Now, we need you to describe what you see when you get there. Watch your voice. You may need to backtrack into the tunnel to avoid being heard. Use your head and report back when it's safe."

Kyle nodded and took the gear. He removed his backpack and crawled into the opening, sliding under the overhang without a problem. Then the dim green glow of the flashlight disappeared into the darkness and the kid was gone.

— 40 —

Hope Torrence
Satan's Gate

"When your time comes to die, be not like those whose hearts are filled with fear of death.
Sing your death song and die like a hero going home."
—TECUMSEH (Shawnee Warrior and Leader)

Hope woke. Her head throbbed as she regained consciousness. The darkness around her was illuminated by a faint, distant light. She tried to remember where she was as she struggled to move. For some reason, her arms and legs were bound together.

She panicked. Was she paralyzed? Was she tied up? Her head was nearly immobilized as well, but she was able to rotate it slightly. She couldn't get her bearings.

Then her memories began to emerge. She remembered tackling Kyle, saving him from the infected creature that was attacking him. She remembered an infected Charlie grabbing her. Poor Charlie. His primal scream had frozen her in place. Then he threw her effortlessly over his shoulder and ran off before she blacked out.

She redoubled her efforts to get free, but whatever was holding her in place was unforgiving. She looked to her left. Her eyes adjusted even more and she could make out a figure on the wall next to her. It was one of the mothers from the Yuma campsite. She was glued to the wall with some hard, white crust that entombed her against the stone. She wasn't moving.

Hope looked more closely at her surroundings. The pinpoint of light was filtering into her area. It was less than a candle in intensity. It showed her enough of the structure around her to realize she was in a cave, and that it was filled with the infected. They clung to the walls of the rocky tube. They were somehow sticking to the limestone and were motionless, like bats hanging from the rafters of a church steeple's belfry.

Hope began to panic. She was glued to the wall inside of some cave, and the only thing she was able to move was her head.

She tried to escape her bonds. It felt like she struggled for hours, but the only thing she accomplished was to flake off some of the crust that bound her head. By the time she quit trying to break free, she could freely rotate her neck but the rest of her remained glued in place. She was exhausted. She fell asleep.

Time passed and she awoke to the stench of rotting flesh. Hope opened her eyes and found two burning yellow orbs staring back at her. She screamed. It was an infected monster, and its face was pressed against hers.

It shrieked back, and its hot, rancid breath nauseated her. She projectile vomited, hitting it in the face.

The creature screamed at her. She could see it rear its hand back, preparing to strike, when another creature crashed into it. The first monster bounced off the nearby wall and rose, stunned.

The second creature roared and approached Hope. It sniffed her, its breath gagging her as well. If she hadn't emptied her stomach already, she'd have brought up even more.

The first creature approached and tried to grab Hope, but the second one screamed at it and the first one backed down.

Then in a flash of barbarity she never could have imagined. The second creature leapt onto the woman next to her and bit off her face. The poor mother never had a chance to scream.

Her body was ripped from its cocoon and flung into the darkness. Dozens of hungry eyes leapt at the corpse and tore it apart. The sounds of their feast were unimaginable.

The second monster lumbered back in front of Hope and stood over her. It sniffed her face and croaked. Several answering sounds came from nearby.

"Fuck you!" Hope yelled. She spit at the two eyes, sending the creature back.

It screamed in anger and she braced for, what she hoped, was a quick and merciful death.

But it leapt away and took a human leg from one of the other creatures. Then it scampered down toward the light and was gone.

The remains of the woman were scooped up by a mass of infected and carried away as well. They joined their apparent leader. She wondered if it had been Charlie she'd spit on.

Hope rolled her head away from the sounds. She couldn't get the smell of the creatures out of head. She looked at the wall nearby and fought back her tears. She decided to die a good death. She wouldn't beg, and she would do what she could to fight. Even if it was just some spittle in their face.

She lay her head silently against the wall. The sounds

of the infected provided a constant background noise of grunts and chirps. But something wasn't the same. There was a sound that wasn't so primal. It was familiar. It was human.

She raised her head from the wall and looked about.

There! Is that a green light?

Hope saw a glowing emerald on the wall to her left. It moved in a circular pattern. She looked about and saw no infected nearby.

"Help!" she hissed.

The light stopped moving then disappeared.

Did she dream it? She wasn't sure. All she knew was she was tired and near death. She didn't know when she'd be the next meal on the menu.

Maybe, she thought, *I should just give in to the exhaustion.*

At least she wouldn't feel death if she was asleep. The poor woman next to her hadn't even made a peep. That was the way to go.

She closed her eyes and passed out. Her last thoughts were of her own demise and how it wouldn't hurt.

Carver

Many minutes went by after Kyle had crawled under the mountain. Carver kept checking his watch, but the time still crept along at its own pace. Gonzalez watched the SEAL pace back and forth. It was driving him crazy.

They were exposed on this side of the canyon, although Shrek was standing guard. The dog could hear a gnat fart from a mile away, so they would have plenty of warning if the Variants came rolling down the hill. Problem was, they weren't a match for the horde that would show up. They didn't have enough bullets to win that battle.

"Hey Chief, I can go get the kid, if you want," Gonzalez offered.

Carver glanced at his watch again. It had been just shy of forty minutes. He should have been back by now.

"Hey!" they heard from the cleft. "Give me a hand."

Carver helped Kyle worm his way out of the hole, and the boy brushed himself off.

"Well?" Carver said impatiently.

"She's alive!" Kyle said. "But I didn't do anything but observe."

"Good. I'm proud of you."

"I would have grabbed her, if I had the chance. Mr. Carver, there are too many of them in there. I wouldn't have had a chance to get her out."

Carver was afraid of that. Even with Shader and his men, they didn't have a full fireteam to combat the Variants.

"Tell me what you saw," Carver said.

"Well, the tunnel widens after you get going. The beginning is the narrowest part."

Kyle described the journey in and gave them an estimate of the Variant strength. Most importantly, with the path from the opening to the back of the cave being fairly straight, Carver could estimate how much cave there was from the mouth in the canyon to the back of the hole.

"I have an idea," Carver said. "But it's going to take good timing."

They quickly made plans and radioed back to the camp. If everything went according to plan, the fireworks would start soon, and they could get Hope out.

Porky Shader
Aboard the V-22 Osprey

Porky had heard of worse plans. Like Operation Liberty that cost them the fleet and most of the country's remaining fighting force.

Potoski was in his normal position, strapped to the bulkhead of the tilt-rotor aircraft, scanning out of the open rear ramp. Behind him was the team they'd rescued from the harbor. The three master-at-arms had enough experience that he trusted them. At least, mostly. But their job was simple, so he didn't worry that they could screw things up if they failed to perform.

The Osprey settled down about half a mile from the canyon, and Shader jumped out along with the three Navy shore patrolmen. The Osprey quickly lifted off and banked to the south, waiting for Carver to give the word. Hopefully, everything would work out.

The four quickly found the canyon and took up position on the ledge above and a quarter of a mile down. They stacked over a dozen full magazines on the ground near each of their positions, and Porky loaded the MK 153 rocket launcher they'd scored from the *Roosevelt*. It was one of the prizes he'd asked to have loaded onto the Osprey the night they made their escape.

He estimated the distance and loaded a tracer round into the attached rifle. He'd shoot the bullet to verify the range to the target then blast the cave opening and bring the mountain down. He'd destroy the opening only after they'd gotten confirmation that the prisoners had been rescued or confirmed dead. Hopefully, that would seal the creatures in a tomb permanently. Then, Lost Valley would become a safe haven once again.

Shader confirmed that the other three were locked and loaded, then radioed Carver that they were ready. Now all they had to do was wait for the fireworks to start.

Carver

Keele and Gonzalez had widened the cave's opening while waiting for Shader to get into position. When the time finally came, Kyle began crawling into the dark hole, followed by Gonzalez. The boy had confirmed that there was enough room to maneuver inside, so both had been outfitted with their firearms. Kyle had his shotgun, while Gonzalez had his M4 battle rifle.

The pair disappeared. Now, Carver just had to wait for confirmation that they'd rescued Hope. The alternative, that they were too late, was not something he could entertain. For him, it was just a matter of time before they were reunited.

About ten minutes after the two entered the cave, Carver looked at Keele. "You're up!"

"I hate this shit," Keele said.

He'd stripped down to a t-shirt and pants. He crawled into the mouth of the cave and squeezed past the overhanging rock. He was their radio relay man. Kyle had tried to contact them on his way out, but the limestone prevented communication.

Keele found the going a bit easier than he thought it would be. In fact, the cool, moist air felt rather refreshing. He flipped his NV monocular down and turned on the IR intensifier. The tunnel did widen, just like Kyle had said. It was tall enough for Keele to sit up and extend his legs. It was, after all, rather comfortable.

Keele waited. It wasn't long.

"We're five minutes out," Gonzalez whispered into his radio.

Both Kyle and he each had their monocular down. So far, the kid had been correct.

They went straight and down. Gonzalez could see a black opening at the base of the descending ramp of stone. It was the back entrance into the cave. They were almost there.

About fifty feet from the hole, a woman screamed. Kyle looked back at Gonzalez in terror.

"It's my mom!" Kyle said before he scrambled toward the hole.

Gonzalez grasped at the kid's leg, trying to keep him from rushing into danger, but he missed.

"NOW!" Gonzalez yelled into his mic. "GO! GO! GO!"

Keele was sitting back against the stone wall, luxuriating in the cool air, when he heard Gonzalez's panicked message.

He crawled back to a bend in the tunnel and transmitted to Carver.

"The shit's hit the fan," Keele said. "It's a go! They sound like they're in trouble."

"Shit!" Carver yelled. Then he got the HAM radio and broadcast to a second portable HAM on the Osprey.

"This is Eagle One. EXECUTE. EXECUTE. EXECUTE. NOW!"

Carver dove into the opening and crawled like his life

depended on it. He passed a stunned Keele and bear-crawled down the slope. He could hear Keele struggle behind him, trying to keep pace. Up ahead, he could hear a shotgun blasting away. As he got closer to the opening, it sounded like the mountain itself had come alive as thousands of voices all roared in a primal, hate-filled scream. It had started, and their fate rested in the hands of a single Osprey and Porky's portable rocket.

All Carver could do now was keep going and pray. As he scrambled toward the sound of battle, the words he'd used many times in preparing his squads for their upcoming missions came rolling into his mind. *Press the fight and keep moving. Because in battle, when you stand still, you die.*

"Keep moving," he grunted to himself. "Keep moving."

He didn't have time to think anymore. Just get to the fight.

Would they make it? Was Hope alive? He would find out soon enough.

41

Hope
Under the Mountain
Satan's Gate

No costly sacrifice nor offerings given
Can change the purpose of the powers of Heaven;
Whatever Fate ordains, danger or hurt,
Our death predestined; nothing can avert.
THEOGNIS
(Greek poet – 6TH Century B.C.)

Hope could smell them coming. She woke from a nightmarish sleep, only to find her worse dreams come true. It was Charlie, of that, she was sure. He had come for her. She was the last of the three still alive.

He stalked around her calcified tomb, snapping his tongue and gnashing his teeth. Around him, dozens of infected hovered and chirped. It reminded her of a religious ceremony, with Charlie as the high priest.

She had no illusions about her fate as the creature, that had once been her friend, stalked around her. She was a totem of their victory, a prize to be had and the high priest was the one to finish her off.

Like the last victim they'd eaten, the monster performed a ceremonial dance. It bent and popped its joints. It raised its deformed arms above its head and snapped its claws down next to Hope's face. It was a killing ritual, but Hope wasn't having any of it.

"Go ahead, you deformed bastards!" Hope yelled.

Her screams of anger and defiance brought screams and chirps from the assemblage. They weren't used to their dinner talking back.

They began to bark in unison. Their bodies swaying back and forth as the Charlie creature smacked its hands on the ground and screamed its demented chant.

Suddenly, there was a collective cry from down at the front of the cave.

The infected monster screamed, and the collective that had been surrounding Hope, rushed down to the entrance of the cave. All but Charlie. It stayed behind and hovered near her, refusing to abandon its meal.

Hope watched as it snapped its tongue back and forth. It bared its teeth in some macabre smile and squatted to launch.

She screamed.

"NO!" came a man's voice.

A shotgun blasted from her left, striking the monster, sending it tumbling into the nearby wall.

She couldn't see who was there, as the fiery blast from the gun's tube temporarily blinded her. She could just make out a figure, a goggle strapped to their head. They rushed by, pumping and firing shots from their gun.

"John!" she yelled.

The figure didn't answer.

A second person appeared.

"Stay still, Hope. We're here to get you out."

"Who are you?" she sobbed, her emotions flooding out.

"Name's Gonzalez, ma'am. United States Marines. Carver sent me and Kyle to get you."

"That's Kyle? Get him out of here!"

"Can't do that, ma'am. He's part of our team."

Hope felt the crust break away as the man ripped the calcifications. She quickly felt her arms unbind then she helped Gonzalez break her out of the lower half.

She was free.

Kyle stepped up to her and hugged her tightly. She couldn't believe he'd come for her. Two more men crawled out of the hole. It was John with another man.

"Hope!" he cried. "LOOK OUT!"

A single-eyed beast flung itself from the ceiling. A lone, yellow orb radiating hate and anger. It was barreling toward Kyle, fangs gnashing and tongue snapping. Carver and the two Marines tried to bring up their rifles, but it was too late. Cyclops was going to get another victim.

A flash leapt over Carver's shoulder. It collided with the infected coyote and knocked it back. It was Shrek. He'd followed them into the cave.

Carver watched as the war dog rebounded from the collision and latched onto the creature's hind leg. Shrek whipped his neck around, smashing Cyclops into the wall.

"No," Carver whispered. One drop of infected blood in the Mal's mouth, and that would be the end of the him.

Keele looked down to the entrance of the cave. He could hear the sound of the Osprey's machine gun rattling outside. He gasped as thousands of creatures poured into the opening. There were far more of them than they had thought.

"We have to go!" Keele said. "There's thousands of them trying to get out. We have to clear the cave."

Carver looked at the two combatants. Keele was right. They had to go. Their radios wouldn't work in here.

Carver looked back at Shrek. He was in a fight for his life. He watched as the Mal dodged and weaved, just staying out of the fangs of the infected creature.

"Let's go!" he heard Gonzalez say.

They'd all jumped up into the hole. Carver was the last one. He tried to take a shot at Cyclops. His laser darted around with the combatants, but there was never a good shot that didn't risk Shrek.

He forced himself to climb into the wall and crawl away. The survivors needed Shader to bring down the mountain on top of the horde. All their lives were at stake if they didn't seal the creatures inside.

A few minutes later, Carver was helped out of the hole.

"Where's your dog?" Keele asked.

Carver just shook his head.

"This is Eagle One. Mission accomplished. We're clear. Send it!" Keele said into the HAM.

In the distance, they heard a *whump!* as the rocket impacted above the cave.

"It's done," Carver said.

"We need to seal this end as well," Gonzalez said, pulling out a couple of frag grenades.

They had backup C4 explosive, if their M67s didn't do the job.

"Say again?" Keele asked, listening to the HAM.

"What is it?" Carver asked.

"The rocket didn't work," Keele said. "Shader said that we're fucked."

Hope flung her arms around Carver. She began to cry.

After all that, they were still going to be overrun. It didn't seem fair.

Shrek

Cyclops is fast. Faster than any enemy I've killed before.

I latch onto his leg and rip it, but the thick armor prevents me from tearing it away. This isn't going to work.

He leaps at me with a speed I can barely avoid. His mouth is full of sharp teeth. He smells of acid. He is poison, and I have no defense.

I see Carver escape into the hole. That's good. At least one of us will live.

I will see this through. Cyclops is to be defeated. It is to be destroyed. I must kill the beast.

An explosion shakes the ground just as Cyclops is about to leap. He falls to the side, and this is my chance. I know I will die from the poison, but I have to kill him. His neck is exposed as he flails for balance. It is mine.

I latch onto his nape and bite as hard as I can. I will grip down harder than I ever have before. I will cut his flesh. I will rip his veins. I will tear his throat. I will kill him.

But his flesh is too thick. It is like leather, too hard to penetrate.

Cyclops screams as he tries to knock me off his back. But I won't let go. I brace the ground and lift his body in the air. I shake my head hard, back and forth, whipping Cyclops from one side to the other.

Still, he screams.

I bash his body against the wall and grip his spine deeper into my jaw.

It reaches up with its sharp back paws to rake me off, but I lift it up once again.

I am tiring.

I have one more thing I can do.

I pin it down on the ground. I re-grip its neck. My front teeth ride over its throat. I leap for the opening that we had used to crawl in here. I land just inside, Cyclops still in my mouth.

I turn back and clench with all my might.

My back teeth find a seam in its spine. I raise it up one last time and snap it down onto the edge of the hole.

I hear its neck crack. It stops moving.

The other creatures are just outside the hole now.

I drag Cyclops with me because I never let go until Carver tells me to.

I am Shrek.

I am the ghost that kills in the night.

I always win.

I won.

Porky Shader
Outside Satan's Gate

The blast from the rocket dislodged a large chunk of the escarpment. It fell at the entrance of the cave, but the rest of the mountain remained. The hole wasn't closed, and the Variants were scampering out.

Potoski rained down lead onto the creatures. Some avoided his fire. The three MOAs poured rifle fire at the climbing Variants, hitting some while others scattered on the wall.

"Eagle One, this is Shader. We're fucked. The entrance is still open. Emergency evac. I say again, emergency evac!"

The Osprey began to turn toward the four of them. They were to be pulled from the edge, then they'd pick up Carver and his men and plan on the defense of the camp.

At least they recovered Hope.

Shader dropped the rocket tube to the ground and gathered a handful of magazines. The four rushed to a flat spot nearby, where Donaldson would pick them up.

The Osprey banked hard overhead and rushed past their pickup.

"What the hell?" Shader yelled.

"Get to cover!" Donaldson yelled into the radio.

Shader had barely hit the ground when a *whoosh* flew by, followed by an SH-60 Seahawk helicopter. Four explosions erupted in the canyon, followed by the unmistakable sound of the door gunner's M134 Minigun. It was spraying the canyon walls at thousands of rounds per minute.

Shader leapt back into his firing position and began to take shots at the surviving Variants. There weren't that many left. The Osprey joined the action, roaming along the cliff-line, taking out anything that escaped Satan's Gate.

Shader looked at the cave's opening. Two Hellfire missiles had brought the mountain down. The Variants were no more.

A few minutes later, Donaldson settled down onto the flat. Shader and the three MOAs boarded, smiles and grins on each man.

The Seahawk maintained overwatch as Donaldson rose and turned to get Carver and his men.

"What the hell happened?" Shader asked.

"Remember the U.S.S. *Spruance*? That was the surviving helicopter."

"That was hours ago. Where were they?"

"I'm not sure where they were, but they found an abandoned airfield and refueled. They spent the night buttoned up, then flew here."

Shader was glad that something had finally gone right. He fell back into a canvas seat and tilted his head back. Finally, things were going their way.

Carver

"We've got to blow the opening," Gonzalez said to Carver. "I can hear the Osprey now."

Carver refused to close off Shrek's point of escape, but with the aircraft inbound, it was time.

Gonzalez grabbed two grenades and bent down. He gripped the handle with one hand, and the pin's ring with the other.

"Sorry, man. That was one good dog," Gonzalez said somberly.

He ripped the arming pin out, keeping his hand grasped around the grenade's handle. The fuse wouldn't light until he let the safety handle pop off. Then he had just seconds to get rid of the explosive.

Carver bent down one more time and stared into the black opening. The cool air had stopped flowing when the cave's entrance was destroyed. Now, it felt like a tomb, with stagnant air and buried bodies.

"SHREK!" he cried out pitifully.

Everyone was moved. Hope began to sob.

"Yip!" echoed out of the hole.

"Holy shit!" Gonzalez said. "Keele, get over here. Help Carver with the dog."

Shrek was backing out of the cave, his hind legs pumping against the sand-covered rock. His butt came out first, followed by his head. Attached to his mouth was the limp body of the infected coyote. It was Cyclops, its lone eye still moving side to side and its tongue wiggling weakly. Shrek had snapped its spine, giving it a high neck break.

"LOS!" Carver yelled to the dog.

Shrek dropped the creature and moved next to his leg.

Carver bent down and inspected Shrek, looking for any cuts or blood. Miraculously, he appeared unhurt and his mouth was clear of fluid.

He looked down at Cyclops. Its brain was still functioning, but its body wouldn't respond. Carver took his KA-BAR and drove it into its eye. He buried it to the ground and twisted it around and around, scrambling any remaining functional brain matter. It stopped its movement. It was dead.

The Osprey began to settle down nearby. Carver left the knife in the creature's skull. It wasn't worth the risk.

Gonzalez finally release the pin and tossed the first grenade into the opening.

WHUMP.

He followed with a second and was rewarded with another explosion.

The ground ahead sank slightly as the tunnel collapsed. Dirt billowed out of the cave opening, followed by a rush of sand and rock.

The cave was sealed.

Carver put his arm around Hope. Kyle was on her

other side. She staggered ahead with them holding her up, her legs weak from the fear and adrenaline dump she'd experienced.

Laura Reedy would do a full body inspection and verify she was clean. Carver didn't want to even think about that. He pretended everything was all right.

Shrek would be chained up to Kinney's porch once again. He would be cleared by tomorrow morning.

The Osprey's ramp closed, and they all sat back for a short ride home. The Seahawk helicopter rode shotgun on their right, the door gunner searching for any Variants that may have escaped. There were none.

When they landed, the rest of the camp gave them all a hearty welcome.

Carver's group had a full body inspection since they'd had close encounters with the Variants. All checked out.

Hope was cleared by Laura and joined them for dinner at Beckham. Carver came in late, having spent time with Shrek back at Kinney's place. He didn't want to leave his friend, but the Mal fell asleep while Carver was brushing the dirt out of his coat. The poor dog was exhausted. He'd defeated his nemesis and deserved the break. Carver left a bowl of food by his side, then joined the others.

It was a good night. They met the pilots of the Seahawk and listened to them describe their adventure. The abandoned airfield was a good find for them. There were tanker trucks that could be filled with aviation fuel and hoisted back to camp by the Osprey. They'd have air cover for almost a year before the fuel went bad. After that, it would be diesel. But that would eventually go bad as well.

They'd have to make some biofuel to run their

vehicles, but all of that was for another day. Now was the time to celebrate. It was important to enjoy the victories because, Lord knows, the bad times were just as plentiful, if not more.

Kyle moved in with Brett Darden. He was happy to have the company. He had never slept alone and with his twin dead, now was not the time to push that issue.

Carver lay back in his bed. Kinney was pulling first shift, guarding the northern side of camp. They were alone.

Hope slipped out of her clothes. The shower felt wonderful and the sheets were fresh. Dinner had been a miracle of tastes and textures. Mr. Morales was a man of many gifts and had created a mole sauce and enchiladas from their long-term food supplies.

She looked at John. His stomach muscles rippled as he lay back against the pillow. Damn, but he looked good. He'd saved her. No one else could have done that.

She found herself needing him. She slid under the sheets and put her arm over his chest. She bent up to him and kissed his neck.

He snored.

Hope lay back and began to chuckle. She rolled over and sighed. She closed her eyes and was asleep in seconds. For the first time in many months, the camp slept soundly. They were safe at last.

For now.

42

Behind Satan's Gate
Charlie

*"You speak my name, I do not mind
To give me credit is so kind
I'm flattered that I have your fear
You wake the sleeping demon here."*
DANZIG
"White Devil Rise"

The dirt begins to rise. A hand shoots out of the ground, grasping at the air. Slowly, a deformed figure pulls itself from the soil. First, its head. Then, its torso. Its single arm pulls and tugs at the dirt, bringing the apparition into the moonlit night.

It tries to scream out, but its throat is coated with rock and sand. It staggers to the base of the hill. It stumbles over a corpse and recognizes the one-eyed creature. A human weapon sticks out from its head. His anger bubbles up, and he tries to scream again. Nothing comes out as its vocal cords are caked with debris.

He hobbles down the slope. It is the path of least resistance. His anger for revenge is muted by his need to feed. He heads for the desert floor, all the while searching for something to consume. Flesh with its wonderful blood. He is possessed.

The thing stumbles and staggers forward. Always down, for that is where it is being pulled. Then onto the desert floor.

The night sky is clear, and it can see many miles away. There is nothing out there. No heat source, no movement. Just sand. Lots and lots of sand. It takes step after step because that is all it knows to do other than consume flesh. Soon, it has gone far away from the mountain, searching for a place to eat and heal. Someday it may be back. But for now, it keeps moving because that's what its brain tells it to do. That is what it does.

Epilogue

Lost Valley

"I will prepare and someday my chance will come."
ABRAHAM LINCOLN

Several weeks had gone by, and life in the Valley developed its own rhythm. Hope and one of the Forum survivors named Claire set up a school for the kids. Of course, the scouts didn't want anything to do with school. In the end, Carver bribed them by including shop classes with Mr. Morales, along with range time and tactical training. It was a fair trade.

Hope moved in with Carver while Kyle stayed with the other boys at the admin building. Work was in progress to change the maintenance garage into a dorm. There were two construction teams operating, now that there were enough bodies to spread the work around. One group was making an open pavilion for the soon-to-be-moved mechanical gear, while the other was modifying the metal garage to handle the many people who needed their own bed. It had been working out well. With plumbing and electricity already being fed to the maintenance building, it was just a matter of putting up walls and redirecting some conduit and four-inch pipes.

Donaldson and Everly were finally able to be open about their relationship. They'd been discrete while serving on the *Roosevelt*, but now they just shared a bed. In some ways, the apocalypse had made their personal lives easier.

The Seahawk and Osprey flew daily, picking up supplies and finding a few more survivors.

The mechanically finicky Osprey and temperamental Seahawk had given them concern, but Morales proved his worth. He gathered maintenance books on one of their first trips out of the Valley and had gone back out to collect parts and equipment. Between Morales and the scouts, the birds continued to function. Eventually, the fuel would run out or spoil with age and both rotor aircraft would be grounded for good. Until then, they were work horses that gave the group some serious mobility and air hauling power. The group's prioritized list of supplies was already half finished. Another month, and they could survive for the rest of their lives up there in the high mountain desert.

Food supplies would eventually run out. The group was gathering seeds and books on how to farm and become self-sustaining. Realizing the value of the bumble bee, several of the Forum survivors were in the process of making hives. The insects were a necessity to pollinate the crops. It would be a short life without them.

They already found some old farming equipment that ran on even the dirtiest of diesel fuel. If they planted the right crops, they could produce bio-diesel that would run the machines. It would make their agricultural work much easier.

Even medicinal plants were on the list, as Chris had begun to bone up on the value of herbs and roots. There was already planning to plant some weeping willows by the lake. The salicylates they could derive from the tree would provide blood thinners and aspirin. They even gave thought to planting poppies for narcotic medication, if any of those could be found.

Several marijuana plants were already growing behind the admin building. No one asked where the seeds came from. They would be used for medicinal purposes only. At least, that was the plan. And while no one had brought up a still yet, once the potatoes and honey started to be produced, it would become an issue. Carver was glad it would be at least a growing cycle away. He needed the peace and quiet right now.

Even little Bella was helping. At seven years old, she was already hard at work in the kitchen, helping Hope and Randy prepare the meals. After, of course, she finished her lessons.

All told, the Valley was supporting nearly fifty people now. There was even talk of setting up a government, or at least, an arbitration system. Nothing serious had come up yet, but it was only a matter of time. Carver thought it was a shame that the bad always came with the good. People were people, and they needed people things to do. That would eventually mean conflict and a loss of the innocence that survival had brought.

It was already a hot and rainless summer. It reminded Carver that on their next trip out of the Valley, they needed to bring back some direct current air conditioners from a camper supply store. That, along with more solar panels and batteries, would help meet the growing demands on the present electric system. The strain of so many people on their grid was already being felt.

Carver sighed and put his hat over his face. He lay

back on Kinney's plastic-covered porch couch and closed his eyes.

He smiled as he thought of his friend. Kinney may have owned this house before the apocalypse, but it was Hope's house now. Kinney bitched about the feminine changes she'd made, like a new throw over his chair and some salvaged pictures on the wall. But he never complained about the clean floors and folded laundry. He was getting the benefits of a woman in the house and seemed to take it in stride, although he loved to complain about it to Carver when they were alone. It helped them bond as friends.

Many nights, the two of them still sat on the house's veranda and talked about what ailed the world and the people in it. They had their opinions on what would make it better, and just as before the Variant virus took hold, it usually ended with boot camp at Parris Island and a good kick in the pants.

Carver reached down and found Shrek lying at his side. As always, the faithful animal was never more than a few feet away. He rubbed the dog's nape then moved up and blindly rubbed him between the eyes. The Mal leaned into him, accepting his affection.

Then Carver drifted off to sleep. His life was as complete as it had ever been, and if the Variants stayed away, he wouldn't complain.

Hope

"If you live to be a hundred, I want to live to be a hundred minus one day, so I never have to live without you."
JOAN POWERS
Pooh's Little Instruction Booklet

"Bella. Would you be a dear and take these cookies to Mr. Carver?" Randy asked.

"Yes, Mr. Thomas," she replied.

"And you can have one too. There are plenty."

The little girl's eyes lit up as she stared down at the platter of sugar cookies. She carefully held the plate as she left to deliver the goodies.

"You know," Hope said. "He's probably taking a nap."

"I've never met a man that would turn down cookies," Randy replied. "I'm sure he'll get over it."

Randy took a half dozen more and put them into a plastic bag. They went into his backpack.

"Stealing cookies now?" Hope chided as she finished drying the pots and pans from lunch. She knew they weren't for him.

"Please. I would never risk this svelte figure on cookies."

"I'll bet your roommates will like them, huh?"

"They might!" he admitted. "Remember, I have four more mouths to keep happy."

Hope smiled. It had to be a dream come true sharing a room with a SEAL and three Marines. The communal bedroom would soon be replaced by more private accommodations once the maintenance building was converted. Until then, Randy was being treated to all the testosterone he could handle.

"They're good people, aren't they?" Hope asked as she hung the final pan on the overhead rack.

"Yeah. They make me feel safe."

"Isn't that the truth." Hope thought of Carver and how he made everything okay.

"Besides," Randy said. "How can you not love a man named Porky?"

Hope laughed. She loved Randy for that. He had made her life bearable when she had worked at that horrible resort job. Now he was making the apocalypse fun for her, as well.

"I have a surprise!" Randy sang. "I've been saving this for a special occasion."

He walked over to one of the storage cabinets and brought out a bottle of Tennessee whiskey.

"No!" Hope said. "You little sneak!"

"Just between you and me," Randy replied.

He poured them each two fingers' worth.

"What's the special occasion?" Hope asked, as she took a sniff of the amber liquid.

"Why, darling. It's Tuesday!"

She laughed again. They each raised their glass for a toast.

"To you and John!" Randy said. "May you live happy and long."

"Thank you, Randy."

"And, to Senior Chief Petty Officer Porky Shader," Randy continued.

"Oh. You like him?" she teased.

"Yes," Randy deadpanned. "But he hasn't found me yet."

"You never know," Hope replied jokingly.

"He's a SEAL, you know. Very serious individual. I've never seen him smile and, you know, I never see him in a pair of pants that fit!"

Hope laughed, nearly spilling her drink.

"Stop!" Randy said, giggling himself. "Don't waste it."

They drank the liquid gold and Hope gave him a hug.

"I'm so glad you're here."

"So am I," Randy replied. "Otherwise, who would tell you about your hair?"

Hope pulled back a loose strand that had fallen from her ponytail.

"Seriously, woman. We have to do something about that mop on your head!"

Shrek

"Why do you like them so much?
Because they stand upon a wall and say,
'Nothing's going to hurt you tonight, not on my watch.'"
A Few Good Men

I lie next to him. The low growl of Carver's snore blends in with the insects in the nearby trees. I sit upright momentarily. I think I smelled something, but it quickly goes away. I never doubt my nose, and there is something out there that makes me uneasy.

I finally settle down and put my head between my outstretched paws. I give the world one last sniff, then drift off to sleep.

I dream of Cyclops and our epic fight. I feel the beast's neck break under my bite. My mind wanders back to time in the Hindu-Kush mountains in Afghanistan, where the enemy would place bombs in the ground. I review all these things before I sleep soundly. At least, as well as a warrior can sleep with one ear on alert and one eye open just enough to be ready for a fight.

I am on always watch.

Because I am Shrek.

I am the ghost that kills in the night.

I always win.

It is who I am.

o — o — o

Thanks for reading!

Please, tell your friends about the series. Promote it on Facebook by visiting my page:

facebook.com/waltbrowning.

Like and follow my page and share some of my posts. You can also sign up for my newsletter on the left side of the Facebook page or visit waltbrowning.com. I will keep you informed of future work, especially more of Carver and Shrek. Their future depends on the readers and anything you can do to help that along would be appreciated.

Continue reading the main storyline with

EXTINCTION HORIZON

book 1 of the Extinction Cycle saga

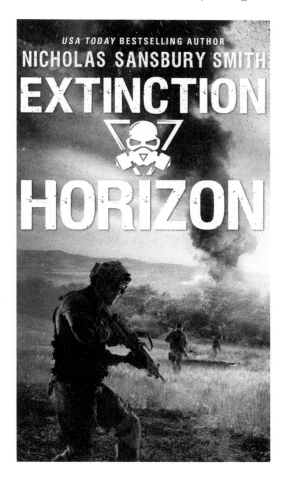

Available wherever books are sold.

Acknowledgements

There are many reasons that a writer puts ink to paper. One may look for fame while another seeks fortune. Regardless of the motivation, good authors pour their souls into the story. What you read should reflect the author's best effort. But the one thing that surprises me is that writing is not a one-man-sport. "Team effort" is such a cliché, but it is absolutely true. The story you just read was created by a group of people that have taken the time and love to help shape it. With this in mind, I would be remiss if I didn't acknowledge the following people.

My wife, Donna. Living with me when I sometimes grow dark and distant for no apparent reason, shows a patience that is beyond expectation. Many times, when a writer is not at the keyboard, their brains are still in the story. When a dark plotline is being created, it doesn't just leave you when you walk away from the desk. It lingers, like a bad odor in the background of your thoughts. She tolerates that. I have to eternally thank her for staying married to me and understanding my multi-leveled brain. She is one of the rare few that can. I love you, Donna.

My editor, Sara. She adapts to my disjointed schedule and never complains. My windows of opportunity to write are sporadic and inconsistent, while deadlines for completion are not. She accommodates me. She backchecks my work and evens out the inconsistencies that occur when you continue a storyline after having left it for weeks. She smooths out the sharp edges of my prose and makes the story flow. Thank you, Sara.

My inspiration, Nicholas Smith. Without him, there is nothing. A good writer steps on the shoulders of past great authors. Exceptional writers blaze their own trail. Nick is a blazer. There are plenty of zombie books out there, all with the same basic story to tell. Nick twisted the genre. He created living zombies using real science. Then, he created a world of characters that brought humanity into that chaos. He is a rare author. I am honored to be chosen to join that world. Thank you, Nick.

My art editor, Tanja at Deranged Doctor Design. What is portrayed on the front of a novel often determines if someone will consider reading it. Covers are critical to success. It is thrilling to give someone a written concept of an idea and then get back an image file that flawlessly gives your words life. To finally see the email with the attached image, arrive in your mailbox, is like Christmas morning. You are a professional and dream maker. Thank you, Tanja.

My publisher, Blackstone Publishing. Thank you for reasonable deadlines and mostly, for believing in my talent. You can't know the pride I feel when I tell people that I am "with a publisher." It is a milestone that many independent writers secretly wish for. You have made mine come true. I will do my best to make you proud. Thank you, Blackstone Publishing.

My readers. I hope I lived up to your expectations. It takes months of work and personal sacrifice to create this series. I am grateful that you took the time to read my story. Thank you.

And so, the story of John Eric Carver and Shrek has ended. At least, for now. I earlier stated that authors write for many reasons. I write for you. This is the truth. Every day, I look at two things. Reviews and sales. I check the reviews first.

Please consider taking a few moments to leave a five-star review of the novel. Not only does it propel more sales, but it encourages my publisher to keep me working. But if I failed to live up to your expectations, all critiques are welcome. It makes me a better writer and shows me that you care.

Again, thank you and stay frosty.

About the Author, Walt Browning

Walt Browning was born in Northeast Ohio. An avid athlete in High School, he went on to play college Rugby and Golf, competing against future PGA professionals John Cook and Paul Azinger. He is a doctor and continues to practice today in Central Florida, where he started his career almost 30 years ago. A personal friend and successful author, Angery American, encouraged him to try his hand at writing. His first book, the highly rated "The Book of Frank: ISIS and the Archangel Platoon", is available on Amazon and led to a collaboration with A.A on the Charlie's Requiem series. Charlie, a 28-year-old drug rep, is caught in Orlando after an EMP destroys the country's electric grid. Her attempts to survive the chaos and horrors of a society destroyed create a fast-paced story of death and redemption. The first book in this series sat at the top of Amazon's dystopian category for over a month.

Walt's future as an author looks bright, with planned novels in the medical mystery/action genre. further dystopian/science fiction novels and of course, the continuation of the Extinction Survival series.

For more information, please visit his website:
WaltBrowning.com
Also, I keep up on Facebook:
facebook.com/waltbrowning

About the Author, Nicholas Sansbury Smith

Nicholas Sansbury Smith is the New York Times and USA Today bestselling author of the Hell Divers series. His other work includes the Extinction Cycle series, the Trackers series, and the Orbs series. He worked for Iowa Homeland Security and Emergency Management in disaster planning and mitigation before switching careers to focus on his one true passion—writing. When he isn't writing or daydreaming about the apocalypse, he enjoys running, biking, spending time with his family, and traveling the world. He is an Ironman triathlete and lives in Iowa with his wife, their dogs, and a house full of books.

Are you a Nicholas Sansbury Smith fan?
Join him on social media.
He would love to hear from you!

Facebook Fan Club: Join the NSS army!
Facebook Author Page: **Nicholas Sansbury Smith**
Twitter: @GreatWaveInk
Website: NicholasSansburySmith.com
Instagram: instagram.com/author_sansbury
Email: Greatwaveink@gmail.com

.

CPSIA information can be obtained
at www.ICGtesting.com
Printed in the USA
BVHW031409150822
644636BV00008B/527

9 781092 871464